S0-ACY-842

Grizzly

Also by Christine Andreae

Trail of Murder

Grizzly

A Mystery

Christine Andreae

St. Martin's Press New York

GRIZZLY Copyright © 1994 by Christine Andreae. All rights reserved. Printed in the United States of America. No part of this book may be used or reproduced in any manner whatsoever without written permission except in the case of brief quotations embodied in critical articles or reviews. For information, address St. Martin's Press, 175 Fifth Avenue, New York, N.Y. 10010.

DESIGN BY JUDITH A. STAGNITTO

Library of Congress Cataloging-in-Publication Data

Andreae, Christine.
Grizzly / Christine Andreae.
p. cm.
"A Thomas Dunne book."
ISBN 0-312-11433-8
1. Women detectives—Montana—Fiction. 2. Dude ranches—Montana—Fiction. I. Title.
PS3551.N4134G75 1994
813'.54—dc20 94-3785
CIP

First edition: November 1994

10 9 8 7 6 5 4 3 2 1

For Andy,
with love

Grizzly

Chapter One

When Dave Fife's wife, Trudi, called me in Washington and asked if I'd pinch-hit as cook at their Montana ranch for a week over Easter, I said I'd get back to her. Last time I was in Montana, I'd hired on as camp cook for a pack trip into the Bob Marshall Wilderness and ended up getting involved in a double murder. They say lightning doesn't strike twice in the same place, but I wasn't feeling very confident. Clint, my ex-husband, had been back in touch for the first time in two years. Rotten memories kept drifting off their moorings.

On the other hand, my memories of the J-E, the Fifes' dude-cum-cattle ranch, glowed golden. During my adolescent years, for a couple of weeks each summer, my parents had taken my older brother and me to stay there. The place had been a teenager's Eden, complete with horses named Cinchfoot and Freckles and wranglers named Slim and Shorty. Recently, my brother had revisited the ranch with his family and come back to report that it hadn't changed. Moreover, the week in question coincided with spring break at the college where I teach.

It was one of my students who tipped the scales and landed me back at the J-E. I've forgotten the student's name, but I remember the moment exactly. It was a Sunday afternoon in late January. I was correcting papers in the library of the Georgetown house I'd been sitting for the past four months, and a freezing rain was pinging against the warped panes of original glass in the tall

Federal-era windows. After every fifth paper I had to get up from the owner's ancestral desk and squeeze out the icy sponges I'd lined up on the windowsills. I'd assigned my English Comp class a division/classification essay, and the results were as depressing as the leaky windows. Reluctantly, I picked up a paper that I'd already put on the bottom of the pile three times. It belonged to a gum-chewing kid who sported a gold chain and a Marine-style crew cut. He defined his life by dividing it into three sections: going to school; working a shift at McDonald's; pumping iron down at the gym. The transitions linking these divisions were identical: "And then I took a shower." I felt a surge of hope in my breast. I was on the verge of declaring the effort a brilliant piece of parody—until I read the last sentence: "And then I took a shower and then I popped my zits and then I went to bed."

And then *I* knew I was going to Montana. I picked up the phone and told Trudi yes.

I flew out of Dulles, then rented a red Escort at the airport in Great Falls and headed west across the rolling plains. Once I'd passed through Choteau, the closest town to the ranch, the smudged blue line of the Eastern Front of Rockies came into sharper focus. Stretching across the wide horizon, the mountains still held spring snow in their creases. I had not seen them snow-covered before, but I recognized their outline against the wash of gray sky. To the south, behind the face of the lift, there was a distant pyramid-shaped peak, almost completely white. To the north rose the mass called Ear Mountain, which, we were told as children, was supposed to resemble a giant ear lying on its side. Seeing it again as an adult, I thought it looked more like a caved-in soufflé, its cavities dusted with confectionery sugar. Of course, this time I was arriving as a cook.

Nonetheless, be it soufflé or Ear-of-the-Earth, the formation was impressive. The Blackfeet Indians who used to hunt buffalo on the plains below it had revered the mountain as a sacred site. The boys of the tribe had climbed to the high, flat summit in search of visions to guide their manhood. More recently, the mountain had inspired the late A. B. "Bud" Guthrie, one of the J-E's neighbors. In the East, Guthrie is not well known, though an occasional film buff will remember him as the author of the screenplay for the classic Alan Ladd movie *Shane*. But in the West, his 1947 novel *The Big Sky* and its Pulitzer Prize–winning companion tale *The Way West* are generally revered as monuments of the region's literature. I had excavated my father's battered paperback copy of *The Big Sky* to read on the plane, but hadn't gotten beyond the first chapter, in which Boone, the hero, brains his belligerent father with a stick of stovewood, steals his gun and his shaving strop (made from the scalp and hide of an Indian), and runs off to seek his fortune. I found myself more concerned about what was going to become of the strop with its tassel of dead hair than about the fate of our hero.

After the hard-surfaced road out of Choteau, I drove about twenty miles chattering along on an improved gravel road that rose and fell between shoulders of arid grazing land—land "so poor we can't even raise hell on it," Guthrie once quipped. I turned off onto an unimproved dirt road and fifteen minutes later jolted across the cattle guard at the J-E's main gate.

The initials stand for "Journey's End." To my ear, the name sounds more like a seaside cottage at the end of a lane than a cattle ranch. But Dave Fife's father, Olwyn, had been a romantic under his stoic facade, and "Journey's End" does have a doomed, poetic ring to it. He incised the name on a long pine plank, hung it over the main gate, and registered his brand as JE. His wife, Cora, who had majored in French at Barnard, declared the letters too egotistical. On her letterhead, she inserted a bar between the J and the E, but no one in the "club" of annual guests ever pronounced the bar. To its multigenerational network of fans, the ranch has always been known simply as "the J.E."

Olwyn and Cora came out to Montana after World War II and settled on the east side the Rockies, up against the massive wall of mountains called the Eastern Front. The scion of a New York family that had made its fortune in footwear, Olwyn used his trust fund to buy a large, rustic lodge and twenty thousand acres on either side of a river called Givens Creek. About half the land was undulating short-grass prairie that reached into the Front Range like an open hand; fingers of grazing land disappeared into the wooded gulches and canyons at the base of the range.

When the Fifes moved into the lodge, the Front's fearsome winter winds had skimmed off most of the roof shingles and half the shutters. The place had been built back in the 1920s by a Wall Street speculator and big-game hunter. He shot elk and deer, bighorn sheep and grizzly. Then, during the crash of '29, he lost courage and shot himself.

Olwyn Fife had his heart set on cattle. He had not counted on running a dude business on the side. But curious friends from back East kept turning up. They seemed to like camping in the lodge's dilapidated servants' wing, and they enjoyed being put to work. They helped Olwyn with fencing and branding and haying. Cora took them out riding, her baby boy in front of her in the saddle. She sent them out on fishing excursions, organized costume parties and evening softball games. After the birth of her second son, she began charging them. Olwyn didn't notice. He was preoccupied with his five hundred head of cattle. By the time he found out, he'd been a silent partner in a flourishing dude business for three years. Cora converted the lodge's servants' wing into offices and built guest cabins back under the pines. Olwyn did not complain. When the price of cattle fell, Cora's dudes from Greenwich, Connecticut, and Main Line Philadelphia kept the ranch afloat.

I followed the road uphill into the pines that sheltered the lodge. It looked exactly the same: same dark timbers, same stone chimneys. Even the giant log pillars that held up the two-story veranda retained their gray crust of bark on the leeward side. *Brigadoon* time. The mountains were like a wall that held off not only warm air and rain from the Pacific, but the breezes of change as well. The only thing I didn't recognize was the shrubs planted under the window boxes, and that may have been due to their leafless state. I half expected Cora, Dragon Lady of the J-E, to appear and scold me for parking in the wrong place.

"You won't believe it," my brother had warned. "It's uncanny." I felt as if I'd come home. The old farmhouse in which we'd grown up in suburban Falls Church had been razed to make way for a shopping mall. But the J-E of my adolescent summers had held fast.

I got out of my rented car. Should I waltz in through the front door like a guest or knock on the kitchen door like an employee? I left my duffel in the backseat, skirted Cora's rock garden, and walked around the side of the lodge to a U-shaped courtyard formed by the kitchen, the garage, and the former servants' wing. A thick new layer of white gravel had been spread to welcome the J-E's first guests of the season. The stones gave under my shoes like a plush carpet. I didn't remember the old stone trough under the office window. Someone had planted it with blue-and-yellow pansies. Not Cora. Not Olwyn.

Olwyn had died almost fifteen years ago of lung cancer. He left the J-E's twenty thousand acres, now debt-free, to Cora with the instruction that she was to keep the land intact. Under no circumstances was she to divide the property between their two sons. According to the grapevine, at the time of his death, Olwyn was estranged from his oldest son, Mac, who had burned his draft card at the University of Montana in Missoula—an institution from which he had dropped out after a semester and a half. The local TV station had attended the protest and caught Mac on camera. He had almost set his own windblown hair on fire as he torched his card over a fifty-gallon steel drum—an overly optimistic size, as it turned out. Mac was one of five card-burners. Thus he made a three-second appearance on the late-night news. Olwyn happened to catch it. Afterward, Mac moved to Canada, where he sat out the Vietnam War. When Jimmy Carter gave amnesty to draft dodgers, he migrated to Kenya, where he learned how to make movies of wild animals.

When Cora died at age seventy (also of lung cancer), it was generally expected that Dave, the younger Fife, would inherit the ranch. He had done his bit for God and country in the Marine Corps, then come home to help his parents run the ranch. But surprise! Cora left the twenty thousand acres to Mac, her prodigal filmmaker. What Dave inherited was a dude-cum-cattle business. The lodge and its old Navajo rugs, the guest cabins and their old iron bedsteads, the tack shed and its dozens of tooled saddles, the corrals and farm machinery—all were Dave's as part of the business.

For use of the land beneath his bequests, he was to pay one dollar per annum to his older brother. Which meant, of course, that Dave had no claim to the land he worked: by the term's of Cora's will, Mac was legally entitled to sell it out from under him.

Certainly Mac had been Cora's favorite. Not that he was a mama's boy. The reverse, in fact. When I was at the J-E in the early sixties, Mac, at fourteen and fifteen, was always in trouble with Cora for riding at breakneck speed or making wisecracks about her guests. (This, of course, made him glamorous among his peers.) The word "cosseted" comes to mind, but that's not exactly right. He wasn't pampered by Cora. She wasn't the pampering sort. Mac was *admired* by his mother.

I don't remember much about Dave. He was probably better-looking than Mac, now that I think of it: he had a nicely shaped head under his sandy crew cut, a square face, Olwyn's blue eyes. It was easy enough to imagine his face on a Marine recruiting poster. But he had none of Mac's break-your-heart appeal. Dave and my brother, Johnny, were the same age, and they used to hang out together. I used to tag along with Mac's followers.

Now he was an eco-star. Over the last couple years, his name kept turning up in coverage of wildlife issues. Most recently, he had been featured in a *Newsweek* cover story called "The War in the West: Fighting for America's Mythic Lands." There was a double-page spread on him, three-quarters of it taken up by a portrait in color of "A Cowboy Who Loves Bears." The caption was set off in a pastel-blue box that picked up the grainy blue sky behind him. Mac looked good: hatless, tanned, friendly wrinkles around his intense dark eyes, mouth firmly set. He wore a khaki shirt rolled up at the sleeves. The khaki matched the color of both his hair and the rolling plains at his back and suggested an attachment to the earth, military strength, the romance of safaris. Maybe I'm reading too much into it.

On the other hand, the accompanying two-column article was headlined "Evan Fife: Jacques Cousteau of the West?" (Evan was Mac's given name. At the J-E, he'd always been Mac—a nickname of unknown origin.) The text, compiled by four stringers, reverently mentioned his early work with lions in Africa (a Belgianproduced film shot in the Ngorongoro Crater), his documentary on the snow leopard (narrated by Peter Matthiessen), and his now famous 1986 PBS special on *Ursus arctos,* the grizzly. At that time, the schoolchildren of Montana were asked to choose the official state animal by ballot. By a landslide vote, they elected the grizzly. However, politicians worried that the kids' choice might champion the grizzly at the expense of the state's economic interests. Timber and oil companies were anxious to "utilize" the bear's pristine turf. Prompted by the industries' lobbies, legislators proposed an amendment switching the state beast to the elk. Mac was there with his film crew when five hundred schoolchildren descended on the state capitol. *Ursus arctos* won the day. And Mac's film, *Bear with Us,* launched his career as an environmental activist.

Mac parlayed a deluge of support letters into grant money and went on to set up a research center called the Sacred Paw Institute "on the family's cattle ranch, which he manages with his brother," according to the article. Mac was described as a "holistic" rancher, a new breed in the state who attempted to "balance the landowner's need for profit with the vegetative needs of both livestock and wildlife." When the Stockman's Association accused him of wanting to have his cake and eat it too, Mac had called a press conference and stated, "Without a dream of Eden in our hearts, our planet will die."

According to *Newsweek,* Mac's largest accomplishment was to unite half a dozen of the state's wildlife and wilderness advocacy groups, all of which had been competing for funding, into one increasingly powerful lobby called the Wildlife Corridor Coalition. Apparently through the force of his personality, Mac had been able to unite disparate nonprofits in a campaign to prevent the exploitation of the Eastern Front by oil and natural gas companies, whose latest geological surveys indicated rich deposits of petroleum. In the northern section of the range, land sacred to the Blackfeet's ancient religion was under siege. But all along the range, from Glacier down to Yellowstone, the habitat of the grizzly, the state's official totem, was also threatened.

Mac. When I had negotiated for the job over the phone with Trudi, I had been too preoccupied with other questions to ask after him. But now, waiting for someone to answer my knock on the J-E's back door, I wondered if he was at the ranch or off doing his environmental thing somewhere. I banged again on the kitchen door, then opened it and went inside.

The kitchen was a large, square room flooded with daylight from high windows over a stainless-steel sink and countertop. The room was warm and smelled not unpleasantly of cooked meats and bacon fat cut by whiffs of bleach. Despite its yards and yards of stainless-steel surfaces, the kitchen seemed more homey than commercial. On one wall, cream-colored shelves held a collection of old yellowware mixing bowls. Blackened cast-iron pans hung from a ceiling rack. "Hello," I called out. "Trudi?"

I walked through the kitchen, into a maze of pantries. I opened a swinging door into a staff dining room where a lone Easter lily sat in a pink foil-wrapped pot halfway down a long vinyl-topped table. I opened another door into a dark corridor paneled in varnished pine.

"Trudi?" I called again. I retreated into the warmth of the kitchen. I was testing the hand crank of an antique cast-iron meat slicer when I heard footsteps coming through the pantries.

A girl in an oversized lavender T-shirt and baggy shorts came into the kitchen. She was about twelve and had the healthy glow of a field hockey player: plump but strong, with fine brown hair falling in her eyes. "Hi," she said. "I thought I heard someone down here. I'm Lynn."

"I'm Lee Squires," I told her. She looked blank. I added, "Cook of the week?"

"Oh yeah. Mom said you were coming. I don't know where she is. I can show you where to put your stuff. We made up the downstairs room for you. Macon's room upstairs is nicer, but he left it full of junk. He doesn't like anyone to touch his stereo while he's gone."

"Macon?" A brother, perhaps?

"He's our chef. Winters, he goes down to Arizona to cook at this resort. Takes off on his Harley. That's why you're here. Mom couldn't get him to come back for just a week." She considered me. "Macon's got this tattoo. A green dragon snaking down one leg.

Sometimes he shaves his leg so you can see it better. He's pretty hairy."

"How's his cooking?" I asked.

Lynn shrugged, uninterested. "It's okay."

"Want to see my tattoo?"

Her eyes widened. "You have one, too?"

Me and Cher. I pulled down the neck of my sweater and leaned toward her so she could see the small red-and-black ladybug below my collarbone.

Lynn moved closer and peered at it. The part on the top of her head was a perfectly straight line. I could smell her shampoo. *Ladybug, ladybug, fly away home.* The tattoo was almost ten years old. I'd gotten it not long after my daughter died of leukemia. Rachel had been four. Now she would have been close to Lynn's age.

At that moment, Mac Fife walked into the kitchen. He looked blankly at us. I tugged my sweater back up.

"She's got a ladybug," Lynn announced to him. She turned back to me and demanded, "You got any others?"

"Not yet."

Mac was preoccupied. "Where's your mom?" he asked his niece.

"Search me," she said.

Mac stood over six feet but somehow looked smaller in person than he appeared in the *Newsweek* portrait. He also looked more worn. In the afternoon light flooding through the kitchen's high windows, the gray in his light brown hair was visible, and the lines at the corners of his mouth looked more sharply etched.

"Hello, Mac," I said. "I'm Lee Squires. I don't know if you'll remember, but I used to—"

"Yes!" he interrupted. Suddenly he was alive, boyish, full of spark and challenge. "I know who you are. I just didn't recognize you! It's been a long time."

We shook hands. His grip was dry and confident.

"Great to see you! Did Trudi tell me you'd been out here before as a cook?"

"Last summer. I subbed as a camp cook on a pack trip in the Bob Marshall. For Pete Bonsecour?"

He frowned. "Don't think I know him." Then it came back to him. "That was the Strand family's trip? A couple of the party were killed, weren't they?"

"Yes."

He looked at me reflectively. His dark eyes were sympathetic.

"What happened?" Lynn demanded.

Mac raised an ironic eyebrow. "They were murdered," he told his niece.

She wrinkled up her nose. "Gross," she said.

"You always did like to be in the thick of things," Mac teased. "We never could shake you."

I smiled. "Not for lack of trying."

He laughed, draped a comradely arm around my shoulders, and gave me an affectionate squeeze. At age twelve, I would have fainted. At age forty, I felt as if he'd finally let me into the gang.

"When we were kids," he said to Lynn, "we used to play keep-away on our horses back up in the gulches. Lee was always *it*. It was the only way we'd let her play. We rode like hell to get away from her. It's amazing none of *us* were killed."

Lynn pushed a strand of hair out of her eyes. "Back in the good old days before insurance," she sassed him. It sounded like the refrain of a song she'd heard too many times before.

CHAPTER TWO

"Insurance" was a dirty word in the Fife household. It would be hard to find an American adult who has no complaint with insurance—be it medical, automotive, or liability. But in Dave and Trudi's case, the insurance business was destroying their livelihood. The guests they'd invited over

Easter were Step One of an emergency family plan to save the ranch—or at least a good part of it. My role in it all was to fatten up the visitors—not as lambs to the slaughter, but as prospective saviors.

After dinner on the evening I arrived, Trudi and I took mugs of tea into the staff dining room and went over the week's menus. Though she was trying hard not to let her anxiety show, I felt as if she were drowning in details. She'd been debating the rice-or-potatoes question for ten minutes when I attempted to lighten things up by asking, "You worry this much over all your menus?"

"Food is critical in this business," she snapped back. Then she let out a breath. "Sorry," she said. She gave me a weary smile. She was a pretty woman with a sturdy build and outdoorsy squint lines at the corners of her eyes, which were blue and made bluer by her eye shadow. She was wearing a bright teal-colored sweatshirt with her jeans. It looked brand-new. She'd put on fresh red lipstick for dinner as well, but now all that was left of it was her liner, and you could see that she'd drawn her lips slightly fuller at the sides than they were. I liked her determination.

She massaged her temples, then pulled a pink plastic comb out of the shoulder-length mass of her tightly permed, uniformly brown hair. She turned the comb over in her hands, frowning at it as if she'd never seen it before. Then she looked up at me. "Would you believe that they've called us everyday and sometimes twice a day for the last two weeks? Once they asked if the orange juice would be freshly squeezed. They just wanted to let me know that they preferred hand-squeezed to machine-pressed."

"What'd you say?" I tried to sound casual instead of alarmed.

"Don't worry, I told them frozen orange juice was part of the Montana experience." She snatched a folder from a pile of papers in front of her. "Look at this." She briskly waved a sheaf of laser-printed papers under my nose, like a nurse applying smelling salts to a fainter. "This is an *hour-by-hour* plan for each day. They weren't happy with 'Breakfast at seven, Morning Ride, Lunch at twelve-thirty.' They wanted to know precisely what time the ride would leave the corral and how many rest stops there'd be along the way and could I send maps of the route for each ride!"

I shook my head in sympathy.

"Lord," she sighed.

"Okay," I announced. "We're alternating. Rice every other meal. Rice, potatoes, rice, pasta."

She said nothing.

"It'll work out," I said.

She stuck the comb back in her hair. "We're counting on it," she said firmly.

She told me part of the story then. Three years before, the J-E had entertained a couple from Boston. They were first-time guests and were coming without children or grandchildren. They had been referred by an old J-E regular who had been at Yale with the husband and had bumped into him again at their twenty-fifth reunion. What the regular didn't know was that since the reunion, his former classmate had gone through a midlife crisis and emerged with a trophy wife.

It was evident from the moment the ranch's dust-caked, elderly van arrived from the airport with them that the new wife was not going to "fit in" at the spartan, family-oriented ranch. She complained about the lack of a swimming pool, and she complained about the resident bat in her cabin. She spent most of the time sunbathing nude on a Hudson's Bay blanket behind her cabin. ("We never could get the coconut oil out of it," Trudi said bitterly.) It took the woman's husband the entire week to coax her up onto a horse. On their last day, he boosted her up into the saddle. She slid off the other side and broke three red fingernails and her wrist.

It was not the first time a dude had fallen off a horse at the J-E. Because guests were allowed to actually ride their horses, to trot and lope instead of plodding along nose to tail in a walk, falls happened rather regularly, especially among the kids, who rode together in one big galloping herd. Nor was it the first time bones had been broken in a fall. Injured riders were swathed in ice packs and driven to the hospital in Choteau and cheerfully thanked God it wasn't worse. For the rest of their stay, they enjoyed the status of soldiers wounded in the line of duty. But Trudi worried about the trophy wife. There was something off about her post-fall gallantry.

Perhaps her smile was a bit thin. Trudi worried through New Year's about it, then, when nothing happened, pushed the incident out of her mind. Almost two years later, the Fifes received notification that they were being sued for $1.3 million. The woman was seeking reimbursement for medical bills and compensation for her mental anguish. Her now ex-husband (because of the anguish, they had gotten divorced) was suing for loss of sex during the year she'd been seeing a psychiatrist.

Adding to Trudi's fury, instead of contesting the claim, the insurance company settled out of court for three times the medical bills—a sum slightly over $100,000. Trudi and Dave protested. Their agent expressed regret. "You're lucky the woman wasn't a concert pianist," he had joked. Neither Trudi nor Dave laughed. The family had been faithfully paying the company's premiums for over twenty-five years, and never before, despite the annual accidents, had they filed a claim. Now not only did the company refuse to do battle on their behalf, it raised their rates in the middle of the season. There was no way they could hike fees to cover the cost. The following year, the premiums tripled to a sum that ate up all profits. When Dave finally managed to get their friendly insurance agent on the other end of the phone, the agent informed him that brain surgeons were better risks than any operation involving dudes and horses.

We sat up talking till past midnight. The next morning at six o'clock, both our faces were slightly puffy after only five hours' sleep—plus, in my case, a stiff nightcap of bourbon from my flask. But Trudi's tongue, unlike mine, was wide awake. She not only rattled food instructions a mile a minute. She went on with her saga of woe, dropping new details here and there, circling around and around as if to unearth some scrap of meaning in the retelling. She watched me measure out coffee into the machine and poked the batch of bread dough I'd set to rise in a huge old ocher-glazed bowl ringed with two blue stripes. (Trudi's recipe for wheat bread, handed down from her father's mother, a rancher herself, called for white sugar instead of molasses and specified lard for shortening.

The sugar didn't bother me, but I winced as I melted huge cholesterol-laden lumps of lard in boiling water and poured it into a well in the flour. A subsequent taste test, however, confirmed something I'd known deep down all along and not wanted to admit: animal fats *really do* taste better.)

Ancestral dough approved, Trudi relaxed maybe half a second, then raced on about how Macon, their regular chef, coped with omelets for forty. (He used a lineup of fifteen bowls, she informed me. His assistant kept them filled, breaking two eggs into ten of them and replenishing the rest with fillings—from the classic bacon-and-cheddar to the daring but tony feta-and-chutney.)

"You've only got four people coming," I reminded her.

"Can you do French toast?" she demanded.

"You like vanilla in the batter?"

"Cut the bread nice and thick. I wonder if they eat French toast."

"Traditionally, it's soup."

"For *breakfast?*"

"Seaweed soup."

"Get outta here."

"Really. They season it with fermented soybean paste. The paste comes in different colors. White for summer, red for winter."

"That's nice." She sounded depressed.

"Don't worry. According to the *Washington Post,* the entire country has switched to corn flakes and scrambled eggs."

"They" were four Japanese businessmen. I didn't mention to Trudi that in Japan, the "morning set" had gained a dish in translation. Cereal, toast, and eggs were served with a tossed salad.

The visit had been arranged through Montana's department of commerce. The Japanese company, NVI (Nippon Vacuum Instruments), was in the process of diversifying and was interested in acquiring a cattle company. (Well-marbled beef—the kind that health-conscious Americans were avoiding—sold in Japan for over a hundred dollars a pound.) NVI's "salarymen" had looked at ranches in Australia and were now arriving in Montana to do some comparison shopping. And although there was better grazing land in other parts of the state, the J-E's cattle operation had one large plus: it was attached to a dude ranch.

According to the man at the state commerce department, recreation was big in Japan. As business investments, golf courses were out (reportedly, the Japanese underworld used them to launder money). Ski resorts were in. But ranches were even more chic. The American West was alive and well in Japan. "They still watch *Bonanza* along with *Twin Peaks,*" the state commerce rep said happily. "Last year they spent over ten million dollars on prefab log homes made right here in Montana."

Apparently, NVI's executives liked the notion of owning both a corporate playground and a working cattle ranch. They also liked the fact that the J-E had been family-owned and -run for two generations. Japanese businessmen, particularly those who could afford Gucci loafers, appreciated authenticity.

"The dude business is not for sale," Dave said firmly.

"It's just a preliminary meeting," soothed the state facilitator.

Trudi had no problem with the nationality of the men from NVI. "There's some people around here still fighting World War II," she commented. "But that don't bother me. As long as their money's good, I can get along with them. I don't care what they look like. We just can't keep on going without a major infusion of capital." She sounded a trifle defensive, as if she were explaining the situation to an audience of loyal dudes. "It's not only the rotten business with the insurance," she pointed out. "It's things like the plumbing. Some of it's over half a century old. The original lead drainpipes are disintegrating. Our handyman, Hil, manages to keep things going, but it's a full-time job in summer. The whole system needs to be replaced. To say nothing of the wiring."

She leaned back against the sink and took a swallow of coffee from an oversized mug that warned "Mom" in giant red letters. It was still dark out, and the high window behind her reflected the kitchen's old ceiling fixtures like a pair of misshapen moons.

I felt a wave of sadness. The time warp was an illusion, after all. Behind the scenes, the old idyll was buckling, about to yield. A new order was waiting in the wings. "You want me to try a batch of French toast now?" I asked. "For your breakfast?"

She thought about it. "Yeah." She sounded encouraged. "Use the white bread. This business?" she went on. "We've never been able to set much aside. But at least until last year we were able to help out our older girls with college."

I studied the kitchen's glass-fronted refrigerator.

"What are you looking for?" Trudi asked.

"Eggs."

"Dairy's in the baker's pantry."

I found six dozen in cardboard cartons on the bottom rack of a cream-colored Westinghouse with rounded corners. It might have marched on cartoon legs out of Little Lulu's kitchen. I took out four eggs and a stainless-steel container of milk from the J-E's cow.

"You're not going to use cream?" Trudi demanded as I splashed the thin blue milk into the eggs.

I looked at her.

She held up her hands. "Okay, okay."

"What about Mac?" I asked her. "How does he fit in all this?"

"It's his idea. He's the one who set us up with the commerce fella in Helena. He's willing to sell them half his land to run the cattle. The other half, the high country, he'll keep the high country for his precious bears."

"But what will happen to this?" I gestured around me.

"If the deal goes through, he's agreed to sell us the land we're sitting on. It's only about ninety acres."

"He won't—" I shut up. It was none of my business.

"What?"

"He wouldn't just give it to you?"

Her eyes narrowed. "It belongs to the bank about three times over. Honey, Cora was barely cold when he started mortgaging this place out from underneath us. Let me tell you, saving grizzly bears ain't cheap," she said sardonically.

"What ain't cheap?" Dave came through the back door, unsnapping his canvas jacket, radiating the good humor of a chronic early riser.

"Your brother's bears," Trudi growled.

Dave's face closed. He washed his hands at the sink. The sky beyond the window had lightened to gray. "I saw Mac and Clare coming off the mountain. I told them to come on down for breakfast." There was a slight question in his voice.

Trudi said nothing.

"No problem," I said. "Who's Clare?"

"Mac's live-in," Trudi answered. "At the moment."

"Trudi," Dave said. It came out sharply, like a rap on the knuckles.

They stared at each other. Then, without taking her eyes off his, Trudi said to me, "Clare works for the Sacred Paw Institute." Her voice was grimly sweet.

Dave let out a sigh of exasperation.

I served breakfast late, at seven-twenty instead of seven, but they were patient, full of encouragement. There was orange juice (frozen) and fresh grapefruit halves (a friend had sent a bushel from Indian River, Florida). Lynn, who appeared with wet hair dripping onto the shoulders of her T-shirt, helped cut the grapefruit and put out boxes of cold cereal, and milk in an old white pitcher whose glaze had crackled. I garnished the French toast with bridges of crisp bacon and served the syrup warm (a touch that surprised them) in a green Depression-glass pitcher. I liked the farmhouse look of the meal: the wash-softened red-and-white-checked cloth, the heavy crockery, the lone Easter lily, its throat dusted with yolk-yellow pollen, staked to attention in the center of the long narrow table. Because it was Good Friday, I'd made a pan of hot cross buns. Their tops were a bit darker than I liked and their sugary X's had melted and dried into thin flakes, but Trudi asked me to repeat them next morning for the benefit of the Japanese, so I felt I was off to an okay start.

I hadn't seen Mac and Dave together since we were children. Back then, it was hard to think of them as related, they were so different: Dave, squarely built, taciturn, guarded; Mac, wiry and vibrant, certain as a crown prince. Now, at midlife, it was as if their brotherness had matured along with them. It wasn't so much a matter of physical resemblance as a similarity of gesture and expression. The wry twist of their smiles was the same. They shared the same turn of voice, the same slight inclination of head and neck. Whatever fierce rivalries had racked their youth, they now seemed settled in with each other. Trudi may have resented Mac for inheriting his mother's twenty thousand acres, but if Dave shared her grudge, it didn't show.

Mac introduced me to Clare. "My assistant," he said. "Clare Jenkins. *Doctor* Jenkins," he teased her.

"Clare," she said simply. She didn't smile. She had waist-long black hair which fell loose down the back of her plaid flannel shirt. At first glance, she looked like a schoolgirl, an Indian schoolgirl, but her black eyes were older. She might have been thirty. Her face was flat, with broad cheekbones. I wondered what tribe she was and whether it was rude to ask.

"Lee's got her doctorate, too," Trudi tossed out.

Oh God, I thought.

"Oh?" said Mac, interested.

"English Renaissance poetry," I said. "Very useful."

He raised his eyebrows and gave me an urbane little nod of compliment.

"More coffee?" I offered, holding up the pot like a shield.

The light from the windows in the staff dining room was still gray, determinedly so. The family ate with little conversation. Dave was reading yesterday's *Wall Street Journal* and Lynn leafed through a paperback titled *Japan-Think, Ameri-Think*. I was replenishing the platter of French toast when she sat up and said, "Listen to this. You know how we call orgasms *coming?*"

Four adult heads turned in her direction.

"Well, the Japanese call it *going.*"

Mac burst out laughing. "God help us!" he exclaimed.

Clare glanced at him sideways, her mouth amused, if not exactly smiling.

"Oh for heaven's sake," Trudi said in disgust.

Dave put his coffee cup down. His face was paternally stern. "*Where* did you find that book?" he demanded.

Lynn gave him a break-your-heart smile. "On your desk, Daddy," she said.

Chapter Three

The guests were due that night for supper. Winging it with a collection of old Fife family recipes, I felt new and nervous, even after my successful baptismal breakfast and a mountainous ranch-style lunch for eight (beef hash, mashed potatoes, sticky buns, white bread, canned pears, and an entire brick of home-grown butter). By two o'clock, I had the kitchen back in order and was ready for a run.

I set out along a dirt truck track that serviced the guest cabins set back in the pines. But at the last cabin, a ranch pickup blocked the way. The truck's original maroon paint had faded to matte pink. In its bed were the black plastic boulders of bagged garbage that Hil, the ranch's handyman, had removed from the kitchen barrel after lunch. Now, one by one, with meticulous slowness, he was loading in a pile of rotting boards torn up from the cabin's porch. From inside the cabin, there was the whine of a power saw. A kid wearing a nail belt stood outside, hands on hips like an overseer in a grade B Biblical. I recognized him from lunch.

"What's your hurry, cookie?" he called as I trotted around the truck.

I stopped. "My name's Lee Squires," I said, trying to keep the frost out of my voice. "I've forgotten yours, I'm afraid."

"Bobby," he said. He was about the age of my English Comp students, and his round face had the same cocky convince-me expression. He wore a yellow Caterpillar cap on his head, a leather bracelet around his wrist, and a red-and-black-checked wool shirt that gaped at his beer belly. Or perhaps I should say butter belly. At lunch I'd watched, fascinated and repelled, as he applied a good two ounces of butter to each slice of his bread.

"Bobby," I repeated.

Hil carefully deposited a board, nail side up, in the back of the pickup. He was taller and skinnier than Bobby, and maybe twice his age. His black eyes, set on either side of a finlike nose, were bloodshot but not unintelligent. In his cheek he held a tumorous-looking lump of "chaw." In terms of Handsome Is, neither Hil nor Bobby measured up to the Marlboro man. I wondered if they'd score higher in the Handsome Does category.

Bobby's eyes moved appraisingly from the scarf tied around my head down to my battered Nikes. In between I was wearing my best sweats and an olive-green diamond-quilted down vest that invariably prompts my mother to ask why I want to go around looking like a hand grenade. "Out for a little jog?" Bobby drawled.

"Good for you," I said. "Very observant. Now, can you tell me where this road goes?"

"Up the canyon." He added with a smirk, "You'll wanta watch out for bears."

"Bears?" I said.

He and Hil exchanged glances. Clearly they thought it incumbent to inject a proper scare into my dudely Eastern heart. They proceeded with elaborate pleasure to tell me how this time of year, the grizzlies were ravenous; how they lumbered out of hibernation in the high country and ate their way down toward the greening plains like dozers cutting separate swaths. Old Short Tail, Hil said admiringly, could break a bull's neck with a single swipe of his front paw. He could tear up an entire hillside, send boulders flying through the air like down pillows, "just to get at a little bitty ground squirrel."

"Really," I said.

They grinned as if it might be fun to see Short Tail get at me.

In addition to such useful facts as "A grizzly now, he'll outrun a horse," Bobby seemed to have an unlimited supply of "true tales" about maulings and death. Just north of us, he informed me, up at Glacier National Park, grizzlies had killed several photographers who had gotten too close. One of them had been dragged down out of a tree. His body was found with the face "clawed off." Down at Yellowstone, a concession employee had gone out hiking and never come back. Not till the end of the season did searchers find his gnawed remains.

Hil grinned. "And there was that lady ranger," he offered.

Bobby shrugged. "She just got her leg ate."

"She played dead," Hil persisted. "Her husband watched the whole thing. Wasn't anything he could do. 'Cept throw his canteen. Alls he had with him was a canteen. That ol' bear charged out of nowhere. They come on like a racecar, cover a hundred feet in two seconds flat."

"It ate her whole leg?" I asked in spite of myself.

Hil nodded solemnly. "They had to amputate. Weren't nothing left worth savin'."

Overhead, a ragged fleet of clouds sailed across a dishwater sky. I was getting cold. I wanted to get moving.

Bobby said, "Good trick, playin' dead with a five-hundred-pound bear tearin' the meat off your legbone." Then his voice slid from awe to scorn. "Heard she wouldn't let them go after it, either. She was one of them tree-hugger types. A art teacher from somewhere out East. That's what she did winters, teach art."

Hil said, "She was on her moon."

"What?"

They avoided my eyes, embarrassed. Then Bobby said delicately, "It was that time of month."

"You mean she was menstruating?"

"Yeah."

"What does that have to do with the price of eggs?"

"It brought on the attack," Hil stated.

I stood there looking at them. Clearly, they were both convinced. "I've got to get moving," I told them. "It's been swell talking to you."

They laughed as if I'd said something clever.

"If you run into any bears," Bobby teased, "be sure to pick a tall enough tree."

"I thought bears went up trees."

The lump in Hil's cheek shifted. "A black bear, he'll climb."

"But not a grizzly."

"Claws too long." Hil opened thumb and forefinger to indicate a length of five inches.

I headed on up the road, ignoring a fork to the left, jogging a couple of miles up into the canyon. Beyond the ranks of pines on either side of the road, walls of wet stone rose into a low shroud of dirty-looking mist. I was glad of my down vest. April in Montana felt like February in Washington, D.C. When I left, the famous cherry trees around the Tidal Basin had already been in leaf and the tourists were out in shorts. But here, high up against the eastern flank of the Rockies, there were no obvious signs of spring, no little glacier lilies piercing the old drifts of snow under the pines, no busy chatter of nesting finches. Except for the distant rush of a creek and the occasional scrape and groan of deadwood in the wind, the forest was silent.

I'd been counting on more gladsome scenery, a Wordsworthian boost to plump up my heart. (Lately, I'd had the nasty suspicion that instead of *pumping,* this vital organ of mine was *scraping*—as if somehow along the way it had been freeze-dried.) When, as a teenager, I'd come out to the J-E during the summer, I'd seen the plains dry and brown. But this time of year, I'd expected to find a lush springtime sea of green rolling toward the thrust of mountains. I'd expected the famous Big Sky to be the way I remembered it: postcard-blue. However, on the long drive from the Great Falls airport, the April sky had been depressingly anemic and the endless landscape as beige as a desert.

A couple of years ago, a Montana friend from Helena had enthused that the Eastern Front was a "spiritual time warp." I wasn't exactly sure what she meant, but the notion had definite appeal. When I bought my ticket to Great Falls, I'd been after green thoughts in a green shade. What I'd forgotten was that classically, spiritual renewal occurs in deserts, not in gardens.

So there I was on the east side of the Rockies, huffing and puffing my way up a socked-in gulch where the tree trunks were as gray as stones and beards of black moss hung from their broken lower branches. Maybe I shouldn't have come, I thought. Maybe I shouldn't have left my mother alone after all. I pushed my guilt aside and kept moving. A sharp wind blowing down the canyon stung my face. I ran past a Dumpster the size of a semi parked in a clearing beside the road. Despite the chill, big blowflies drifted around it. The top was open, but it was screened with heavy-duty metal mesh.

Finally, I hit snow, a solid blanket of mush that covered the road. I stopped, glad of the excuse, and turned back. The road was not steep, but my blood was pounding in my temples and my mouth felt dry. Clearly it was going to take a couple days to adjust to the higher altitude.

I left the road and walked into the woods toward the noise of the creek with the idea of hiking back along its (durst I hope mossy?) banks. The forest was fairly open. Between clumps of pine trees, patches of ground were littered with dry deadfall, pale rocks, and faded clumps of beargrass.

I'm not sure how far I walked, but however far it was, the babble of the creek never came nearer. A trick of the canyon's walls, I decided. I closed my eyes and marveled: the rushing water, wherever it was, sounded exactly like the whoosh of tires on asphalt. I might have been standing back in my little walled Georgetown garden listening to the flow of traffic on Wisconsin Avenue.

But I wasn't. I was wandering through a drab pine forest. The pines all seemed to be the same variety, all tall and narrow and ragged as worn-out bottle brushes. I thought of Dante's *selva oscura*—the dark wood where he found himself lost at midlife. The only way out was down, through the nine concentric circles of Hell. Not an encouraging thought.

I checked my watch. I'd left the J-E's kitchen less than an hour ago. It seemed longer. I heard a rustling behind me and turned. It stopped. I started walking again, placing my feet carefully, listening for sounds I wasn't making. More rustling. Something large was moving behind me in the underbrush. I turned around and peered through the tree trunks but saw nothing. A deer, I told myself. An elk, maybe. Nonetheless, I felt a prickle of vulnerability, the same scratch of fear that quickens the step on city streets at night. I began checking out the trees, rating their climbability. At the same time, I was annoyed at myself for allowing Bobby's death-by-bear stories to get to me. No doubt he'd picked them up from the sort of manly magazine found in barber shops. As for the "fact" that the smell of menstrual blood could provoke an attack, it seemed too bizarre to be true. Nonetheless, the tales nagged in the creases of my consciousness like the monsters that hide in the dark corners of childhood.

I stopped at the edge of a small clearing, the kind of place lost children come upon in fairy tales. There was no gingerbread cottage, but a bunch of crows and ravens in the trees on the far side of the clearing were making enough racket for a coven of wicked witches. A fly buzzed heavily at my shoulder. I brushed it away. Had I gotten turned around? Was I close to the Dumpster?

The clearing was about thirty yards across, a natural minimeadow of damp blond grasses. The grass was well trampled and, in places, matted down, suggesting deer or elk beds. I looked over at the crows flapping and squawking in the trees and saw, half hidden in the shrubbery below them, what appeared to be a naked body. It had the blackened, pebbled look of the corpses of Iraqi soldiers killed by our "smart bombs" during Operation Desert Storm. In the photographs published after the war, all that was left of their uniforms was shreds stuck to their forearms and knees.

You're hallucinating, I told myself.

It is hard to say which was more terrifying: what I was seeing or the idea that I wasn't really seeing it. I was unable to move so much as my big toe, but my mind kept ticking along like an alarm clock. It's a log, I insisted to myself. A log caked with black mud. But if it was a log, it was a hefty one, bigger in diameter than any of the trees in the vicinity. And why was it mud-coated? Had something been rolling it around in the muck under the shrubs? Had a grizzly been after some small animal hiding beneath it?

It's just a log, I decided firmly. But I felt no relief. The thing persisted in looking like the torso of a person lying on his side in a circle of mud, back toward me, head hidden under a spreading bush.

I moved sideways, angling for a different view, tripped over a gray boulder, fell and banged my left knee against it. I was electrified by a sharp squirt of pain. I cursed, and rocked back and forth, and waited for it to subside. Beside the offending rock, in a half-melted patch of snow, I spotted a partial print. It was a bare foot. A very large bare foot. It looked wide enough for a quadruple E. The print was blurry around the toes, but I counted five of them. How odd, I thought. Had someone sat down on the rock and taken off his boots? I stood up, tested my knee. Then suddenly the wind abated and I smelled it.

Now there was no question. With my hand clamped over my nose, I limped a couple of paces closer. The corpse's back was broad and long-waisted. The legs were short, but beneath the caked mud and pine needles, buttocks and thighs were massively muscled. In places where the mud had washed thin, I could see skeins and cords in bas-relief, like the muscles and veins of a power lifter oiled for competition. I could also see that its head was missing. And so were its hands and feet.

I don't know how long I stood there staring before I turned and bolted. Perhaps it was only a second or two, but it seemed an eternity. Everything felt nightmarishly slow, as if I were running through taffy.

Miraculously, I found the road. Things began to speed up. I kept on running. When I spotted the pink pickup, I felt leaky with relief. Hil was still there. I can't recall when I had been so glad to see someone. I ran up to him. "Hey," I gasped. I grabbed the side of the pickup for support.

Hil backed away. It took me several tries before I could get the words out. "There's a body in the woods," I croaked.

"What?" he said.

I tried to swallow. My mouth felt as dry as sandpaper. "I found a body," I repeated.

Perhaps I was screaming. Bobby and another man came out of the cabin. They stood there staring at me.

"I'm telling you," I insisted, "there's a dead man out there!"

I searched Hil's blank, reddened eyes and saw something shift. He was home.

"Where?" he asked.

"Its head is gone," I said. Then something hard and wet welled up in my throat.

The men exchanged glances.

"Where's it at?" Hil demanded.

I knew that if I tried to speak, I'd cry. I kept my mouth shut.

"Maybe you could show us?" said the man with Bobby.

I nodded.

"You ride with Hil," he ordered. "We'll follow."

So Hil and I led the way in a bouncing, matte-pink garbage truck to the site of—what? Not your ordinary shoot-out, certainly. Why was the victim naked? And why had his body been mutilated? I saw the legs casually bent at the knee as if they belonged to a sleeper who had lost his feet in a bad dream. They had been cut off above the ankle, and the remaining stumps of calf were ragged. Some small animal had been gnawing at them.

I felt nauseated. Hil's truck didn't help. The cab had a sweetish, boozy smell, punctuated by whiffs of something that smelled like rotting fish. I twisted around and looked through the dust-speckled rear window. The bed of the truck was empty. Hil must have made one trip to the Dumpster and returned to the cabins for more. Behind us, the carpenters drove a new blue-and-gray Chevy pickup with metal racks and a black metal tool chest in the bed.

I tried out my voice. "Who's that with Bobby?" I asked Hil.

"His daddy."

"They live here?"

He shook his head. "Choteau."

The plastic seat was cold. I began to shiver. Hil was in no hurry, perhaps out of deference to the truck's extreme age. Or maybe he'd had a postprandial hit of red-eye. In any case, his leisurely, unflappable attitude was oddly reassuring. I glanced at him. The bump of tobacco was still in his cheek, but he was looking handsomer by the minute. Maybe it was his beaklike nose that persuaded me. It gave him a slightly dangerous, raptorial look, but then, I've never been drawn to "safe" men. Nor men with small noses, either.

We got out of the trucks at the snow line. Bobby's dad told me his name was Pick. He had a genial voice. On the window of his truck, an American flag decal announced, "These colors don't run." On the rear bumper, a yellow-and-black sticker said, "Never argue with a sick mind." I puzzled that one over while Pick folded back the front seat and selected a big Winchester from a metal rack welded to the back of the cab. It also held a .22.

Bobby looked at the .22, then looked at his dad. "How come I get the pop gun?" he demanded.

Grim-faced, Pick handed the Winchester to Bobby, then took out two boxes of shells and a revolver from the glove compartment. The revolver looked big enough for Dirty Harry. They loaded up.

Pick strapped a holster around his waist, but kept the revolver in his hand. He went first, following my tracks into the woods. "Keep together now," he ordered. I had the feeling he'd done this before. Maybe in the jungles of Vietnam. Bobby looked excited. "Let's get a move on," he said.

Hil and I kept a safe distance behind them. Nothing looked familiar. "I was looking for the creek," I babbled nervously to Hil. "And I found this clearing." I felt a wave of panic. *What if it hadn't really been there after all?*

But it was there. Bobby walked right up to it. "Jesus Christ," he said. He poked at it with his boot. The boot slid sickeningly. He jerked his head away from the stink he'd released. Then, from a less intimate distance, he inspected the body, waving at the flies. "Big guy," he remarked. "See here, a bear's opened him up."

His dad took a step closer and peered at the neck. "No bear did that. His head's been *cut off.*"

Bobby giggled. "That ain't all."

"What?" Pick demanded sharply.

"They took his equipment, too." Bobby gave me a sly glance. "Look here," he invited.

Instead I studied the ground at my feet. The carpet of pine needles was light and dry and unreadable. "I don't get it," I said.

Bobby giggled again, a mirthless sound. "Maybe he put it in the wrong place."

I moved away. "Look at this," I said. I showed Hil the footprint I'd found by the rock.

Hil nodded. "Bare," he said.

"But why?"

"Reckon he was hungry."

"So he takes off his shoes?"

The men looked at me as if I were mad.

Bobby cracked, "Never heard of a b'ar wearing shoes."

"Wait a minute," I said. I peered at the print. "What made this track?"

Pick came over and hunkered down beside it with his shotgun. I heard his knees crack. "Grizzly," he pronounced. He pointed to several punctures in the mud, gouged dots about three inches beyond the toes. "That's its claws."

"Oh," I said.

He stood, pushing himself off the ground with his rifle, and glanced back at the mutilated body. "Poor devil," he said.

Bobby said nothing. His glee had subsided along with his color. He looked greenish.

"You think the rest of him's around here somewhere?" I asked them. Bobby turned, took three jerky steps, and threw up. Hil studied the pointed toes of his cowboy boots.

Pick suggested, "Let's have a look."

"Maybe we should wait for someone," I suggested.

"Like who?"

"The sheriff?"

Pick dismissed the idea with a shrug.

But I didn't want to stay there any longer. It wasn't only the smell, which seemed to come and go in waves, or the malevolent, random buzz of stray flies. It was the terrible sense of flatness I had. "I've got to get back and start supper," I told them.

The mention of food seemed to stun them. I turned and started across the clearing.

"I'll take her back," I heard Hil offer.

Pick grunted. "Get Dave to call the sheriff," he ordered.

I sat in the truck waiting for Hil, staring through the windshield at the snow on the road and seeing the severed neck bone, which was brighter and whiter than the snow. The muddy flesh around it had been torn by carrion eaters, but the cut through the vertebrae was expert. The knife had been sharp. It occurred to me that with the head and hands missing, identification of the victim was virtually impossible. But what was the point of taking the feet? And why the genitals? Had a psychopath kept them as souvenirs? And why did the loss of genitals seem more obscene than the loss of a head?

Hil opened the door of the truck and climbed in. He put both hands on the steering wheel. I waited for him to start the ignition, but instead he reached across my knees, opened the glove compartment, and took out a half pint of gin—Tanqueray, of all things. The green bottle was unmistakable. He unscrewed the top and offered it to me. "You look like you could use something," he said.

I thought twice about sharing a bottle with a tobacco-sucker, but the label was reassuring. I took a swig. It was cold and went down smoothly. The smell of it brought back summer evenings from my childhood. I saw my father sitting on our porch in his shirt sleeves with his martini in a stemmed glass and the evening paper. I could almost smell the boxwood through the screens. I took another, longer swallow.

When we got back to the J-E, Hil offered me a breath mint. I accepted that, too. He winked at me. "Ya gotta watch it around Trudi," he said.

"Thanks," I said.

He shrugged it off. "I better go tell Dave." He sounded resigned. He might have been going off to report a clogged toilet.

CHAPTER FOUR

Dave had already left to meet the guests' plane in Great Falls when Hil and I arrived back at the lodge to report the body. Hil, at a slow but steady pace, went off to find Trudi, and I, after waiting around in the kitchen for I'm not sure what, went to my room. It was located at the end of the corridor in the old servants' wing off the kitchen. Lynn told me they sometimes used it as an extra guest room when the cabins overflowed. The walls were papered with a cottagey print of yellow roses. There were two small windows, two narrow beds with iron steads painted white, two dressers enameled red, and one stuffed chair, a bit too large for the room. I took off my down vest and smelled it. I took off my sneakers and smelled them. Then I took off my sweats. I had my nose in them when Trudi burst through the door. Lynn's frightened face was behind her.

"What the hell's going on?" Trudi demanded. "Hil comes to me, half in the bag, and says you tripped over a corpse behind the Dumpster?"

"It was in the woods." Hugging the damp ball of my sweat clothes to my chest, I told her what I had seen. For Lynn's sake, I left out the part about the missing genitals.

They stared at me, horrified. "Oh my God," Trudi said.

"Hil was okay when we got back here," I offered with a twinge of guilt.

"He wasn't when I talked to him," she snapped. "Really, he's hopeless. I keep telling Dave."

The floral coziness of the room provided no comfort. The house seemed very empty. For a moment we listened to it, as if gauging the strength of its timbers, the width of cracks between window and sash.

"I don't think we've ever locked up here," Trudi said. "There's always been someone home. I don't even know if we have keys!"

"It didn't just happen," I reassured her. "I mean, it had been there a while. Whoever did it is probably long gone."

"Sweet Jesus," Trudi said.

I started shivering. I dropped my sweats on the floor, tugged a patchwork quilt off the foot of the bed, and wrapped it around me Indian-style. The worn cotton felt cool and soft against my skin. "I've got to get in the shower," I said. "I keep smelling it." But I didn't move.

Lynn made a small frightened noise. "Ma?" she wailed.

Trudi drew herself up. "Don't be silly. Lee's right. Whatever happened, happened. It's over with. It's got nothing to do with us. I'm going to call Mac. He can talk to Pick and Bobby and call the sheriff. We've still got beds to make up."

The quilt around me was beginning to warm up. I didn't really want them to leave. Perhaps I was afraid of what might look in the window when they were gone.

"Take your shower," Trudi scolded, as if it were all my fault. "You are not to breathe a *word* of this to our guests, you understand?"

I guess she thought I might pop my head out of the kitchen and go, "Psst, hey fellas, guess what I found?"

There was an abundance of hot water, and I used more than my share, but the shower didn't help much. I came out of it feeling spacey, as if the line between dreaming and waking were dissolving. I dried off and found blood on the towel—two weeks early. It's the altitude, I told myself. I pushed away the thought of a bear attack and pulled on jeans and an old Black Watch flannel shirt that had belonged to my father. I had rescued it from a giveaway box my mother had packed after his death. It had been a shock to see it there, neatly folded among all his button-downs, and I had felt a stab of betrayal, as if she were giving away all the autumn Saturdays he'd worn it. I was careful not to wear it around my mother.

I looked at my watch. It was only four-thirty. Back in Washington, it was two-thirty. As good a time as any to call my mother. The phone for guests' outgoing calls was in the lodge's Big Room, a vast, two-story log living room used mostly on rainy days and cold evenings. At one end of the room there was a walk-in stone fireplace; at the other, a library nook under a minstrel gallery. The room was furnished with oversized sofas and chairs upholstered either in old cracked leather or new maroon vinyl. The islands of furniture were lit by rickety parchment-shaded standing lamps. A scattering of buffalo skins and Indian rugs lay on the dark, polished floor. Above the windows in the dim upper regions of the room hung the disembodied heads of animals bagged by the ranch's original owner. Over the years, a number of these trophies had been decorated by high-spirited guests. A cigarette dangled from the heavy lips of a moose head, several billed caps and a dusty felt fedora hung on the ten-point rack of a deer, a mountain goat's yellowing beard sported a faded pink bow.

The phone was located on a maplewood desk under a row of windows that faced west. By design, the phone was exposed. Cora Fife had disapproved of men who could not leave their offices behind, and the lack of privacy tended to discourage lengthy business calls. Trudi, supported by the wives, had seen no reason to change this arrangement, and the phone itself was still a black rotary model, circa 1950.

My mother's phone rang four times, clicked, and played her all too familiar message: "You have reached the office of Dr. Marcella Romann-Squires. I cannot take your call at this time. . . ."

My mom the psychotherapist. Her voice is warm, sympathetic, encouraging. She even has the slightest hint of an accent, or perhaps it's her intonation. Whatever, her voice suggests a pre–World War Europe where cures were expected to be leisurely rather than immediate, where disturbed patients writhed on solitary couches, not in groups on the floor. Her Dr. Jung lilt, I call it. It is, in fact, deceptive, because my mother actually prefers groups, and not only in her work. She lives with a group on Capitol Hill in a townhouse whose basement serves as her office. It is a curious assortment of friends, this second family of her choice. Each of them is an "ex" of one sort or another: an ex-priest who teaches accounting at UDC, an ex–mental patient (St. Elizabeth's) who is now licensed as a massage therapist, and an ex–battered wife who drives a cab and sings in a gospel choir on Sundays.

I can't deny that they are loyal friends to my mother—who often subsidizes their shares of the rent. Moreover, if it weren't for their devotion, I would not have been calling my mother from Montana. I would have been camping on the couch in her office. Back in February, she had gone skating at the rink down on the Mall and broken her left leg. It was a nasty spiral break that refused to heal and required two operations to scrape out infection around the pins. She'd had the last operation the week before I left, and she was scheduled to come home from the hospital on the same day I was scheduled to fly out of Dulles at seven in the morning. My brother refused to disrupt his family's spring skiing trip to bring her home—even though I had been with her throughout both operations. So it was partly annoyance at him that allowed me to be persuaded by both my mother and her housemates to use my nonrefundable ticket.

"That's what friends are for," my mother said with a sly smile from her pillow, and Opal, who had chauffeured me to the hospital in her cab, had erupted into her wonderfully deep, operatic laugh. It was the kind of laugh that made patients down the hall get out of bed and wander down the corridor to join the party. Nurses were constantly shooing people out of my mother's room, then lingering themselves. It would have driven me crazy, but my mother liked all the company. "I sleep very little at night," she told me. "I have all the solitude I need."

I wasn't worried about her care. Opal and Tommy, the New Age masseur, had proved themselves excellent home nurses. They could get her up and down the stairs without having her go ashy, in and out of the bathroom promptly, and even do her hair to her satisfaction—not that it requires much doing. My sixty-five-year-old mother's hair is still thick and mostly black and cut in an elegant cap. In fact, my mother's housemates were more skilled at seeing to her comforts than either my brother or I.

Perhaps deep down, I resented them, worried that they were

getting "too close" to my mother. But up on the surface, I was giving priority to the worry that her leg seemed to resist healing. It bothered her too. My mother, however, saw the whole business as a spiritual, not a physical, crisis. "I don't believe in accidents," she said. "I went *skating* and I *fell* and I broke my *left* leg." Her priestly friend Al nodded sagely at this.

I said nothing.

From the pillows, she gave me one of her gnomic smiles. "My body is sending me a message," she explained.

I didn't buy it. What kind of message had my daughter Rachel's cancer been? And who was it for? For her? Or for me and Clint?

My mother's canned message lilted across the continent. "If you kindly will leave your name and phone number, I shall return your call promptly. Thank you." A moment later, the line dinged.

"Mom," I said, "it's me, Lee." I could hear my voice echoing in the room. "It's—uh, Friday afternoon, Good Friday actually, and I just wanted to see how you're doing and if you got home okay. Tommy? Al? Opal? If one of you is there, please pick up. I want to know what's going on. Is anyone home?" I tried to keep the irritation out of my voice. "Anyway, Mom, I hope you're on the mend. I'll try and call later tonight—it depends how soon I get through in the kitchen. I don't want to wake you up, so maybe I'll try in the morning instead. Talk to you soon—I hope."

I hung up.

Where was my mother? Had she not come home from the hospital after all? I sat in the darkening room, gazing out the window over the desk. The wide lawn around the lodge was still brown. Beyond it, over the dark tops of the pines, banks of gray clouds opened slightly, like a crowd relaxing, and revealed a molten gold lining.

I heard the front door slam and hurried footsteps in the hall. I stayed put, monitoring the widening crack in the clouds. A moment later, whoever it was came back into the hall.

"Lee?" A male voice. "Lee!" he called up the stairs.

I pushed the chair back from the desk. Its legs squealed. I stood up.

"Oh, there you are." It was Mac. He was standing in the wide doorway, the light in the hall behind him. He strode over to me. He looked drawn, middle-aged, familiar. His dark eyes were concerned. "Are you all right?"

Suddenly I was. "I was just making a phone call. To my mom. I left her home with a broken leg that's gotten infected."

"And you've got the guilts."

"Only mildly, at the moment, thank you."

He smiled. "I was always a bit afraid of your mother."

"Sort of like she could see through you and zip, right out the other side?"

"Maybe that's what it was." But he was distracted, agreeing to be agreeable. "I talked to Pick about the body."

"Have you—uh, seen it?" I asked.

He shook his head. "Trudi asked me to stay here. At least till Dave gets back. . . ." His voice trailed off. "I called the sheriff's office, but he wasn't there. There's an accident down on 287. Some kids flew off the road in a pickup. The dispatcher said the sheriff's out there picking up the pieces. I told her it wasn't an emergency, that we'd call back."

His appraisal surprised me. But he was right. There was no emergency now. Even if it felt like one. "I guess it's not going anywhere," I agreed reluctantly.

"You okay?" he asked again.

I nodded. We were standing Metro-crush close in the big empty room. I could see the stitching on the pointed collar of his blue-checked Western-cut shirt. I could see lines like the lines on an open palm crossing his Adam's apple. I felt an urge to reach out and trace them, to feel his tanned skin under a light finger. Instead, I shifted my feet, opened up the space between us. "I've got to get back to work," I said. I felt my hair. It was virtually dry. In the space of twenty minutes. In Washington's humidity, air drying took hours—despite the fact that my hair was the fine, Nordic variety.

"Pick said there was evidence of bear activity?" Mac asked.

"We saw a couple prints."

"All the same bear?"

"You're asking me? Didn't they tell you? I thought the prints had been made by a barefooted hiker."

"How big was the print? Do you remember?"

"About like this." I measured a space with my forefingers.

"We got a sow we've been monitoring in that quadrant. But that looks big for her."

"I might be wrong."

He looked at his watch and let out a small snort of frustration. "I wonder where the hell Dave is. It's really getting too late to go up there now."

"Why?"

"Well, the Front grizzlies are pretty much nocturnal animals. It may be an adaptive evolution, we don't really know. Out on the plains, grizzlies would have been more vulnerable to hunters than bears in the back country. Maybe they learned that night was safer. In any case, they start moving around twilight. You don't want to get in their way—particularly in a feeding area."

"But what about the body?"

"If they've already been at it, another night isn't going to matter. It's just not worth the risk. We don't want to have to end up killing one of them. We've got enough trouble as it is with whatever happened back in there. Throw in a dead grizzly, and you'll get half the county driving out here for a look."

"Trudi's afraid of scaring off your guests."

"I think Dave can get the sheriff to handle it quietly. Ed Becker's not going to want it broadcast that someone's going around chopping off heads—and sundry parts. He's not going to want to deal with a panic any more than we do. My guess is he'll call in the state homicide people from Helena."

"Mac? What do you think happened?"

He thought about it a moment. Then he said cautiously, "Pick seemed to think there was a ritual quality about it."

"Yeah," I agreed.

"Jesus," he said. "Sounds like something out of a samurai comic." He made swishing noises as he sliced his hand back and forth through the air. "The Japanese probably have a poetic name for it." He looked at me. "Sorry. My son went through an oriental violence stage a couple years ago."

"I didn't know you had a son."

"He lives with his mother. In London."

"How old?"

"Sixteen. He's coming out here this summer. First time, for all practical purposes. He was a baby when Marsha left."

She left. "I've got an appointment with a roast," I announced. I picked my clip up off the desk and twisted my hair up onto the back of my head.

"Don't," he said.

"What?"

"Leave it down."

I thought of Clare's long, loose black hair. Amused, I snapped in the clip with my free hand. "You don't want my hairs in your popovers."

He put his right hand over his heart and recited, 'In thy golden snare, my heart is strangled . . .' "

I frowned. "Very Petrarchan."

"Yes, Professor?"

"Do I get another line?"

" 'Fair Tigress tell, contents it not thy taste?' "

"Wyatt?" I guessed, though the diction wasn't quite right.

"Nope." His dark eyes flashed.

"I give up. Who?"

"My father."

"Olwyn?"

Mac smiled at my surprise. "He liked sonnets. He worked on them the way some people work crosswords. Mother had a little book of them printed up."

"I didn't know he wrote poetry."

"Most people didn't."

"I'd like to see a copy."

A shaft of light slanted through the window. It coppered the hairs of the buffalo skin at our feet. The room heaved softly, as if we were afloat. Mac said, "Back when we were kids?"

"Yes?"

"I thought you were something else."

"Did you?" I kept my voice light, skeptical. "You could have fooled me."

"You were only twelve."

"Fourteen, the last summer," I corrected.

"I kept waiting for you to come back all grown up." His eyes held me. I felt his hand on my shoulder. His finger drew a soft stroke behind my ear that raised the fine little hairs on my neck.

I brushed his hand away. "Why did your wife leave?" I asked.

He smiled at my rudeness. "She couldn't hack it out here."

I tied my bandanna around my head and marched off to the kitchen.

There is a reason why women cook in the presence of death; why we bake hams and zucchini bread and cupcakes brightly dotted with M&M's for the children. It not only grounds us in the deepest rhythms of life. It is also a discipline, and like any discipline, it can serve as a shield. On that particular night at the J-E, I embraced the dinner prep as a shield against the rotting human meat I had stumbled over in the clearing; and more—a shield against the live impulse I'd discovered in the Big Room.

Mac's move had caught me by surprise. But upon reflection, I had to admit I was not all *that* surprised. When I met him again in the kitchen of the J-E after half a lifetime, an instinctual part of me had reached—or been pulled—toward him. I was familiar with the feeling—a subterranean yearning I'd tried to dissect in any number of my poems, a dark mix of maternity and sexuality, of pity and desire. But I was not familiar with its present incarnation.

As a man, Mac was a virtual stranger. Did he hold, as Pushkin allegedly held, that a man cannot possibly have all the women in the world but is obligated to try? Certainly he was not deflated by my no. Perhaps he was simply employing that litmus test of the woolly West: "Are you a Good Girl or a Slut?" Testing, testing, one, two, three, testing. I'd learned the hard way that you can't ace this peculiar test. It has a built-in failure factor. Everyone loses out.

Anyway. Said Good Girl peeled and rinsed and chopped and contemplated the delights of Slutdom with Mac Fife—certainly a distraction from the mutilated thing in the clearing. I worked on keeping fingers out of the way, tuned in to each vegetable, muttering their names over and over like holy names in a litany. *Potato, carrot, save us from Darkness.*

To welcome the guests, Trudi had provided an impressive cut of J-E–grown prime beef. It was to be the centerpiece of an American culinary triptych: on the left-hand panel, there were popovers, white rolls, roasted potatoes, and a sprinkling of frozen green peas; on the right-hand panel, an apple pie in a deep tin dish and a scoop releasing balls of vanilla ice cream.

I moved from potatoes to piecrust. While my hands measured out flour and checked the temperature of eggs, I tried to keep my mind's eye focused on the mandala of a perfectly pink roasted loin of beef—this on my own pet theory that the magic of visualization works as well for cooks as it does for athletes. Of course, my concentration faltered. (Where was my mother? Had she been in the bathroom?) But gradually the kitchen became warmer, safer. The roast released its deep, rich scent into a vegetable steam. Boss Trudi popped in and out with news updates. Mac had called the sheriff again. He was on his way home from the accident. Dave had called from a Western outfitter's in a Great Falls shopping mall. As planned, he had driven the Japanese there directly from the plane, but they would be later than expected getting back to the ranch. "He said they were having a ball buying the place out," Trudi reported. "So far so good, I guess."

"What?" Lynn asked, coming into the kitchen with her paperback West-meets-East manual.

"Your dad called. He says our guests like to shop. They think five hundred dollars for boots is real cheap."

"Did you tell him?"

"Yeah," Trudi said.

"So what'd he say?"

"He said, 'Huh.' "

"That's it?"

She let out an exasperated sigh. "He asked if we were okay and I said yes, we were fine and dandy." She gave Lynn's sagging T-shirt an appraising look. "You're going to change, aren't you?"

Lynn ignored the question. She held up her book like a preacher holding up the Bible. "You're supposed to bow to them," she announced. "The more important the guy is, the deeper the bow."

Trudi rolled her eyes to the ceiling. "I don't want to hear this."

"Men bow with their hands on their thighs. Women are supposed to keep their hands together. Like this." She put the open book facedown on the counter next to a pile of carrots I'd cut for crudités. She crossed her hands in front of her like a Venus protecting her crotch, then dove into a bow.

"Honey, they *can't* do it like that," Trudi protested.

Lynn straightened. "What's the matter with it?" she demanded.

Trudi giggled. "Your butt sticks up like a duck's—you look like you're bobbing for fish!"

"So let's see you do it!" Lynn challenged.

Trudi folded her hands together and, with great dignity, inclined her head and shoulders in a bow that Queen Victoria might have used to acknowledge her subjects.

"Not low enough, Ma."

"It's low enough for me, sweetheart."

Lynn scowled, snatched a carrot up along with her book, and strode out of the kitchen.

Trudi gave me wry smile. "She's all right." Her voice was proud.

We heard Dave's van driving up, and Trudy went out to meet it. Through the window over the sink, I saw them embrace, hard and quickly. Dave had already dropped off the guests at their cabins, and he and Trudi stood talking a long while against the side of the van. Then they came in.

"You okay?" Dave asked me. He sounded just like Mac.

"Jim-dandy," I said.

He stared at me, as if seeing me for the first time.

"She's fine," Trudi said impatiently.

Dave's blue eyes were uncertain.

"I'm fine," I told him. "Honestly." I wondered if my tongue was turning black.

* * *

The presence of the Japanese was anticlimactic, at least from my viewpoint in the kitchen. Under the fluorescent glare of fixtures in the staff dining room, the Fifes' visitors did not look like a powerhouse of commerce that could make or break the J-E. They looked like a quartet of tired tourists who smiled as if their lives depended on it. Trudi had decided to feed them along with the family rather than isolate them in the summer dining room. This was a cavernous room with dark varnished floors and blond varnished tables. Proportionally, it mirrored the Big Room and was linked to it by the lodge's entrance hall.

Certainly the staff dining room, with its green-painted wainscoting and cream walls, bare save for a school-type clock and a lumberyard calendar, was friendlier than the empty formal dining room. Nonetheless, to my eye, the staff dining room, though pleasingly austere at breakfast time, was a bit bleak for dinner. I suggested bringing down a couple of the emergency kerosene lanterns I'd seen lined up on the top shelf of the pantry and dining by lamplight instead of fluorescent tube. This was not well received. "You'll stink up the whole dinner!" Trudi exclaimed.

I didn't bother suggesting she serve a good Cabernet with the roast. We were being authentic here, and coffee was the authentic Westerner's mealtime beverage of choice. Liquor was served before dinner, in the Big Room. Lynn, who had changed her T-shirt for a lace-trimmed calico shirtwaist, which she wore with black jeans, carried in my tray of crudités and a turquoise Fiesta ware platter of smoked trout garnished not at all cleverly with lemon. Nonetheless, the yellow wedges against the plate's blue glaze pleased me.

Mac and his raven-haired assistant, Clare, joined the party late. They had not changed, and the knees of their jeans were mud-stained. There was also a younger man with a waxed mustache who wore a black silk bandanna around his neck. He had brought along his guitar and his wife. His name was Cass and he'd been invited to sing cowboys songs after dinner.

Despite my failures in concentration, the roast turned out well enough. Trudi, flushed from cocktails, was pleased. There were more smiles than conversation, but they all cleaned their plates at least once. There were no sirens, no red lights spinning through the windows and around the room's clean, bare walls. Lynn and Clare helped clear, then fed the dishes into the commercial machine. It had a smaller capacity than home dishwashers, but ran a load in five minutes.

We were waiting for the scalded dishes to cool enough to handle when the phone rang. The three of us looked at each other. It rang again. I plucked it off the wall.

"J-E," I said.

An abrupt voice barked, "Sheriff Becker here."

"Just a moment please, Sheriff." I nodded at Lynn, and she sprang lightly through the swinging door. "Dave Fife has been trying to reach you."

A moment later, I heard Dave's footsteps in the hallway. When his voice came on the line, I hung up. "I'll finish up," I told Clare. I put away the plates, loaded my pots, and bundled up the garbage. There was no sign of Hil, though I'd saved a heaping plate for him in the warming oven. According to Trudi, I was supposed to feed him in the kitchen. (Pick and Bobby, who lived in town, went home for dinner.) In return for his supper, Hil was supposed to help out with the dirty dishes, then make an evening run to the Dumpster.

Maybe he was sleeping it off. I scraped his plate into the garbage, cringing at the waste, and left the bag inside the door. I didn't know if the Front had raccoons and rats, as D.C. did, but I'd already seen enough of what bears could do. I slipped into the Big Room.

The fire in the baronial stone fireplace sent humpy shadows up the high log walls and lit the glass eyes of the animal heads. Cass stood on the hearth singing something Hank Snowish to chords strummed on his guitar. His hip lifted as he tapped time with the heel of his boot. I moved to the makeshift bar, a card table covered with a cross-stitched cloth. The Japanese were drinking scotch—if the level of the J&B bottle was any indication. I poured myself a nice fat bourbon.

The guests were sitting with Trudi, their hostess, all squashed together on the long sofa that faced the fire. Trudi looked a little stiff, as if she could have used some elbow room, but the men relaxed against each other, swaying to the guitar, their after-dinner glasses of whiskey firmly in hand. The two older men wore dark business suits, white shirts, and smoothly gartered socks with black Italian shoes. The stockier one, with thick receding silver hair and a round face, sported a string tie whose silver-and-turquoise bola sat neatly, if incongruously, between the wings of his French collar. He was Mr. Yamaguchi, the senior member of the group and the head of NVI's foreign investments. His first name was Mitsuhide, but the Fifes were playing it safe with "Mr. Yamaguchi." The other older man, Mr. Tanaka, was Yamaguchi's "secretary"—though he looked more like a secretary of state than a clerk/typist. He was thin and elegant-looking, with large thin-rimmed glasses, and wore a discreet paisley silk tie with his serge suit.

The younger two, both in their thirties, were more casually dressed. The group's arranger and chief translator had gone all out and was wearing jeans and boots with a brilliantly striped Western shirt. The shirt still had the store's creases in it, but his jeans and boots looked well worn. He had spent two years in Philadelphia, where he had acquired an M.B.A. from Wharton and the nickname Sam. His colleague in NVI's finance department was going by Kaz—an Americanization of Kazuhiro, his first name. Kaz's black hair stood straight up on top like a soft, overlong crew cut. He looked like a golfer, in pleated slacks and an apricot knit shirt under a designer windbreaker.

The family sat spread out around them in the Big Room. Dave, back from his phone call, sat in a large stuffed chair. Lynn perched on its arm. She slumped against her father like an affectionate puppy seeking reassurance. Clare and the singer's wife took either end of a side sofa. Mac straddled a cowhide footstool, drinking a beer from its brown bottle. His dark eyes latched onto mine. With some effort, I looked away.

Cass segued into John Denver's "Country Road," and the Japanese grinned and chattered a little, then burst into song. After their own fashion, they knew the words. Trudi and Lynn added their soprano. Their faces glowed in the firelight, and when the song was finished, everyone clapped and laughed.

Maybe it will be okay, I thought. They were a nice, hardworking family. Maybe the thing lying out there in the dark had nothing to do with them. I took a sip of bourbon. Let it be okay, I petitioned.

Chapter Five

Ed Becker had been sheriff in Teton County for fifteen years, and during that time there had been only one homicide: a domestic case in which a wife shot her husband—justifiably, in the eyes of the court. So by city standards, Sheriff Becker's experience in murder was nonexistent. His department was small (six men) and his jurisdiction comparatively large (some 2,389 square miles). Yet despite the miles, in rural communities news of disaster spreads far faster than it does in the city, where everyone prefers *not* to know what is going on down the street.

Friday night, while we sang around the fireplace, Sheriff Becker heard Dave out on the phone and concluded that until they knew what they had on their hands, there was nothing to be gained by getting folks all stirred up. Nosir. He appreciated Dave's situation and would impress upon his people the importance of holding their tongues. At the same time, Becker was determined to go by the book. He told Dave he'd send a couple of the boys out to secure the body. He himself had just come in to get cleaned up—he still had to notify a dead boy's momma. It didn't rain, it poured. He'd be out there first light. No, he didn't need to talk to Dave's foreigners, not right off, anyhow. But he'd need a statement from the gal who found it.

At five-thirty the next morning, I gave Dave a thermos of coffee and a bag of sandwiches to take to the men who had spent the night sitting in their truck back in the canyon guarding the victim's remains. It seemed a futile, belated action. Mac, who was worried about the combo of armed deputies and hungry grizzlies, had objected strongly. Dave, however, insisted that he wasn't going to tell Becker his business.

Hil showed up in the kitchen at six to collect the garbage of the night before. His black hair had grooves from his comb and his faded flannel shirt was clean, but the whites of his eyes were startlingly red—they looked as if they might glow in the dark. He ate his stack of pancakes (topped with two fried eggs and half a cup of syrup) standing by the kitchen sink. If he had a hangover, it had no effect on his appetite.

As per Trudi's order of the day, the men from NVI paraded into the staff dining room at exactly seven o'clock. Like Secret Service agents securing a president's path, the younger men cleared the way for their silver-haired boss, Mr. Yamaguchi. We were ready for them. The frozen OJ was cold and the coffee hot.

"Good morning," Trudi greeted cheerily.

Dave looked them over. "Pretty spiffy," he approved.

They were outfitted in new prewashed designer jeans, belts with gleaming silver buckles, and new canvas bush shirts in bright solids and stripes. Kaz, the one whose black hair stood up like brush, was sporting ostrich-skin boots, but the others' new boots were plain enough for the Brooks Brothers crowd: the toes were rounded, the stitching subdued. They didn't look all that different from the old fifty-dollar pair I had in my duffel upstairs. Except mine were bigger.

"At home on the range, huh?" Sam joked, presenting his compatriots with a sweep of the arm, as if he were personally responsible for their transformation into cowboys.

"Very nice," Trudi said, indicating their clothes.

"Thank you, thank you," they said, acknowledging her compliment with good humor.

Sam and Kaz hovered around Mr. Yamaguchi, pulling out his chair for him and all but unfolding his napkin. In his magenta shirt, with his silver hair and round face, Mr. Yamaguchi might have been taken for a Native American chief. Following their lead, I poured his coffee first.

"Would anyone like oatmeal this morning?" I asked the table.

"Oatmeal?" Trudi repeated half a decibel louder. "Porridge?" she tried.

The men discussed it in Japanese. "For tomorrow morning, please?" Mr. Yamaguchi suggested.

"Fine," I agreed.

There was more discussion in Japanese. Sam offered that Mr. Yamaguchi had eaten oatmeal on a trip to Scotland.

"You've been to Scotland?" Trudi asked him.

"On a fishing trip," Sam answered. Mr. Yamaguchi nodded vigorously, then mimed a cast.

Dave perked up. "You like to fish?" he asked.

Mr. Yamaguchi did indeed like to fish. Dave proposed an expedition, and Mr. Yamaguchi accepted. Sam and Kaz looked worried. They whipped out their schedules. Dave waved the printouts away. "We'll work it out," he said firmly. He and Mr. Yamaguchi smiled at each other. The rest of the meal was spent in a linguistic struggle over the subject of native cutthroat trout.

Trudi's Holy Saturday schedule included a morning ride back into the canyon up a trail where, as she promised in pamphlet prose, "we will share the beauty of the wilderness with mule and white-tailed deer and perhaps be treated to glimpses of a golden eagle or bighorn sheep." But to keep the Japanese out of the sheriff's direction, Dave announced a horseback tour of the cattle operation. After breakfast, he and Trudi took the guests down to the corral to get fitted for saddles. Lynn went off with fresh towels and a mop to do up their cabins. Hil stuck a lump of tobacco in his cheek, wrapped a cook's apron around his narrow hips, and cleared the table.

"I'll take care of the dishes," I told him. I wanted the kitchen to myself. His presence made me uncomfortable. If I'd cast him as a rescuer the afternoon before, endowed him with the sharp, inarticulate glamour of a hawk, this morning he was merely sour.

"It's my job," he said. In the dishwashing pantry off the kitchen, he banged and clattered the plates and flatware, announcing his discontent, if not the cause of it. During a momentary lull, I heard him hawk and spit. My stomach turned. Exactly *where* was he spitting? The machine started up with a grinding noise, then coasted into a loud, continuous grumble. Detergent-scented steam seeped into the kitchen. Hil came out of the pantry and settled in against the island counter, watching my movements like a barracuda monitoring a snorkeler.

"You done?" I asked.

"I'm supposed to wait on the sherf."

I went into the Big Room to try my mother on the phone. The recorded message hadn't changed. "It's Lee again, Mom," I said after the ding. "Hope everything's okay."

Back in the kitchen, the only part of Hil that had budged was his eyelids: they had lowered a fraction. Like a captive raptor, he made it hard to tell how alert he was. I poured myself a fourth cup of coffee and took it into the dining room. It felt good to sit down. I started plotting dinner. Trudi had managed to find a salmon that looked every bit as impressive as her roast.

At nine-fifteen, Sheriff Becker banged at the back door. I let him in. He stepped across the threshold, politely holding his white Stetson over his midriff. He was a man of medium height with a determinedly trim build. His seamed face was weather-beaten, but his sizable bald spot was as pink and vulnerable-looking as a baby's bottom. He made no attempt at a comb-over; the remaining band of iron-colored hair had been clipped short. There was a military preciseness about him. It was not only the haircut. His uniform, a cotton-poly twill, looked as if it had been starched. There were knife-sharp creases in the short sleeves and also along the legs of his trousers. His badge twinkled in the kitchen light.

He told me he was just about finished up there and would Hil and I mind retracing our footsteps with him. No problem, I said. Then I realized Hil was gone. I checked the pantries, the hallway, the office off it, and gave up. It was Becker's problem, not mine. I ducked into my bedroom, pulled a sweater over my T-shirt, and grabbed my vest. The sheriff wasn't wearing a jacket. Clearly he thought it was spring.

"I can't find Hil," I told him. "He knew you were coming. I don't know where he went."

Becker let out a small puff of contempt. "Métis." (*Metee,* he pronounced it.)

"What?"

"Métis. Half-breeds." He shook his head. "Old-timers like Olwyn Fife swore they were the best trackers around, but—" He broke off and gave a skeptical shrug.

"Half what?"

"Cree and French, mostly. Used to be a whole tribe of them, came down out of Canada with the Canadian army at their heels. They went 'agin the government,' and a bunch of them ended up hiding out along the Front. Never set foot in town—afraid the Mounties would get them and take them back to hang."

"When was this?"

Ed Becker shook his head. "You got me there. Sometime in the last century, I reckon. All I know is, the few of them left around here ain't worth a damn." He glanced at his watch, black-faced with fluorescent green numbers and an expandable steel band. "You ready?" he asked politely.

The weather hadn't improved overnight. There was the same flat, gray light, the same stinging wind, a bit colder perhaps. At the end of the road, most of the snow had melted under the tires of official vehicles. We ambled casually through the woods. In addition to his sidearm, Becker carried shotgun, but there was none of the tension of yesterday when Pick and Bobby, tracking my footsteps in a half-crouch, had led the way in.

Three Teton County deputies rustled slowly around the perimeter of the clearing, still searching for severed parts. The body to which they had belonged was gone. It had been photographed from every angle on both Polaroid and 35mm film. Then, under the supervision of a state medical examiner from Missoula, the deputies had pulled on rubber gloves and maneuvered the remains out of the muck into a special zippered bag. It was the kind of unattractive job that, in some societies, turns the people who do it into "untouchables." In ours, after a real stinker we feel kindly toward those who clean up, and, for a day or so at least, we don't complain about local taxes.

In any case, what was left of the victim had been driven off to Missoula in a state van. The clearing was now defined with yellow crime-scene tape. Someone had stretched it from tree to tree, wrapping it around slender trunks, as if to corral a herd of clues. A blue tarp had been anchored with rocks over the place where the body had lain. The Crayola colors, the bright blue, the sunshine yellow, were reassuring. There was a certain innocence about these pieces of plastic. I wanted to believe that they could erase whatever evil they outlined.

Becker called for one of the deputies to bring the camera. We ducked under the tape. While the deputy filmed, I showed where I had stood at various times, where Pick and Bobby and Hil had stood. We moved from spot to spot, and now and again I caught the stink of something dead. Becker seemed not to notice. Had the deputies left scraps under the tarp? Given the condition of the body, it might have been hard to avoid.

Becker was patient and thorough. I could imagine him listening attentively to a woman go on about her cat or jawing with the boys down at the feed store. His listening skills probably kept him in office. But out here, at the scene of no one knew exactly what, his eyes were distracted. They kept scanning the woods around us.

I asked him about the autopsy. His voice was grim. "The doc's talking about doing it first thing Monday. But the lab work takes time. We may not have a full report till sometime next week—next month, if they do a genetic fingerprint."

A rustling in the woods made all three of us turn. Becker and his camera-toting deputy looked at each other. "Russell?" called the sheriff. "Sonny?"

"I think they're back behind us, Sheriff," the deputy said.

The rustling was persistent. Whatever was moving through the woods, it was definitely coming our way, and at a good clip. Becker raised his shotgun. The deputy and I stepped back.

"Keep together," the sheriff ordered. "Who's that?" he called again. He settled his cheek against the stock of his gun.

"He-ey," someone called.

Becker raised his head and lowered his gun. A man was climbing up out of a ravine on the far side of the clearing. He waved. "Hey, Sheriff." He ducked under the yellow tape and walked over with an energetic spring in his step. He was young, late twenties maybe, wearing hiking boots, jeans, and a gray shirt.

"You could have got yourself shot, son," Becker said.

"Sorry, Sheriff," he said. "Mac said I could find you up here." On the sleeve of his shirt there was a machine-embroidered patch. I squinted and made out the words: "Fish and Wildlife."

Becker was still annoyed. "You almost bought yourself a pine box," he said.

Fish and Wildlife's eyes were friendly. "Y'know, you can't buy a plain pine box these days?" he asked conversationally. "They make 'em out of particle board. Leastwise the cheap ones."

Becker gave a curt nod, as if the young man had just buried someone cheaply. Then he said, "This here's Lee Squires. She's the one who found it."

"Walt Surrey," he said. He was hatless, and his auburn hair, longish and in need of a wash, curled above his shirt collar. He had the kind of milky white skin you see in portraits of Renaissance youth. What saved him from being pretty was a pair of severe black eyebrows set like hyphens over his eyes.

I asked, "You're working on the killing, too?"

"That's the sheriff's department. Fish and Wildlife investigates bears."

He turned to Becker. "Looks like a male and female. We took measurements of the prints, and Mac is over at his place running them through the computer. I'll pick up some scat samples to take back with me, but I can tell you right now they've been eating meat. The scat is black and loose."

Becker wasn't interested. "Didn't see your truck," he said to Walt Surrey. He still sounded annoyed.

"Came up the other way."

"Sheriff!" a voice called from the woods. "Over here!"

Becker and his deputy strode off. I'm ready to go now, I thought. "How did you come in?" I asked Surrey.

"There's an old logging road just below here, this side of the creek."

"So whoever was up here wouldn't have had to drive past the lodge?"

"No, ma'am, you took a long cut. My truck's parked not two hundred feet from here. The killer could've driven in with no one the wiser."

"Or killers."

Surrey nodded.

"Is it marked on the map, the logging road?"

"No, ma'am," Surrey answered.

"Then they'd have to have known where it was. I mean, would they end up here by accident?"

Walt Surrey considered it. "Well," he objected, "any local hiker or hunter could know it. And anyone involved in the census."

"What census?"

"The Eastern Front grizzly bear census. It's Mac Fife's baby. He got it off the ground, a ten-year study involving Fish and Wildlife and private landowners along the Front—the J-E, the Pine Butte Preserve, the Boone and Crockett people, a bunch of others. The goal is to develop a method of identifying every individual bear in our study area. That way we can have an accurate population count to work with. If we can find out how often young are being born, if we can document litter size, survival rate, and so on, then we can determine whether the reproductive rate is healthy or not."

"And if it isn't?"

He gave me an ironic look. "Then we'll have the scientific data to prove that we're wiping out the species."

"I take it you don't knock on den doors for this census?" I asked.

Obligingly, Surrey looked amused. "We use cameras and carcasses." He raised his head slightly, as if sniffing. "Smell that?"

"It's not leftovers?"

"It's a ripe horse. We've got a feeding station down in the draw there. We bring in the carcass and set up heat-activated cameras. Mac's developing the film we had on the horse. Between that and the prints here, we should be able to identify which bears were involved here."

The sheriff walked back to us alone and unarmed, carrying a small plastic bag in his right hand. "Found a shell," he announced. His voice was almost cheerful. He took out a pair of half-frames from a case in his breast pocket. The case was made of tooled leather, its edges whipped together with beige plastic cord. A grandchild might have made it on a rainy day at 4-H camp. Becker put on his glasses and read the bottom of the cartridge casing through the plastic bag.

"A .338," he said. He held up the bag so we could admire it. The brass was still bright enough to catch the light. It looked big enough to stop an elephant.

"Any others?" Surrey asked.

"Just the one. So far. We're not done yet." He rolled the plastic bag around the cartridge casing and slipped the packet into his breast pocket. "So," he said to Walt Surrey, "you think we got a couple of rogue bears involved here?"

"No sir," Surrey said firmly. "The bears were minding their own business. That body was just carrion. If it hadn't been so close to the horse, I doubt there'd be as much of it left as there was. I'm guessing they had their fill at the horse, so they weren't all that interested in what they found up here. Rolled it around a bit, but from what I saw, it looked like coyotes did more damage. Next to whoever used the knife."

The sheriff's face remained expressionless.

"The horse was there when it happened?" I asked.

"Looks that way."

"How long has it been there?"

"About a month. Mac brought it in on a lift at the end of March. I'd have to check for the exact date."

"What if the killer or killers used the logging road to get up here—would they be on your candid camera?"

"Not unless they went within six feet on either side of it." He turned to Becker. "If something shows up on the film, we'll send it over."

Becker nodded.

"Are you a warden?" I asked Surrey.

"A biologist," he said. "I started out with the Forest Service, but I didn't much like the way they did things there. I've been with Fish and Wildlife for the last two years."

"How long has your census study been going on?"

"Mac got the funding last spring. We started with five cameras. This year we added another five."

"You keep the same sites? I mean, how long have you been using this one?"

"Just since March. We don't use the same station twice. The idea is to count the bears, not feed them. We don't want to set up a new series of boneyards. It's hard enough getting people to close their old ones."

"A *boneyard?*"

"A dump for dead animals," Surrey explained. "Every winter, ranchers lose some of their stock, especially during calving. They used to dump the carcasses in an open pit. Now they call us and we distribute them at various remote sites. Back when the buffalo were still around, the grizzlies would come out on the plains to feed on the herd's winterkill. That's the model we're using."

The sheriff shook his head. "A lot of trouble for nothing," he grumbled. "We've gotten along just fine for millions of years without the dinosaurs. I'll bet we can do just fine without grizzly bears."

Surrey nodded sagely. "A lot of folks feel that way."

The sheriff let out a small grunt of satisfaction.

Walt Surrey's job may have been bear management, but he wasn't half bad with people. Then it occurred to me that human beings were part of the ecosystem, too. Elementary, my dear Squires.

Chapter Six

I came back from the woods, stirred my Senate bean soup for lunch, and went into the Big Room to try my mother again. It was about eleven o'clock in Montana, one in the afternoon in D.C. The telephone desk in the Big Room was gone and the rotary phone sat on the floor. While I'd been out with the sheriff, Hil and Dave's cattle manager, a man named Roy whom I had yet to meet, had moved half the furniture and rugs out of the Big Room, leaving an open expanse of scuffed floorboards. Trudi had decided to entertain the Japanese with a Saturday-night dance. In addition to an assortment of neighbors, she had invited a caller/DJ and his boom box.

I squatted under the window and dialed my mother's number. The line was busy. A good sign. I stood up and browsed along the bookcases under the minstrel gallery. Most of the books were hardbacks in their jackets. There were some duplicates, though not together on the shelves. The J-E's guests had left behind a haphazard library of best-sellers.

The sharp click of the front door unlatching made me start. A woman's voice called out, "Hello? Hello, Mac?" I relaxed. It was not a knife-wielding psychopath. It was someone who knew Mac. "Yoo-hoo! Is anyone home?" the voice insisted loudly. I went out into the hallway.

"Oh," she said. The woman was carrying a trench coat, a squashy silvery nylon overnight bag, and an expensive-looking briefcase made of "British tan" calfskin. She was wearing a black knit tunic, black knit leggings, and what looked like black combat boots. She also wore large purple plastic hoops in her earlobes, and her carrot-colored hair was in an aggressive Colette-type frizz. She didn't look very Montana, but for all I knew, she could have been the Front's version of the girl next door all dressed up for the dance.

"I'm Monica," she announced as if she expected me to know who she was. She gave me a big smile. It matched her big hair: both had thrust.

"Lee Squires," I said.

She kept her smile turned on. "Monica Leeds," she added helpfully, as she advanced into the hallway.

"Sorry," I said. "I'm new on the block."

She deposited her coat and bags on a bench. "I'm the one who did the *New York Times* piece on Mac. Is he around? I tried over at his institute, but no one was there. He wasn't in his trailer, either. Something's come up. I've got to talk to him." There was an excitement in her voice, and an authority. She looked about thirty: confident, fashionable, and about as stoppable as a tank—

not that there was anything tanklike about her body. She was slim under her supple black knits, with high, tidy breasts. Her figure was prettier than her face, which was long and had a horsey quality—perhaps it was all those square teeth when she smiled. "It really is crucial," she pleaded.

"I don't know where Mac is, but Dave and Trudi will be back at lunchtime."

"Now tell me who they are," she asked. Her voice was easily chummy, as if I were an old friend and confidante.

"Dave Fife is Mac's brother."

"Oh, of course."

"You want me to call down to the farm office? Maybe someone there knows where he is."

"Listen, that would be great. If you don't mind?" she asked, suddenly humble.

"Not at all," I said formally. I felt as stiff as a butler.

I went into Trudi's office, which was off the corridor to my bedroom. The walls were paneled in pine and hung with colored photographs of Lynn and Trudi and Dave's two older daughters. There was also a poster-sized calendar that looked as if it might have been ordered from the Museum of Modern Art catalog, and, over a tweed recliner, a framed Bev Dolittle print of piebald Indian ponies in the snow. Two desks, one with a computer, the other with a fax machine, sat under the windows that overlooked the back courtyard. I found the number for the farm office on a card taped to the desk. I dialed, and the phone rang once. "J-E Cattle Company," answered a woman. Her voice was startlingly vampish.

"Uh, this is Lee Squires—the cook up at the lodge," I said. "I'm trying to find Mac Fife. There's someone here to see him."

A giggle made me suspicious. "Who's this?" I demanded.

"Lee?"

"Lynn? What are you doing there?"

"Checking out the new calves. Are we talking *cute*? You should come down and see them!"

"Do you know where Mac is? Some reporter's showed up."

"Oh-oh," she said, her voice serious. "Dad's not going to be happy. Can't you get rid of him?"

"Her. I doubt it. See if you can find Mac, will you? Tell him *The New York Times* wants him."

I went back into the Big Room and found Monica Leeds reading the guest book. It sat on a massive table that usually stood in the center of the room but had been pushed against a wall and barricaded by a bank of sofas. Monica sat astride one of the sofa backs, flipping through the pages. "Nils Westfield," she said to me. *"The* Nils Westfield, the guy who wrote that book on Vietnam?"

It was. My brother had met him here last year. "I don't know," I told Monica.

"He won a Pulitzer for that book." There was awe in her voice.

"Mac should be along shortly," I announced. "You can wait here for him."

She snapped the guest book shut, tucked it under her arm, swung a black knit leg over the back of the sofa, and dismounted. Her combat boots made an emphatic thud on the wooden floor. "So," she said cheerfully, "tell me about this body someone found. Was it you, by any chance?"

"You'll have to excuse me," I said. I walked into the hallway, past the stairway, through the swinging pantry door. She followed me into the kitchen. I could feel my face getting hot. (How many times have I wished for thicker, darker skin!) I turned to confront her.

"It was you, wasn't it?" She smiled as if I had done something cute.

I indicated the book under her arm. "I don't believe that's for public consumption."

"Oh," she said airily, "what's-her-name won't mind. What *is* her name?"

"Trudi Fife."

"I'm just going to copy out a few names and addresses."

I thought about it for a moment. Then I nodded. "Did you find Michael Jackson?"

"He came *here?"*

I have to give her credit. Michael Jackson at the J-E was a real stretch. "Came with a bunch of bodyguards. Never took off his white gloves. I think it was two years ago. Here, I'll find it for you." I held out my hand.

She gave me the guest book.

"Thanks," I said. I tucked it under my arm. We stood facing each other across the island counter of stainless steel. I noticed that Monica Leeds plucked her eyebrows. Beneath her balloon of orange hair, they were thin, 1920-ish arcs. They emphasized the look of surprise on her long face. Then she laughed. "Where did they find you?" she asked.

"A stork brought me."

"Yeah, like a big silver one maybe. You aren't local."

"I'm the cook. I really do have to get to work." Standing on tiptoe, I slid the guest book between yellowware bowls on a top shelf. "Have a seat." I gestured to a stool, but she wouldn't sit down. She dogged my steps to and from the refrigerator, the pantry, the ovens, asking questions nonstop—despite the fact that I didn't answer any of them. She was not offended. She seemed propelled by kinetic excitement. When Mac came in the back door, she jumped at him with a yelp like a delighted hound dog.

"Monica," Mac said. "Well, well."

They grinned at each other.

"Dare I ask what brings you out this way?" he said.

"Not your shitty Montana weather, I can tell you that. I could be in the Bahamas." She let out a mock sigh.

"But you aren't."

"No. I got an assignment from *Vanity Fair,* interviewing Jane and Ted."

He waited.

"Turner's busy dozing off the top of a mountain that blocks the view from his porch. You glad to see me?" she asked. Her expression was coy. It was unbecoming.

I moved away into the baker's pantry, punched down a roll of dough, and began forming it into small balls. The old marble slab set into the wooden countertop felt cool and soothing.

"What do you want?" I heard Mac say bluntly.

Her voice changed. She was serious, professional. "I heard somebody butchered somebody back in your woods."

There was a silence. Then Mac said pleasantly, "That's not true. What's your source?"

Silence.

"Somebody's mixed up," Mac told her. "Remember that story last year about how wolves killed two skiers? Turned out the dispatcher said 'two steers'?"

"No one's garbled this. My information is good. I've got direct confirmation from, shall we say, official-but-not-for-attribution sources. I'm going to cover this, Mac, one way or another, so you might as well lie back and enjoy it."

Silence.

Monica let out a little snort. "Unfortunate phrasing. Look, trust me. I'm not going to fuck you. The *Times* piece was virtually a puff. I'm on your team—in case you've forgotten. And I'm not budging from here until you talk to me."

I kept on rolling dough balls. The marble was pale gray and blurry, its veins obscured by years of scrubbing and bleach.

"Believe it," Monica said. "You'll have to call the sheriff to get rid of me, and I promise you, I'll have the story out of him before we're halfway to Choteau."

"I'll bet you will," Mac said bitterly.

"Jealous?" Her voice was amused.

I picked up a greased muffin tin from the wooden section of the counter, held it half an inch over the marble, and let it drop. It landed with a metallic ring. The conversation out in the kitchen stopped. Maybe they were miming and pointing in my direction. I hoped so. I started putting my dough balls in the tin, three to a cup.

"We've got a group of visitors," Mac resumed. It sounded half-objection, half-plea.

"Yes?" she prompted.

Don't, I urged silently. But he did. He told her about the men from NVI. "We're wooing their support for the Sacred Paw Institute" was how he put it. He also told her about the body I'd found and the cartridge casing the sheriff's men had found. "But right now, we don't even know if the guy was shot," he said. He also told her that the Japanese did not know about the death.

"And you'd prefer they didn't know," Monica stated.

"Talking to them's like being lost in a mine field. We don't need a bomb as well."

"Nice," Monica said appreciatively.

"Jesus, put that away. This is all off the record. Deep background."

"I like it."

"Like what?"

"The Jap angle."

"You are not going to use any of this, not one word, until they've gone."

"Okay," she agreed. There was a pause. "It's okay," she coaxed. "I promise. Cross my heart and hope to die, swear to God on a stack of Bibles, Korans, whatever you want."

Mac's voice was hard. "Don't blow this deal on me, Monica," he said.

"Mac. Listen to this." A bubble of excitement surfaced in her voice. "I talked to my agent this morning, just before I left Bozeman. I said I thought there was a big story out here, don't twitch, I didn't say anything, I just said it involved you. And she said she could sell a book on you."

"A book?"

"She's with a top agency. She knows the markets. She says the wilderness is warming up. Let me hang around, take a few notes, do a discreet Boswell number, see what develops with your corpse."

"You *discreet?*"

"If it leaks, don't look at me. You think I want to jump-start someone like Calvin Trillin into action? *I* want to be the one to write it for *The New Yorker*. But you aren't going to be able to fend off the local press for long. Not after the autopsy, anyway."

"There's a dance here tonight for the Japanese." Mac sounded dubious.

"Baby doll, I love to dance!"

"This is country dancing, Monica."

"Hey. Do-si-do and away we go!" The floorboards in the pantry shook. Her footwork sounded like a platoon on the run.

"Lee," Mac bellowed over the racket.

I took my time. I plopped the last balls into the tin, covered them with a floured tea towel, and wiped my hands on my apron. The stomping stopped.

"Lee?" Mac called.

I carried my tray into the kitchen. "Yes?" I said sweetly. I set the rolls to rise on the back of the range. Monica moved out of my way. She was flushed and slightly out of breath after her demo. I was willing to bet she wouldn't make it all the way through a Virginia reel.

"Monica's going to stay over for the dance. She'll be here for dinner."

"No problem," I said. Stiff smiles all around. "What about lunch?"

"Clare will get us something at the trailer. Tell Trudi, will you?" Mac instructed. "Get her to make up one of the cabins with a desk. Monica's going to write a book about me." He didn't exactly strut. It was more a matter of buoyancy, as if he were keeping the lid on his pleasure and it had puffed him up.

"Have laptop, will travel," Monica said brightly.

"Come on," he said. His boyish vitality had returned, and along with it, his magnetism. He was back in control again. He shepherded Monica toward the door. I felt a pang of abandonment. "Clare will be glad to see you," he told Monica.

I'll bet, I thought.

Dave and Trudi strode into the kitchen after their ride looking anxious. "What'd the sheriff say?" they demanded in unison.

"Nothing new." I broke the news about Monica. They ushered me out of the kitchen, down the hall into Trudi's office, and shut the door. Trudi went to the coffee-maker and poured two mugs. "Coffee?" she offered. I shook my head. I was still feeling a high-octane jag from my morning dose. Caffeine was clearly the fuel of choice behind scenes at the J-E. Even the most inept wicked witch could drop the entire ranch into a hundred-year sleep by substituting decaf.

"Monica Leeds," Dave said. "I don't believe it. As if a dead body wasn't enough. Now we've got her snooping around."

Trudi let out an angry snort. "If your brother tipped her off . . ." she threatened.

Dave said nothing.

"Why'd you let her in?" Trudi demanded of me.

"I didn't. She let herself in."

They stared at their mugs.

"What was the article like?" I asked. "When did it come out? I didn't see it."

"Last fall," Dave said wearily. "She's a clever writer." He shrugged. "The article served its purpose."

"Mac ate it up," Trudi said with disgust. "But she used Dave's quotes and put them into Mac's mouth. I guess you could call it creative journalism."

"She doesn't let facts get in her way," Dave agreed.

"She says she's going to do a book on Mac," I told them.

It was like watching a stop-action sequence of unfolding flowers: slowly, wordlessly, the two of them seemed to bloom. Their shoulders dropped a degree. The corners of their mouths softened. Perhaps like Mac, they were seduced by the notion of a book. I remembered the alienated hero of Walker Percy's *The Moviegoer* who argues that only when one's hometown is seen in the movies does it become real. In the same way, perhaps "being in a book" confirms one's existence. And who doesn't need a little confirmation from time to time?

On the other hand, the Fifes' acceptance of Monica's intrusion might simply be a manifestation of the kind of stoic fatalism common to farmers and ranchers. Sometimes hailstorms wreck your corn. Sometimes brucellosis destroys your herd. There was no point in moaning and groaning about it. At least the invasion of the press offered the hope of damage control.

"She goes in with you," Trudi decided.

"What do you mean?"

"I'm not going to have her upstairs sharing a bathroom with the three of us. She can have the other bed in your room. I'll get you the linen and she can make it up."

"No," I told Trudi.

"Pardon?"

"No. You can't put her in with me. She takes up too much space. I need my privacy. Write it off to my artistic temperament, but no way."

They said nothing. Their faces hardened again into a stone wall.

"I'll throw a snit fit if it'll make it easier for you."

"This I gotta see," Dave said.

"Put her in one of the cabins," I suggested.

Trudi shook her head. "They aren't ready. The water's off. Besides, I don't want her snooping around the Japanese for bits of color like what brand of toothpaste they use. What if they catch her peeping in their windows?"

"Maybe they'll be titillated. A tale to tell over sake with the boys."

"It's just for one night," Trudi said.

"No."

"We need you to keep an eye on her," Dave said.

"Sorry, friends," I said. "Not in the contract." I glanced at my watch. "Speaking of which, lunch will be ready in twenty minutes."

CHAPTER SEVEN

Cowboys exude a mythic aura in our culture, but the cows that keep them in business do not. Few tourists in search of the "real" American West have any interest in seeing cows, but the Fifes' visitors were an exception. All during lunch, the Japanese visitors chatted with Dave about his crossbred herd of Black Angus/Hereford. While I had spent the morning learning about counting bears, they had happily counted calves.

At the J-E, from the end of February to mid-April, some four hundred cows had "dropped" their calves. (Apparently, calves are not "born" on ranches; they "drop"—like manna from heaven.) The Japanese had inspected Dave's windfall—from their velvety pink noses to their encrusted tails—and had been duly impressed. Despite their awkward English, they seemed to have no problem grasping the mathematical intricacies of Dave's computerized breeding program.

After the guests departed to their cabins for naps, Dave and Trudi and Lynn lingered in the kitchen.

"They sure've done their homework," Dave commented.

"And not just math, either," Trudi added. She stretched her jaw, as if she'd been smiling too hard. "They all took riding lessons before they came. But get this: they say they learned on electric horses. There's not enough space in Tokyo for real horses, so they go to a special studio where they saddle up robot horses and trot in place. They even have computer-coordinated videos so they can plug into trails around the world."

"No way," Lynn said.

"That's what they said. At least, I *think* that's what they said. They can't get over all the space here," she told us. "They keep wanting to know where all the people are. Did you know the average Japanese family lives in a space smaller than our kitchen? How many square feet did he say?" she asked Dave.

"Two hundred and eighty-two."

We shook our heads in disbelief.

"So what did Becker have to say?" Trudi asked.

I filled them in on my morning while Dave absent-mindedly polished off the leftover cornbread I'd made to go with the soup. I'd been counting on a piece for my own lunch.

At three, Dave picked up his guests in his Blazer for a tour of Mac's turf. Trudi, in her mother-hen mode, sent me along. "You need a break," she clucked. "Besides, with Mac, the more the merrier. He likes an audience." I didn't protest.

Dave drove down past the corrals, bumped over the cattle

guard at the front gate, and turned north on the gravel road I'd driven in on. Mr. Yamaguchi and Sam were in front with Dave. I sat in the backseat between Mr. Tanaka and Kaz. We nodded and smiled at each other. Mr. Tanaka smelled of cologne under his new Stetson. "Did you have a good ride this morning?" I asked them.

"Like *City Slickers,*" Kaz said with a grin. "We are Billy Crystal! We refresh ourselves from the stresses of work."

Mr. Tanaka smiled in agreement.

In the space between Dave's and Mr. Yamaguchi's heads, I could make out Ear Mountain through the windshield. My memory of it was summertime: as a twelve-year-old, I'd seen the folds of its base carpeted with dark green vegetation which, from the distance, looked as soft and lush as velvet. I remembered working out an excruciating conceit about how some princeling had carelessly tossed his cape over the mountain's "roots." All very romantic in iambic tetrameter. But now I was a grown-up, supposedly, and the mountain was bare, its rocky shins exposed, its summit hidden in the low cloud ceiling. It loomed ahead of us, a bruise-colored mass rising from a fringe of black pine forest, then slid out of view as we turned at a sign I'd missed on the way in: a weathered gray board with neat, newly painted blue letters that announced, "THE SACRED PAW INSTITUTE 2.7 MI."

Mac, after inheriting his mother's land, had hauled a trailer into a stubby, thumb-shaped drainage along the southern border of the wildlife management area below Ear Mountain. There was no need to build a road—the tractor that hauled in the mobile home had impressed a serviceable two-track scar into the land's tawny crust. The place was wind-scoured and barren—no trees stood higher than my shoulder—but private. Mac had parked his trailer down in the lee of a bench. Then he dug an outhouse behind it and moved in with a tank of propane for heat, half a dozen gallon milk jugs filled with water, and a truckload of his film cans.

Ten years later, the potholes in the track had been filled with grapefruit-sized stones, the trailer had been given plumbing and skirted with plyboard, and Mac had moved his office into a new log building whose outside walls were still golden and glossy with polyurethane. From the low-slung porch, you couldn't see much of the sky—the high wall of the Front blocked most of it out—but the wind was determined. Out on the ocean, the same breeze would make one think about taking a reef in the mainsail.

Inside, however, the low ceiling and varnished pine paneling created a below-deck coziness. Pale green topographical maps and LANDSAT images in fuchsia, orange, and yellow decorated the walls. Beige "Berber" carpeting covered the floor. A Swedish wood stove heated the central open work space, where Dr. Clare Jenkins sat at one of several Japanese-made computers. She greeted us solemnly. She had changed out of her jeans for the occasion. In her crisp white shirt and calf-length navy skirt, she might have been a nun of science. As she led us through the desk area into a meeting room, her long black hair swayed against her straight back like a heavy veil. All she needed was a crucifix tapping her midriff.

The meeting room was no-frills, convincingly nonprofit. The chairs were chrome and molded plastic, and the long table had a vinyl "butcher-block" top. A coffeepot sat on a built-in pine cabinet. What drew the eye was the collection of Indian artifacts mounted along the walls: beadwork parfleches and moccasins, a feathered pipe, flint war points. These were displayed in museum-quality Plexiglas shadow frames which reverently turned them from something once used into something once crafted.

Clare took orders for coffee and served us in lumpy, ecologically correct stoneware mugs while we milled around waiting for Mac, who she said was on the phone to Belgium. I browsed along the wall, studying the collected fragments of a bygone culture. The white man had swept the Great Plains like a hundred-year hurricane, then picked up pretty pieces from the rubble: a shoe here, an antler-handled knife there. Were these pieces better saved and displayed or buried? I couldn't decide. I studied a toy-sized beaded turtle with yellow and blue diamonds on its back. It looked familiar. Somewhere I'd seen it before.

Mac made his entrance with a shopping bag. Monica came into the room behind him, but slipped off to the side. Her unobtrusiveness surprised me.

Mac welcomed the visitors with a brief we-are-honored speech. He towered over them, and when he shook hands all around, he had to stoop slightly. He presented the men with four identical packages, each handsomely wrapped in marbleized paper and tied with gilt cord. The visitors thanked Mac profusely but didn't open their gifts. They respectfully set them on the table beside their mugs of coffee.

"What'd you give them?" I asked Dave, who had drifted to the back of the room.

"Sacred Paw T-shirts," he said. "They're supposed to like T-shirts. The state guy advised us to wrap them up like they were the crown jewels. Otherwise they'd be insulted. And he told us they might not open them on the spot. Apparently *they* worry about insulting *us* by not having the right expression on their faces when they see what the gift is."

"Pretty complicated."

He gave a live-and-let-live shrug. I had the feeling that somewhere along the line, he'd learned the trick of letting worry run off his back like water off a duck's.

I indicated the beaded turtle on the wall behind us. "Dave, what's this one?"

He turned to look. "An amulet. They used them to hold a baby's umbilical cord. They'd pin it to the child's cradleboard, turtles for girls, lizards for boys. Lizards were considered tough, hard to kill."

"And turtles aren't?"

He smiled, the father of three daughters. "The turtle carried the world on her back."

Mac strode over to us. "I guess we're off on the right foot," he said to his brother. But his eyes were on me. "Glad you came," he said.

Thhh-UMP, went my heart. Stop it, I ordered. To Mac, I said, "We're talking turtles. I keep thinking I've seen this amulet before."

"You probably have. It was part of my father's collection. Do you know how he got it?"

"No," I said.

Clare and Sam drifted over like a of pair sheepdogs about to collect a stray. Mac ignored them. "There was this old Indian woman he used to go visit and talk about the old days. Mrs. Davies, her name was. She had a house outside Choteau. Anyway, one time she showed Dad this amulet, which he duly admired. It had belonged to her grandmother. When he went to go, he handed it back to her, but she said, 'No, keep it.' And he said, 'Mrs. Davies, I can't do that. This has been in your family for generations.' And she told him, 'Keep it, if you want it. I don't care about all that Indian stuff.' He said he got out of there as fast as he could, before she could change her mind!"

He smiled at Clare, as if the story had special meaning for her.

"Perhaps we should get started?" she suggested.

"Clare's Blackfeet," Mac announced.

"Oh?" I said.

For a moment, she said nothing. Her face was quiet. Not even her eyes moved. Then she said to us, "My father was full-blooded Blackfeet. But I'm not an enrolled member of the tribe." Her severe lips twitched in a ironic smile. "Mac, on the other hand, had been initiated into a tribal warrior society."

"A token white," Mac said modestly. But there was pride in his voice.

Clare explained, "His Blackfeet friends are traditionalists who want to keep the oil companies off their sacred lands. But he's also made some enemies among the rest of the tribe, who want oil money." She turned to Mac. "You going to cover Badger-Two Medicine?"

"We'll see how the time goes. I suppose we ought to get started." He turned to Sam. "I'll stop for you every paragraph or so. If I start running on too long, give me a signal."

"Excuse me?" Sam asked.

"Aren't you going to translate?"

Sam looked taken aback. "Translation is not necessary."

"It's not?"

"They understand English."

Mac looked skeptical. "I'm going to be covering some complex issues here."

There was an awkward moment of silence. Then Sam said, "It would not be polite to suggest their understanding is less than perfect."

"Jesus Christ," Mac muttered in exasperation. "So they're

going to sit there and *pretend* they understand?" he demanded. "I mean, why bother?"

Sam didn't answer. His face was bland and impenetrable, like that of a teenager hooked up to a Walkman.

"Just do it," Dave said. He hadn't raised his voice, but it was hard.

"This is the stupidest thing I ever heard!" Mac bristled. The men at the table turned their heads.

Sam looked at the floor.

"I apologize for my brother's rudeness," Dave said formally to Sam.

Sam gave an embarrassed nod, avoiding Dave's eyes.

But Mac was quick on the uptake. "Hell," he said cheerfully. "I apologize for myself." He clapped a hand on Sam's shoulder. "I didn't mean to offend." He grinned. "I'm just an ignorant paleface."

Maybe it was a line he used to good effect on the reservation. Regardless, it worked fine on Sam. He beamed back at Mac. "No problem," he said.

"Butter-stinker," Clare corrected. "An ignorant butter-stinker. That's what the Japanese called the first Europeans they saw—or I should say smelled."

Mac perked up with interest. "You still say it—'butter-stinker'?" he asked Sam.

Sam waved the epithet away. "No, no, no," he objected. "No one says it anymore."

Mac moved to the head of the table. He grinned like a naughty boy. "We've been talking about butter-stinkers," he announced. Then he paused. His audience looked slightly alarmed, but they smiled back at him. "And it occurred to me that as our diets evolve—as Japan consumes more beef and we consume more fish—we will share the same stink." The men laughed nervously and murmured to each other in their own language.

"Seriously," Mac said, commanding their attention. "The ties between this land and yours predate the arrival of Commodore Perry's black ships in Tokyo harbor. Our connection is aboriginal. Japan, as you know, was once linked by bridges of dry land to Korea and Siberia. Your Stone Age ancestors were cousins of the hunters and gatherers who walked from Asia into what is now Alaska and eventually migrated southward into the Great Plains. Then, as now, our technologies were similar." He gestured toward a display of points. Heads swiveled. "Ancient arrowheads made on both sides of the ocean are virtually indistinguishable. The same is true of harpoons and fishhooks. In fact," he continued, scanning the polite faces around the table, "our lands share a similarity that predates *Homo sapiens.* Like Japan, during the Cretaceous period, the Rocky Mountain Front had sea on both sides—the Pacific Ocean to the west, and on the eastern side, a vast inland sea that divided our continent. Are you going to visit Egg Mountain, our local dinosaur dig?" The men looked confused. Mac looked to his brother.

Dave said, "It's a possibility."

Mac turned back to his guests. "Well, back when half of eastern Montana was under water, herds of dinosaurs grazed along the shore. Today cattle graze the same land."

He paused, still trying to gauge his audience. Were their minds appropriately boggled by the juxtaposition of cows and dinosaurs? It was hard to tell. Mac plunged on. "Now, I know it was your interest in cattle that brought you here. But in the next half hour or so, I'd like to persuade you that the J-E has far more to offer than prime beef. It can offer you a pioneering role in the preservation of an American Serengeti. Together we can forge a paradigm for a truly—and I stress the word *truly*—holistic use of this section of what we like to call 'the last best place.'

"The earth is our mother," Mac continued, shifting smoothly from the didactic mode into the poetic. "When you think of the earth as mother, you walk differently on her." He gestured toward the small pair of windows at the end of the room. "The Blackfeet believe that these mountains out here are her backbone." He paused. "The Rockies are her backbone," he repeated softly, as if his words were caressing fingers.

I felt a shiver run up my own spine. I wanted to be on his team. I wanted to show him that I too loved my mother. For a nod of his approval, I'd lick a hundred thousand stamps. Well—maybe not. I became distracted trying to think exactly what I would do (and not do) to prove myself worthy. Paste his bumper sticker on my car? I was not really a bumper-sticker sort of person, even if I had a car.

I glanced across the room at Monica sitting in a folding chair, hunched over her notepad. She scribbled quietly away, completely focused on Mac and his speech.

I tuned back in. Mac had pulled a map down out of the ceiling. It showed Montana's Rockies running from the Canadian border down to the western corner of Wyoming. "Nature doesn't recognize state lines," he said. "It pays no attention to park boundaries. The earth has its own jurisdictions. Now, we are located in a jurisdiction called the Northern Continental Divide Ecosystem." He drew a hand along the upper neck of the mountains. He might have been soothing a nervous horse. Then he patted the flank, a southern patch called the Greater Yellowstone Ecosystem.

"Our mountains and meadows form a crucial linkage zone for wildlife migrations between the protected habitats of Glacier Park in the north and Yellowstone in the south. These migrations of endangered species, of the grizzly bear and the gray wolf, are essential to their preservation. For a healthy gene pool, these animals need a pristine wilderness where the biggest and the boldest members of the species can roam freely and reproduce. They need a wilderness where they can live purely, drawing on thousands of years of evolution." He tapped the map at Glacier and Yellowstone. "In parks, the big, aggressive grizzlies are the ones who don't shy away from tourists. They end up being destroyed. But without them, the grizzly will no longer be a true grizzly. Isolated and inbred, this great animal will be reduced to something we can manage: a shy, scaled-down version, a Pooh bear playing to tourists' videocams."

Mac had stopped taking fixes on the Japanese's bland faces. Now he was coasting along on his own passion. He described the grizzly as a "canary"—that environment indicator once used by miners. Of all endangered species in the lower forty-eight, he said, the grizzly was the most sensitive to impact from humans. "A stable bear population is the measure of a healthy wilderness," he declared.

"In a real wilderness," he went on earnestly, "we are not guardians, but observers. Native Americans, from Maine to Alaska, watched bears and regarded them as teachers, as guides to the year's ripenings. The black bear, the brown bear, the grizzly—they all know where to find the early spring greens. They know where the berries are, when the salmon run, and when the acorns are ripe. More amazing, the grizzly knows how to live without these foods. During the winter, he descends into the 'little death' of hibernation. His 'rebirth' in the spring is a metaphor of transfiguration that informed not only Native American spirituality, but the early mythologies of ancient Greece, of Scandinavia, of Asia. The bear knows the great secret of descent into darkness and resurrection into light."

Clare, who was sitting next to me against the wall, cleared her throat. Monica looked up expectantly.

Mac acknowledged Clare with a pleasant nod. He considered the men at the table. "My staff often accuse me of getting mystical," he confided. "They'd rather talk about 'reservoirs of information' than 'secrets.' But imagine if we could discover the bear's secrets! The bear, for example, suspends excretion during hibernation. It does not soil its den. Nor does it poison itself with its own wastes. What is the mechanism here? Is there a hormonal control that our medical doctors can use to prevent kidney failure? Some of the bear's metabolic adjustments during hibernation are far more refined than those of smaller hibernators. Who knows what gifts the bear has yet to give? Perhaps someday we will be able to hibernate through surgery—or even through prolonged space travel."

He checked his watch. "Now," he said, coming back to earth, "in a few minutes, we're going to take you out to a grizzly feeding station. This is part of the Sacred Paw's wildlife management program, which I'll explain on the way. But before we go, I'd like you to see a few slides of the creature we're talking about. Don't expect to see a grizzly during your stay here. One of the thrusts of our management program is to avoid grizzly-human contact—for the safety of both species."

It was hard to tell what the Japanese made of all this. The language dilemma reminded me of a family story about my grandmother and a new chauffeur. She'd allowed him to drive her for hours in the wrong direction because she hadn't wanted to hurt his feelings by pointing out the correct turn. Every family has stories like this, private parables pulled up from communal memory as examples of behavior to emulate or avoid. But watching the Japanese sit through Mac's speech put a new, more positive spin on the legend of my grandmother's courtesy. Perhaps something more intelligent than exquisite manners had been in play. Perhaps her patience had been an investment in her future—and a shrewd one at that. The chauffeur, a Portuguese named Alberto, remained devoted to her until she died.

In any case, Mac's slides elicited more response than his speech. In the darkened room his audience, like lovers who turn out the light, apparently felt freer to express themselves. They joked and chatted, tossed out questions via Sam or Kaz, made guttural noises of admiration and appreciation as the slides clicked and changed on the screen. There was no voice-over accompanying the images, no background score, and this gave the presentation both intimacy and immediacy. Mac's bears weren't made for TV. They were as real as a home slide show. We were separated from the grizzlies only by the length of a telephoto lens. We saw them through the eye of one person crouching below the brow of a hill. Or at least that was the illusion. Later I learned that most of the slides were stills cut from Mac's famous documentary *Bear with Us.*

The frames, of course, were stunning. There were backlit grizzlies with fur like golden fire, grizzlies wet as dogs hooking cutthroat trout out of streams, silver-brown cubs rolling in green grass, their black footpads exposed to a deep blue sky. What surprised me was the anthropomorphic quality of these pictures. There were few shots of bears on all fours. One bear sat on a rock, back to the camera, peering over its shoulder as if caught on a toilet. (This was greeted with much hilarity.) Another bear sat with one leg casually crossed over its knee, shoulders slumped like a teenager's. A pair of boars faced off, mouths open like enraged neighbors screaming across a fence. Cubs draped their chins on their sleeping mother's back, or their paws on each other's shoulders.

Evidently the "sacred paw" was more dexterous than it looked. One slide showed a sow delicately holding a branch of berries, and Mac noted that a scientist friend of his claimed to have observed a bear playing with a feather. Certainly, in Mac's collection of slides, the ursine postures were amazingly humanlike. They suggested playfulness, humor, affection, anger. Even Mac's prize sequence, a mother taking down an elk in a streambed, was oddly unbestial: the three cubs watching from the bank were as attentive as Little Leaguers watching a pro at bat.

The show didn't take long, maybe ten, fifteen minutes, and toward the end, perhaps to reemphasize mutual ties, Mac showed several slides obtained from a Japanese bear researcher in the mountainous Akita district of northern Honshu. These showed the Asian black bear, also called the "moon bear" because of the white crescent marking across its chest. Its ears were round, like mice ears, and in one snarling shot, its snout managed to look almost piglike. There was no mistaking the Japanese reaction: they greeted the moon bear with snorts of contempt, derisive hisses.

"This bear is a pest," Sam declared. "Extremely vicious. Every year, many people die from attacks."

Mr. Yamaguchi said something in a rapid, guttural staccato.

Sam translated, "Mr. Yamaguchi suggests that the situation is entirely different in Japan."

"The moon bear's death toll is high," Mac conceded. "Two or three a year. Considerably higher than the grizzly's. But your population is more dense. In either country, however, you are far more likely to get killed by lightning than by a bear attack. Human deaths are not really the issue. The conflict is basically economic. The moon bear destroys your tree plantations. The grizzly destroys livestock, especially sheep. Out here, ranchers lose around twenty sheep a year to bear activity."

"And cows?" asked Mr. Tanaka.

"Not so many—one or two."

"The moon bear kills sheep also," Kaz observed.

Mac clicked the remote, banishing the moon bear. A slide of the Front under an early-morning sky illuminated the screen. In the hazy light, the rock face was cream-colored, the creases a soft gray-blue. Below the mountains, the plain was golden. It was easy enough to imagine the stretch of grassland dotted with herds of antelope and bison. It was a utopian image, but Mac ignored it.

"I believe our conflict with the bear can be resolved," he argued. "For example, here we have a foundation that reimburses ranchers for losses due to grizzlies." He clicked again. The screen went white. "That's it. Lights?"

Clare rustled over to the switch and turned on the overhead. The Japanese sat blinking, as if surprised to find themselves in cowboy suits.

"The real threat to the grizzly," Mac persisted, "is not agriculture. Of all extractive uses of the Front, agriculture is the most compatible with its wildlife. The real threat comes from oil and gas exploration. If we allow Chevron or FINA to banish the grizzly from our mountains, we will have cut our link to a power source far more valuable than oil or gas."

He paused, as if about to conclude, but couldn't resist a parting volley. "The Rocky Mountain Front is the latest beachhead of international oil companies," he insisted. "These companies are racist oligarchies. They are determined to destroy not only the grizzly, but an entire network of ecosystems. And they have our government in their pocket! The Bureau of Land Management, for example, has just granted FINA Oil permission to drill in Badger-Two Medicine—land that borders the Blackfeet reservation and is a mere two miles from Glacier National Park!"

Mac's face was flushed. He conjured up dynamite and polluted runoff, blowouts of deadly gas, burn-off turning the night sky orange. But the speech went beyond apocalyptic images. It was propelled by an anger that seemed not quite tamed. No one stirred. Clare made no effort to intervene. She listened attentively, her face solemn, her hands folded in her lap. She might have been in church.

I glanced over at Monica. She had stopped taking notes and was sitting back in her chair, observing Mac with the look of a satisfied cat.

Chapter Eight

If the Eastern Front had been seashore during the age of the dinosaurs, some millions of years later the retreating glaciers of the Ice Age scoured the former sea bottom into flat plains and left lakes of melted ice whose overflowing waters carved new riverbeds. More unexpectedly—at least from a twentieth-century perspective—in isolated pockets at the foot of the Rockies, the glaciers also left swamps. Not your brackish, steamy, southern kind of swamp, but what Mac called a "boreal fen." The J-E's Bear Paw Swamp looked like a small lake. Its rippled, shallow waters were open to the sky and bordered by dense thickets of shrubs. The peaty meadows around the swamp were solid enough to drive over; in places the peat was twelve feet deep. At the same time, they were wet enough to support an island of flora rare to the Front's highlands but common to the woods north of Edmonton, Canada. Later in the season, Mac assured us, we would find gentians and sedges and even yellow lady's slippers.

In late April, however, the new growth around both Bear Paw Swamp and Pine Butte Swamp to the north (owned by the Nature Conservancy) was virtually invisible. Nonetheless, it drew the grizzly down out of the mountains to forage for its spring breakfast of sprouting grasses, bulbs, tubers, and roots. The day before, the attraction had become more than vegetable: in a stand of leafless cottonwood, Mac and the Fish and Wildlife man, Walt Surrey, had deposited the bloated carcass of a black cow.

When we drove up in Dave's Blazer, Mac following with Clare and Monica in the institute's pickup, Walt was up a ladder against a tree. He was fiddling with a black box mounted on the trunk above him. Inside the box, Mac explained to us, were a battery and a camera triggered by a heat sensor. The visitors were interested. Kaz asked if he could climb up for a look, whereupon Dave asked Walt to bring the camera box down so Mr. Yamaguchi and the others could inspect it. This took some time. Mac found a screwdriver in Walt's truck and took it up the ladder, then Walt dropped a wing nut and the visitors joined in hunting for it in the dry grass around the base of the tree.

Meanwhile, the cow was stinking. It had the same stink as the decomposing corpse the sheriff's men had removed that morning. No one else seemed bothered by the smell. There were also a lot of flies. They made a map around the cow's swollen anus. They flew lazily out her nose and settled like a sloppy mascara around the rims of her dead eyes. They also polka-dotted the engine-warmed hoods and fenders of the parked vehicles. Mac unsheathed the knife he wore at his belt and slit the cow's dirty white belly. The rush of liquid sounded like a horse's stream.

I walked upwind for a look at the swamp. The place would have suited Andrew Wyeth's palette—a color-blind wash of grays and browns. The cottonwoods were mottled white and beige, beyond them the expanse of swamp water was a wind-hammered pewter, and in the distance the mountains were gray-blue beneath their loads of snow. You had to work hard for color, to sort through yards of dark brown tangle to find a bright red twig of dogwood. You had to peer deeply into the blond clumps of grasses to find short blades of green. I made a mental note: the more painstaking the process of discovery, the more intense the pleasure. Deep within, I felt the slight hum of a poem—more of a vibration than a song. I fingered a length of twig, supple and red as an artery. Would it fit itself into words? Would the stink of dead flesh that seemed to be following me around waft its way into a poem?

A mewing sound drew my eye upward. The sky was still threatening, but not delivering. A white-and-gray bird flew jerkily into the wind. It was a sea gull. A *sea gull*? I walked back to the group. Kaz and Walt, who was now on the ground, were talking film types and ASAs. The camera was back up in the tree, and Mac was on the ladder. Sam and Monica, on Mac's instructions, were taking turns walking up to the cow. Mr. Yamaguchi and his secretary, Mr. Tanaka, were recording the exercise with nifty-looking little videocams. Clare stood leaning against a truck, arms crossed.

"What's going on?" I asked.

"They're trying to get the focus set so it'll go off. The heat sensors are tricky. You've got to get it set up just right, and even then, it's not always reliable. We've processed a couple of dud rolls that were triggered by the carcass heating up in the sun."

A flash came from the tree. A cheer went up from the men. Sam was standing over the cow. Like a victorious bullfighter, he made a sweeping bow. Monica blew him a kiss.

"You use a flash?" I asked Clare. "Doesn't that scare them away?"

"It doesn't seem to. The camera has a crystal display that dates and times each frame. Our films show the same animals coming back night after night to feed."

"Okay," Mac called down. "Let's try that again."

Sam yielded to Mr. Yamaguchi, who solemnly marched up to the cow, but triggered no flash.

Clare invited, "Come on, I'll show you something." I followed her around behind the parked trucks. We hopped over a ditch. The walls of it were peaty, and there was water in its bottom. We might have been walking across an Irish moor. But only a few feet farther, camouflaged in a thicket of saplings, was a miniature log cabin. The peak of the shingled roof couldn't have been more than seven feet high; the top of the doorway, which was closed off with a sheet of plywood, was level with my forehead.

"There used to be a homestead here," Clare explained. "The wife's still alive in a nursing home in Choteau. She must be over ninety. Back in the twenties, she and her husband raised eleven kids here. One of them's buried back in here somewhere, and she used to come back to visit the grave once a year. The husband made a living trapping beaver and muskrat in the swamp. This is all that's left. The other buildings burned down. A bunch of hunters were camping in the house."

"But what is it?" I asked her. "A storeroom?"

"I don't think so. Look, there's a window here on the side."

The window wasn't much bigger than an open encyclopedia, and like the doorway, it was sealed against trespassers with plywood. I looked up at the roof and saw the stub of a stovepipe. "There was heat in it," I said.

"I think maybe it was built for some of the children. Maybe they couldn't all fit in the house."

We wandered off to inspect the foundations. There were still chunks of charred log strewn in the depression. Clare was right. It had been a small house, about fifteen by thirty feet. It had stood about a hundred feet from the child-sized cabin—the mother would not have heard any of them crying in the night.

"Do you know how the child died?" I asked.

"No," she said.

I felt a bond with the mother—and a surge of awe. How had she managed out here in this desolate northern swamp without a telephone, without a doctor, and with all the other children underfoot—perhaps a baby at her breast and another on her hip? I thought of Rachel, my child beyond cockcrow. The night she died, I sat with her body till dawn. And after Clint, her father, called the funeral home, I sat some more with her in its morgue. I sat with her till I noticed that the blue in her irises had faded away. I never did close her eyes.

I stared at a chunk of charred log at my feet. Had the mother who lived in this house been able to press down her dead child's eyelids?

Clare picked a burr off her long skirt. "How do you think it went?" she wondered.

I was taken aback. "You mean the child's dying?"

She looked shocked. "I meant Mac's speech."

"Oh," I said. It took me a moment to shift gears. "Well, they didn't go for the moon bear, did they? That much was obvious. Hard to tell what they got out of the rest."

"They hunt the moon bear in their national parks—with a government stamp of approval. Another ten, twenty years, the moon bear will be extinct. Mac couldn't resist bringing it up."

"What about the grizzly? I thought it was legal to hunt them in Montana."

"It used to be. Now the grizzly's got federal 'threatened' status, but that hasn't stopped the annual death toll. A hundred years ago, the grizzly population in the continental United States was estimated at around a hundred thousand. Today it's below a thousand. Somewhere between nine hundred and six hundred. No one's certain. That's why the census is so crucial."

She picked another burr off her hem, then looked up at me. "What did *you* think of the presentation?" Her face was unexpectedly pliant, as if she'd lowered a mask.

"I was moved," I admitted. "The pictures are phenomenal, and Mac's a persuasive speaker. But you don't need me to tell you that."

She caught my eyes and held on to them. "He's good." There was nothing nunlike about her tone of voice. It suggested rumpled sheets, musky smells. Her black eyes challenged.

Annoyed, I swerved back to Mac's speech. "Actually," I told her, "his admonition about being observers, not guardians, of mother earth struck me as disingenuous. That's what's he's doing, isn't it? All his lobbying, all the media exposure. He's *guarding* his patch of wilderness."

She considered the objection. "When you're *in* a real wilderness, you're not a guardian, you're trying to survive. There's a difference between the experience of wilderness and the work we do to preserve the actual place." She paused thoughtfully. "Once upon a time, way back when, we used to be a codominant species with the grizzly. But now we're dominant, so there're management issues involved. That's what the Sacred Paw institute's about, working out the economic, social, and political management of the grizzly. Mac is tuned in to that—he wouldn't have gotten very far if he hadn't been. He's a brilliant manager. But at the same time, he'd like to believe that *he* is being managed by the grizzly. That the grizzly has a kind of spiritual power and can save *us* instead of vice versa. It's more than a head game. He's really into all this Indian stuff. He's got this fantasy about a purer, simpler time. It's like he's looking for paradise lost."

"Aren't we all."

"We can't go back to Eden," Clare said sharply. "Whatever

we end up with as a designated critical habitat, it's going to have to be managed. And to be effective, that management must be based on a scientific knowledge of the grizzly's biology and life cycle. Folklore isn't going to cut it."

We walked back toward the miniature cabin. "Speaking of folklore," I said, "there's something I want to ask you." I stopped, embarrassed by my ignorance.

She looked at me. "What?"

"Hil and Bobby—that carpenter kid?"

"Yeah?"

"They told me some story about a ranger who got attacked by a grizzly. They said it was because she was 'on her moon.' "

To my surprise, she didn't scoff. "There are a number of stories like that. One of the most famous cases happened back in the late sixties, a young woman killed up at Glacier. Grizzly dragged her off in her sleeping bag. They think maybe the zipper was stuck. Her friends got out of their bags and climbed trees. They were sleeping out in the open, no tent, and that was probably a factor. But she had her period and had been using pads, and that got more attention than the other circumstances."

She paused, then reflected, "It's interesting. A lot of native belief systems posit a special connection between women and bears. The Lakota believed that if a menstruating woman tanned a bear skin, she would herself become a bear. In many different cultures, there are stories about bears abducting and mating with women. Not just Native American cultures. There was a bishop of Paris back in the sixteenth century named William of Auvergne. He maintained that bear semen was very like a man's and that it was possible for a human mother to carry a bear's child. The myths are abundant. And there's always the temptation to connect them to an actual physiological phenomenon. But the data on menstruation are inconclusive."

"You mean there are *studies?*"

"Oh, sure. Some scientists up in Manitoba ran a series of field experiments with polar bears and found more response to used pads than to other animal odors. But polar bears are far more carnivorous than either grizzly or black bears, so you can't really extrapolate. Someone else at the University of Montana did an analysis of grizzly-bear-inflicted injury and found no significant correlation between attacks on women and their menses. But it's probably not a bad idea to wear a tampon in bear country."

"Like out here," I said.

She smiled. "As Mac said, you're more likely to get hit by lightning. Of all the hundreds of thousands of people that visit Yellowstone each year, there have only been five or six grizzly bear fatalities since 1872—and most of the those occurred in the late sixties after they closed the garbage dumps and the bears started wandering into people's camps."

"One more question. You've got *sea gulls* out here along with your bears?"

She brightened. "Did you see one?"

"I don't know what else it could have been."

"They migrate down along the Front from Seattle. A sign of spring."

We searched the sky. It was still gray and swollen. A blast of wind rattled the bone-white tops of the cottonwoods. A shower of twigs clattered against the roof of the abandoned children's cabin. Clare's long hair blew across her face. She looked like a heroine on a moor, unworried about snarls or the painful, time-consuming nuisance of combing them out. I ran a hand across the rough-cut lintel of the cabin's boarded-up doorway. What had the children seen from their threshold? Now, between the trunks of two larger trees, there was a clear sightline of the dead cow. The men were still playing with their cameras. I checked my watch.

"I've got to get back. Trudi's got this gorgeous salmon and we haven't decided yet what to do with it. Any suggestions?" I asked her. She and Mac were coming for dinner again.

"I don't cook," she announced. She sounded almost proud—like an expensive cleaning woman proclaiming, "I don't do windows."

"You eat." Did Mac do the cooking? Or did Trudi feed them both?

But she wasn't interested in my menu. "Take the pickup," she said. "Walt will give us a lift back."

* * *

Her directions were simple: follow the track, take the left fork back to the road, and turn left. But alone in the truck, I found the way back longer than I remembered, and I kept wondering if I'd missed the turn. The track from the abandoned cabin to the road was about five miles, and the J-E's gate was another three. A respectable half-day hike and you still hadn't reached the lodge. I could imagine becoming addicted to that kind of space. I wondered if the Japanese found all the elbow room soul-expanding or threatening.

Back in the J-E's kitchen, Trudi and I considered the defrosting salmon. The theme of the week was East-meets-West. I'd done enough homework before I left to know that even if all the ingredients had been available, faking a goodwill romp through Japanese cuisine was out of the question. At the same time, I didn't want to go totally chuck-wagon. I wanted some familiar islands for them—the equivalent of an American burger in the wilds of Siberia. The challenge was finding foods and preparations common to both Japan and Montana. Hence the salmon. Trudi wanted me to bake it *en croute*. Her visitors, she pointed out, were both partial to French cooking and appreciative of presentation. "They're more sophisticated than most of our visitors," she argued.

"Exactly," I said. "So they'll be delighted we aren't doing it up like a Marriott banquet. Have you ever seen anyone actually *eat* the crust? No. It's sodden on the inside and bulletproof on the outside and it invariably remains in polite little piles on the side of everyone's plate."

We settled on broiled steaks topped with béarnaise. There would be plain rice with lightly steamed vegetables on the side, and for starters, as the Brits say, a light, peppery watercress/spinach soup made with beef stock instead of cream. I'd made the soup in the morning, and julienned the carrots, celery, and green beans, and that afternoon, Lynn had made "fail-safe" Girl Scout chocolate mousses for dessert.

My only real worry was the plain white rice. I'd xeroxed a recipe for *gohan*—Japanese for steamed rice—in a Time-Life cookbook. It involved a sequence of rinsing, soaking, boiling, simmering, resting, fluffing. When it comes to cooking (and probably other things as well), pulling off Plain is often more demanding than doing it up Fancy, and you couldn't get much plainer than steamed long-grain rice.

"Just cook it," Trudi said impatiently.

"Right," I said.

CHAPTER NINE

The next morning, Easter Sunday, I slept late. Instead of breakfast as usual, in order to give everyone a chance to recover from the Saturday-night dance, Trudi had scheduled an eleven-o'clock picnic brunch, with coffee and sticky buns available at eight. I expected to wake at five, as I'd been doing—five in Montana was seven back home. But either my body clock had clicked into the new time zone or the steady flow of beer and high-impact polkas had taken their toll. I woke up slightly dehydrated and cold. Without opening my eyes, I groped around for the quilt. It had disappeared. I curled into a ball inside my flannel nightgown. I didn't get any warmer. I squinted at my Timex on the bedside table. It said six fifty-five. Then I heard breathing. Oh, yes. It was Monica Leeds, in the next bed beneath her quilt—and mine.

I had been admirably assertive (I thought) in my refusal to share my room with her. I had said no, no, and no, pleasantly, patiently, and firmly. And here she was in my room, and it was my own doing.

If Trudi and Dave Fife had shown a flash of resentment at my refusal I would have stuck to my guns. But they had pulled back, acquiesced. "I can't say I blame you," Trudi had admitted. They had politely swallowed their disappointment. I felt a distance grow between us. I suppose I was attempting to bridge it—no act of charity is totally unselfish—so I had agreed. Not very gracefully, I'll grant. I grumbled enough to tarnish my halo, though later, Saturday night, when I watched her at the dance, I felt better about it, less of a chump. She jumped right into the party with both black boots. She pulled the Japanese men, one after the other, out of their seats and onto the floor. She hooted as the whining fiddles on the caller's tape picked up speed and gave high fives. She allemanded her way around a circle of "Oh, Johnny, Oh!" and when the music stopped, she laughed between gasps for air and gave her "salarymen" triumphant hugs. Her homely face glowed. She flirted with them, teased them, matched them beer for beer. They loved her.

She disappeared early, during one of the caller's breaks, but by that time, the ice had been broken and the men from NVI and the other guests, about a dozen or so neighbors, were all in comradely high spirits. I danced with Sam and with Mr. Tanaka and felt like a galloping giantess. Mr. Yamaguchi complimented me on the dinner, so that was nice. After a couple of beers, I felt brave enough to discuss the intricacies of my rice recipe with Kaz. He seemed mystified. Finally I asked, "How do *you* cook rice?"

He shook his head and smiled apologetically.

I tried again. "Does your wife cook rice?"

Yes, of course she cooked rice.

"How does she cook rice?" I persisted. I could almost see a cartoon balloon over the top of his spiky black hair. In it, his thoughts read, "Extremely weird here."

What he said was, "In electric rice cooker."

"Oh," I said.

Moving right along, I tried, "So, Kaz, what do you do for fun?" Not a good choice. The question was more trouble than *gohan* recipes. "Hobby?" I tried. "Vacation?" The concepts seemed alien. I tried "leisure time," and he got it. His miming was eloquent. He put down his beer and squinted through an imaginary camera. His hands fluttered gracefully. Then he flapped his arms in slow motion. He managed to make it look as if there were no bones in his sleeve. He smiled dreamily. What he liked to do was photograph birds. Big ones. He made a talon out of one hand. Raptors? Eagles? Hawks? Yes, yes! Relieved, we raised our plastic cups of beer to each other.

Mac and I (in cowboy boots and sneakers, respectively) made it all the way through a wild "Golden Slippers" without maiming anyone, though by the end we were going so fast that my braid was as dangerous as a whip. Afterward, as the room stopped spinning, we held on to each other longer than strictly necessary and I saw Trudi appraising us from the sidelines.

I also met Roy, the J-E's cattle manager, and his wife. They both had round, weather-reddened faces that sat like polished apples on their square bodies. Roy was wearing a string tie and green-checked gingham shirt that matched his wife's full skirt. She wore several stiff, frilled petticoats so the skirt stood out above her knees like Shirley Temple's. Out on the floor, they looked professional, twirling in perfect unison. Their daughter was about Lynn's age, and both girls wore summer dresses of flowered cotton. The strapless bodices were sculpted around breasts that jutted out like offerings. With their painted lips and lifted chins, the girls looked like twin figureheads on a ship about to brave the sea.

Walt Surrey, auburn hair slicked back, was there with his wife and their new baby, who obligingly slept through the evening cocooned in his plastic car seat. Bobby and Pick were there, and we said hello to each other a bit awkwardly—no one wanted to mention the matter up in the woods, but it was hard to think of another topic. "Good party," we agreed. The only one I didn't see was Hil.

The party ended at midnight with a Virginia reel. The head couples led their lines of dancers out the front door and around the lodge to the side lawn, where Dave, by the light of a Coleman lantern, was cooking half-pound hamburgers on a gas grill big enough to roast a pig. I went to my room, thinking Monica would be asleep.

I tiptoed down the hallway, took some seconds silently turning the doorknob, and opened the door to be hit by an explosion of yellow wallpaper roses and gamy heat. Every light in the room was on. It was also stifling. I might just as well have opened the door of an oven—an oven cooking dirty socks. Monica was sitting naked on the bed, legs crossed. She didn't look up. She was lost in the laptop on a pillow in front of her.

I turned off the heat, an electric baseboard unit under the dresser, and opened the window over my bed. As I pushed up the sash, I thought I caught a movement sliding through the dark outside the window. I felt a stab of alarm. I cupped my hands against the screen and peered out. The screen had a dusty metallic smell. I heard distant voices and laughter from the hamburger eaters. I could see nothing through the screen, but I had the creepy sensation of a presence in the blackness. I pulled back into the bright room and coaxed the flimsy curtains along the rod till they overlapped.

Had someone been peeping at Monica? Her fingers kept up a delicate tattoo on her keyboard. She looked less healthy naked than clothed. Her ribs and shoulder blades and the bumps of her spine protruded harshly under her pale skin. Her breasts were mostly brown nipple. I wondered if she suffered from an eating disorder. In the glare of the overhead fixture, she might have been a cruel sketch by Toulouse-Lautrec, although she lacked the lassitude of his models. Her posture was concave, but determined. Her bones were on edge. She had the intensity of a starved cat about to spring.

"Mind if I turn out the overhead?" I asked.

"Huh?" she said without looking up.

I repeated the question.

Her fingers stopped. "Yeah, okay."

I clicked off the wall switch and left the lamp between the beds on. "Can you see okay?"

"Mmm." Click-click-click went her fingers.

I recognized her condition. I worked with a yellow pad and pencil, but my tune-out capacity was every bit as strong. Not long after Clint and I were married, he came home while I was lost working on one of my poems. Perhaps I said "Hi." I don't remember. But an hour later, I looked around and saw a bunch of pink roses in waxy green tissue lying on the floor. Clint was not around. I still feel guilty about that one.

But back to Monica Leeds. I went to sleep feeling not exactly comradely toward her, but at least benign. Six hours later, I felt less benign. I was not about to get out of bed and do my stretches on the cold floor with her snoozing snugly under my quilt. I thought about snatching it back, then settled for banging a sticky dresser drawer and singing "Vesti la giubba" in the shower on the other side of the wall beside her bed. I knew all the words, right down to Pagliacci's final sobs. I'd memorized them in college to impress an Italian professor with soulful brown eyes. Unfortunately, singing is not among my abilities. When I walked back into the bedroom, Monica eased her head out from under the covers. The electric frizz of her orange hair had a dent in it. Her eyes were open and annoyed. "Morning," I said cheerfully. She closed her eyes and dropped her head back onto her pillow.

After a solitary cup of coffee in the warm kitchen, I felt pretty decent. I called my mother from the Big Room. The furniture had already been reassembled. Someone, probably Hil, had lit a fire in the vast stone hearth, but it burned listlessly, giving off more smoke than warmth. The room was cold enough for a jacket, and beneath the chill there was the faint morning-after smell of beer.

"Lee, darling," my mother said. Hearing her calm voice, live from D.C., I felt my eyes sting with tears. I hadn't realized I was so tightly wound. "I'm so glad you called," she said. She sounded bright and happy. "I'm just having my second cup of coffee." I pictured her propped up against the pillows, her small, dark head alert as a bird's, her shoulders draped in the red-and-gold paisley shawl she used as a bed jacket. Her coffee would be too sweet and lukewarm. Tommy, her holistic masseur, would have brought it upstairs in one of the useless little painted porcelain cups he insisted she use. They were part of a Sèvres tea set that had belonged to my grandmother, and were too shallow to keep anything hot after the first swallow. In her kitchen cupboard, my own stoneware mug stood bullishly amid the fragile nests of her cups and saucers. For the first time in a long time, I felt homesick.

"Happy Easter," I said brightly.

"I had the most wonderful Easter present!" she bubbled. I winced. I'd forgotten to send her something, anything.

"Early this morning," she went on, "I had a dream. I was on

a street, perhaps in Paris or Rome, a foreign country, and a bag lady approached me. There was something vaguely familiar about her. She told me she had something for me. She took me down into a huge basement and started rustling around through all these plastic garbage bags. Then she pulled out a gold lamé dress—something Marilyn Monroe might have worn! And she said—"

Here my mother paused theatrically. "She said, *'I've been saving it for you.'* "

"Huh," I said. "Did the dress fit?"

"Oh, Lee, don't be so literal! Sometimes I find it hard to believe you're a poet."

I let it go. If it had been my dream, the zipper would have gotten stuck and become part of a long, tedious nightmare—the kind that makes you scream from sheer boredom.

"Don't you see?" she insisted. "It was a dream about my *healing!*"

"Who was the bag lady?"

"The Wise Woman," my mother said.

"That's nice." I tried to sound upbeat, but I really didn't feel like chatting about Jungian archetypes. I had grown up in a family which dissected dreams over corn flakes. When my friends spent the night, they were intrigued and flattered by my mother's interest in the state of their psyches, but the older I got, the more embarrassing and intrusive I found this breakfast pastime. I didn't want to dish up my soul's nightly workouts for the amusement of my family—or for my mother's beady clinical eye. My brother and my father innocently polished up their dreams and deposited them in her apron like rivals tossing golden apples into a goddess's lap. But by the time I was twelve, I'd bowed out of the contest. I'd grab a piece of toast and run.

Although she had worked hard to hide it, my mother was disappointed in my lack of interest then, and I could feel the same disappointment now. I ignored a prickle of anger. "Mom," I said sincerely, "I'm really glad you're on the mend. I was worried about you."

"I was too," she admitted ruefully. We laughed. Truce. We talked about what the surgeon had said, what her doctor had said, her various medications. Then she asked, "How are *you?*"

"Fine. Everything's fine. You having Easter dinner there?"

"We decided to skip the dinner and have hors d'oeuvres instead. Shrimp and Brie. And champagne."

"No ham?"

"Certainly not!" she said gaily. "I've finished with hams!"

We had always had a ham at Easter. And jelly beans and dyed eggs. The eggs would always come out of their dark, vinegary baths paler than expected: pink instead of red, lavender instead of purple, mint instead of emerald. My brother and I would hunt them in navy-blue flannel coats from Best & Company. They had brass buttons down the front. "I remember a hat you bought me one Easter," I reminisced. "A picture hat, dark navy straw, very finely woven, and there was a circle of lilies of the valley around the crown. Remember?"

She hesitated. "Yes, I remember it." But her voice was no longer carefree and girlish. She had shifted into a more somber mode. "Lee, what's going on out there?"

"Mom, stop it!" I snapped.

"Stop what?" she prodded carefully.

"Your Delphic oracle act."

Her voice was calm, professional. "I hear you talking wistfully about a hat you had when you were nine. Lee, you *hated* that hat."

I looked through the window over the desk. White bands of ground fog floated eerily above the lawn, and the sky above the old pines was white also, but the cloud cover was high and seemed to be diluting. The day wasn't going to be a sparkler, but it looked as if our al fresco brunch was on.

"There's been a killing," I told her. "I was out running and I found the body back in the canyon behind the lodge."

"Oh, Lee." Her voice was immensely sorrowful. "Not again?" As if I were an addict confessing a relapse.

"You make it sound like it's my fault."

The line was quiet. I heard the echo of my complaint. I looked up at the heads of dead deer and antelope. "Mom?"

"Yes," she said.

I outlined the story for her. "Problem is, I keep smelling it. I keep sniffing myself, but it's not on my skin. Is there such a thing as an olfactory hallucination?

"Yes. Not common, though. If I remember correctly, it's associated with hebephrenic schizophrenia."

"Great."

She didn't sound very worried. "Would it help you to know more?"

"I don't know."

"Have you tried irrigating your nasal passages?" she asked.

This is an unattractive yoga trick which involves snuffing warm water up your nose till it trickles down your tonsils. It was my mother's version of "Take two aspirin." And yes, I'd tried it. "It didn't do any good," I reported.

"Well," she advised, "don't just ignore this smell of yours. Pay attention. The Unconscious likes to pun. Follow your nose, as it were. See where it leads you."

"Mom, I know where it leads me. And I don't want to go back there, thank you very much."

"Hmm," she said sympathetically.

I tried to joke. "At least it's not sabotaging my cooking."

"I will do some homework and call you this evening," she decided.

"You going to lay out the tarot for me?"

Silence.

"Just kidding, Mom. You know, a little therapeutic humor?"

"I'm going to try to reach a friend. He teaches psychiatry at Georgetown." She paused. "And then I'm going to consult the *I Ching.*" She was serious.

We hung up. I felt both exasperated and reassured. Having a witchy mother isn't always easy. But at least she's on my team.

At ten I loaded the pickup with folding tables, coolers, water jugs, plastic crates, wicker hampers with cracked leather hinges (they looked like props for a *Brideshead Revisited* set), firewood, and grill top. Then with the help of Trudi's hand-drawn map, I drove to the picnic site. We were to rendezvous up on a ridge about three miles out on the prairie. Trudi and Dave and the guests had already headed out on horseback. Mac and Clare would bring Monica

Leeds in their truck. Lynn planned to mount up one of the ranch-use ATV's and drive out to the ridge. ("You are *not* to spook the horses, understand?" Trudi had instructed severely. "Ma, gimme a break," Lynn had retorted.)

The top of the ridge was a broad plateau dotted with twisted, wind-stunted pines that, like bonsai, played games with scale. Walking along the ridge, head over hundred-year-old trees, felt lordly if not godlike. The view helped. Like all high views, it encouraged illusions of omnipotence. To the west, the Front's snowy ridges stretched across a pale blue horizon like a great empire's wall. To the east, as far as the eye could see, rolled the khaki prairie. The only landmarks were isolated, flat-topped buttes in the distance. They might have been neighboring castles on a medieval plain. It took me a while to find Bear Paw Swamp, a series of irregular silvery patches surrounded by blotches of dark mauve vegetation. It was too far away to distinguish trees from brush or to spot the children's cabin. Even the road out to the swamp was scarcely visible, an old scar in the prairie's tawny skin. It was a relief to be outside in full daylight, to be able to see into the distance in every direction. The lodge's dark corners and high shadows were beginning to get to me. It was not only the occasional whiffs of death I smelled. Every time I moved out of the security of the kitchen, I felt as if there were something at my back. My own fear, no doubt.

I unpacked the truck and started the fire inside an existing ring of blackened rocks. I set up the tables and gathered stones to slip into the pockets Trudi had sewn in the tablecloths to keep them from flying away. Between the tufts of dry grasses, the top of the ridge was as stony as a northern beach. Again, upon close inspection, I discovered astonishing colors: I picked up gray stones covered with pale green rosettes of lichen, purple-brown stones covered with velvety orange lichen, black pebbles smooth and rounded as pieces of sea glass, white pebbles porous as weathered bones.

I tried some artful arrangements of my collection on Trudi's navy-blue calico tablecloths, but they persisted in looking like a three-year-old's pile of pretend cookies. "One for you, one for you, three for me . . ." I dumped the stones. The food would have to stand alone. I wasn't very happy about "doing brunch". I wholly agreed with the late James Beard's objection that brunch was a neither/nor sort of meal. I had tried to talk Trudi into a Virginia-hunt-type breakfast of glazed ham and biscuits with a big pot of beans cooked over the open fire. But she seemed to think her guests might die without a dose of eggs before noon. She was thinking champagne and crab quiches. I was thinking scrambled eggs and bacon. I had no objection to the champagne: it reminded me of Karen von Blixen, who served midmorning champagne in crystal goblets in the African forest. But quiches struck me as off-base. Mind you, I'm not into Real Man food, bloody haunches of elk or pinto beans burned in their can. The reverse, in fact. I wanted Mother food: the comfort of buttery scrambled eggs on a dark, rainy night; the tempting smell of bacon on a cold morning.

Less is more, I argued. Trudi was skeptical. I reminded her of the salmon's success. I lectured her on the two S's of menu planning: simplicity and suitability. "You wouldn't serve asparagus with barbecue, would you?" I asked.

"Why not?"

I switched tactics. "Don't forget we're going to be outside. Factor in the fresh-air phenomenon. Outdoors, plain food tastes better than fancy. You could serve PB&Js and win."

"The last time I served peanut butter sandwiches to our guests was after a new 'chef' boiled a standing rib roast. No one could believe it, never mind eat it. The guy had references, too."

"Hard to get good help."

She looked at me sideways.

In the end we compromised on an upscale ranch-style breakfast: iced California bubbly and heated Bloody Marys; eggs and bacon and potatoes in a sheepherder's version of a frittata (Trudi called it a "pie"); biscuits and huckleberry jam; fried apples.

The guests arrived in the mood for a feast, and I started pan-slinging. Trudi's recipe for shepherd's pie had belonged to her Scottish grandmother, whose family employed emigrant Basques on their sheep range. The dish was seasoned with thyme, which the Basques probably picked wild on their native hillsides, but the only thing growing among the dry grasses on the ridge was a patch or two of *Douglasia,* a tiny mountain pink, so I was using generous pinches of the supermarket variety. Like any home-on-the-range meal, it was a one-pan operation: first the bacon, then the potatoes (very thinly sliced) in a spoonful of the bacon fat, then the beaten eggs. The trick to any egg dish is low heat, so when I poured in the eggs, I hefted the giant-sized cast-iron pan off the fire, covered it, and let its own heat slowly set the eggs. This made room for my pan of apples. The biscuits I had made earlier that morning in the J-E's kitchen. (Trudi told me that her grandmother, when out on the range, would mix her biscuits right in the flour sack, pouring bacon grease in on top, adding baking power and milk, and stirring up flour from below until the dough was the right consistency. I was impressed.)

I didn't have much time for conversation, but I do remember that Trudi was worried about the ranch's telephone. She filled a blue enameled tin cup from the coffeepot on the Coleman. "Something's wrong with the answering machine," she said. "The message light was blinking, but when I pushed replay, I got this weird electronic noise. It must have gone on for five minutes. It's never happened before." She made it sound ominous.

"The phone works?"

"Yeah." She blew ripples across her coffee and took a tentative sip. "I just wondered if the sheriff was trying to reach us."

"You could call."

"It was probably just one of the girls calling to say Happy Easter." She went on about her older daughters. I picked up the lid of my pan and carefully stirred the potatoes. So far, so good. They were browning, not burning. I leaned forward to inhale their steam, then decided on more thyme. Trudi snitched a piece of bacon. I snapped my spatula at her hand but she was too quick.

"Get outta here!" I ordered.

The guests milled around my fire. Monica was wearing her black leggings and boots, but topped with a cream-colored nubby-knit turtleneck and an artfully bleached denim jacket. Its red plaid lining had been faded to an orange that matched the lollipop of her hair. Monica's skin was Pre-Raphaelite pale, her mouth carmine. The look was Lady-of-Shallot-shops-J. Crew. Clare was in jeans and wore a battered canvas field coat over her loose black hair, so that it gathered around her collar in a pageboy effect and made her look younger and happier. Both of them were drinking hot Bloody Marys—along with the Japanese. As it happened, I was the only one into the champagne, and although I usually prefer my bubbles drier, its yeasty, almost peachy sweetness went down very smoothly with the wood smoke from my fire. The glasses Trudi had packed—shallow dishes on stems—were precarious. According to enological legend, their shape had been molded on Marie Antoinette's breast. Drinking out of her shoe would have been easier. Nonetheless, as I squatted over the fire, maneuvering my glass away from stray boots, I managed to polish off half the bottle.

Thanks to the champagne, I had to work to keep my pans in focus, so I wasn't paying much attention to the general conversation. However, an exchange between Clare and Monica piqued my interest. Over my head I heard Monica say, "It's not the same. I need to see one."

I glanced up. Clare was frowning. "I've been here three years, working with Mac in the field, and I don't think we've seen more than two or three in that time."

"I want a grizzly for my lead. Not a footprint. Not a piece of its shit."

"First-person thrills and chills, huh?" Clare said sardonically.

"Look, I'm thinking *Esquire*. You stick to monographs."

"Go up to Glacier if you want to see bears," Clare said firmly.

"Which brings us to a key question," Monica sailed on. "Why save the grizzly in Montana when the species is flourishing in Canada and Alaska? Bears don't have a critical role in the ecology. No other species depends on them. They're like us. You could wipe both bears and humans off the face of the earth and it wouldn't be a disaster. Nature would be fine without us. Better off, even."

Clare smiled. "You sound like a Wise Use parrot." Sam the Translator was standing beside her, listening with interest.

"Spare me," Monica said.

"Well, wherever you got it from, you're right," Clare conceded. "Ecologically speaking, we don't need the grizzly." She paused. "Mac would say we need the bear precisely because it is like us."

"And what do you say?" Monica demanded.

She reflected a moment. Then she said slowly, "I don't think it's an arguable premise. Like the existence of God. You can argue till you're blue in the face, but it's really not the province of logic. It's a matter of belief."

Sam interjected, "Belief and knowledge are often reflections of each other."

The two women stared at him. "How inscrutable," Monica cracked.

Clare ignored her and turned to Sam. "Yes, belief and knowledge go hand in hand. And my research leads me to preferences. I'd rather have the grizzly on the Front than Chevron."

Monica smiled a *Mona Lisa* smile.

Sam's dark eyes flitted back and forth between their faces. "You got oil in them thar hills?" he joked. He gestured in the direction of the J-E.

Clare acknowledged his mastery of the idiom with a smile. "Probably," she answered. "Or natural gas. We're right on what geologists call the Overthrust Belt. It was formed about the time of the dinosaurs and runs from the Arctic end of the Canadian Rockies all the way down into Central America. Back in the late seventies, there were some major strikes along the Alberta and Wyoming portions of the belt. Now there's a lot of interest in our section of it."

"From Chevron?" Sam wondered.

"Among others. The Gulf War's given oil companies a new incentive to drill at home."

"How much oil are we talking about?" Monica demanded.

"Up in Badger-Two Medicine, government geologists estimate between one and ten million barrels—maybe enough to run the country for half a day. And destroy the habitat in the process."

Sam looked thoughtful.

The next time I looked up, Sam had moved away from the fire and was deep in conference with his boss, Mr. Yamaguchi, and Yamaguchi's secretary/assistant, Mr. Tanaka. The three of them stood apart from the group, by an outcropping of gray rock. They talked rapidly in their own language, nodding intently, but not smiling. They could have been coming to consensus on where to go pee. But I was willing to bet they were talking oil and gas.

* * *

Later, when the meal was over, and the guests stood together admiring the long views and postponing the discomfort of getting back on their horses, Mac pointed out a segment of the prehistoric Great North Trail, which, he told them, started up in the Bering Strait and ran down along the Rockies all the way to Mexico. Then he traced the boundaries of the J-E. He stood against the vast vault of hazy sky with his arm extended like a prophet pointing to the Promised Land. The Japanese, small as minor figures in a fresco, followed Mac's finger with their binoculars. "Well, gentlemen," Mac asked, "are you tempted? Is this the kind of place you're looking for?"

Under the brim of his Stetson, Mr. Yamaguchi's mouth smiled. "Yes," he said. He turned to his colleagues. They were smiling, too. "Yes," they echoed.

Chapter Ten

The problem with any group is that if you do not belong, it becomes a "they." The word itself has power, a collective authority: for some mysterious reason, "they say" carries more weight than "we say." "They" provokes unease, if not paranoia. ("They're out to get me.") So perhaps it was only an attack of the theys that gave me the sinister feeling that the Japanese would happily dot the J-E with oil wells. Perhaps if I had known them as individuals, if I had had time to sit up till the wee hours talking with Sam or spend an afternoon fishing with Mr. Yamaguchi, I would have trusted them more.

Certainly Japan's ecological consciousness had been raised

since the seventies, when *National Geographic* ran pictures of victims deformed by a diet of mercury-poisoned fish and pedestrians masked against air pollution. Today, Tokyo has less air pollution than New York City. Nonetheless, I worried. I worried that the Japanese would buy the J-E. I worried that they wouldn't buy it. And underneath the discordant sharps of these dueling worries there was the dark bass-line worry of the butchered body I'd found back in the canyon.

After we got back from the picnic brunch, I took another run, this time down the drive and out a couple of miles across open sagebrush. As I huffed and puffed back up to the lodge, I saw not one but two red Escorts parked in the kitchen yard. One was Monica's, I guessed. The rental company at the Bozeman airport must have given her the same model car I'd rented at the Great Falls airport. I strode through the kitchen and down the hallway to Trudi's office. She was sitting at her computer staring at a spreadsheet, nibbling at the side of her forefinger.

"Hey," I said from the doorway.

Trudi swiveled around from the monitor. "What's the matter?" she said.

I gestured with my thumb in the direction of my room. "She's still here?"

Trudi let out a resigned sigh. "Yeah."

"Do you know when she's leaving?" I inquired coldly.

"No. But probably not until after we hear about the autopsy. Dave called the pathologist's office in Missoula. They said it's scheduled for tomorrow afternoon." Trudi hesitated, then announced, "I talked to both my girls. They didn't leave any messages on my machine."

"So you think it was the sheriff."

"I don't know."

"So call him."

She winced. "I hate to bother him. I'm mean—it's Easter Sunday."

Irritated, I changed the subject. "I need an extra blanket."

Trudi looked at me. I didn't explain. She picked a bunch of keys off her desk. "No problem," she said briskly.

I followed her down the hallway to the ranch's linen closet, a narrow, unheated room under the eaves. At the end of the room, a dark green shade was pulled down over the single window. Silver light flared at its sides. Trudi flicked on the overhead. The ceiling-high shelves were stacked with a domestic arsenal of neatly folded linens, towels, and extra pillows. One wall displayed a veritable museum of coverlets and blankets: tufted cotton Depression-era spreads in apple green; summer-weight wool blankets yellowed with age; Hudson's Bay blankets heavy enough to flatten a restless sleeper. I felt as if I'd been admitted to a general's private storeroom—the general being the late Cora Fife. Her red-bordered labels still stuck to the edges of the shelves. "Cabin 1," she had ordered with a steel-tipped pen. "Upstrs double." "Cabin 5."

Trudi handed me a red wool blanket. It smelled faintly of cleaning chemicals. We lingered, savoring the systematized abundance of the room. "Originally," Trudi explained, "all the rooms in this wing were this size—cells for the great white dude's servants. Cora knocked out the walls between three of them for her office. She used two for your room." Idly, she scratched at the edge of a label. Her fingernail was short, polished red and as round as a child's. It made no inroad on the label. Clearly the only way to get them off was sandpaper.

"Does Cora walk at midnight if you put sheets in the wrong place?" I asked.

She smiled wryly. "I don't put the sheets in the wrong place." She paused. "But I can tell you she's been giving Dave hell in his dreams. A couple of times I woke him up, but he didn't appreciate it a whole lot, so now I lie there and listen to him groaning." She sighed. "I'll be glad when this whole business is settled, one way or another. I'm almost past caring what happens to the place at this point."

Back in my room, Monica was sitting on her bed, clothed this time, but still locked into her laptop. Maybe she'd washed her socks, because the air had improved, and I noticed that she had folded my quilt over the foot of my bed, but the room still wasn't big enough for both us. After I showered and changed, I took my red blanket and my travel alarm into the Big Room and climbed the stairs up to the balcony for a nap before the dinner prep. The bookcases up there were filled with jacketless best-sellers from an earlier era. John P. Marquand. Francis Parkinson Keyes. John Gunther. I picked up an Edna Ferber, set my alarm for four-thirty, and lay down on a cracked leather sofa with Trudi's red blanket. I didn't get past the first sentence. The book emitted a dry-attic smell that knocked me into sleep like ether.

The telephone on the desk downstairs woke me. It pierced my oblivion with an unkind grinding that I mistook for a kitchen appliance. After three rings I remembered where I was. On the fourth ring, it stopped. I lay there with my eyes shut. My legs felt like lead. I wasn't sure I was strong enough to move them. I started to drift off but was interrupted by the unmistakable clatter of Monica's boots. Bang-bang-bang, she came into the Big Room at a run, stopped short below my balcony, and snatched up the phone.

"Yes?" she demanded breathlessly. "Yes, this is Monica Leeds. Right. Right. No, I'm freelance. I appreciate your calling back. I was talking with Jim Moffit and he told me you might have something for me."

She listened. "Wait a second," she interrupted. "Let me get this down. What? What do you mean, 'off the record'?" she demanded. "If you don't want it in print, why talk to me?"

She went "hmm" a couple times, then said, "Yeah, well, let's make it 'not for attribution' then. But if it's as hot as you think, I'm going to need confirmation from other sources."

I peeked at my alarm clock. It was just after four. In the afternoon. I'd been asleep for only fifteen minutes. I closed my eyes again and heard the impatience in Monica's voice. "Look," she said, "I just told you I wouldn't use your name. Yeah. Right. I understand. So what's the big tip?" She sounded skeptical.

There were several seconds of silence. "Jesus," she swore softly. "I don't believe this."

More silence. Then a quick rattle of paper. She'd turned a page in her notebook. "Wait," she said sharply. "What was that click? Was that your line?"

"Shit," she muttered. She raised her voice and demanded, "Is someone on the line? Hello? No, listen," she told her caller, "it's okay. Yeah, I got that. Ford, like the car." She paused. "You better believe I'm gonna check it out." She flipped another notebook page. "You got a number for this guy?"

She listened. "That's okay, I can look it up. Yeah, well—" Another pause. "Thanks," she said quickly. "Bye." She replaced the receiver.

I waited under my blanket without moving. I heard a brief rustle of paper. For a long moment the room below me was still. Then she expelled an excited blast of air. It reminded me of the way deer snort in the woods. She left the room. The echo of her boots was surprising light and sharp.

A food writer might accurately describe my Easter Sunday dinner as "a postmodern mélange of Montana ingredients, Japanese seasonings, and French techniques." I wasn't sure it would work. Moreover, because I cook in freelance spurts, not as a full-time quotidian grind, at the outset of any job I invariably feel stiff and edgy, like a skier on the first snow of the season. I tend to rely on luck as much as skill, and for this meal, neither failed me. Trudi produced two brace of wild ducks frozen in blocks of ice inside half-gallon milk cartons (the gift of a shooting friend) and two legs of spring lamb weighing no more than four pounds each (from a local sheep rancher). I cut the breasts from the ducks and butterflied the legs of lamb. Then I marinated both and grilled them over a charcoal fire Hil started for me out in the courtyard. I basted the duck breasts with a sweet teriyaki sauce and took them off the grill while they were still as rare as roast beef. Then I carved them into slices and garnished them with a slaw of red cabbage, shaved and blanched and dressed with rice wine vinegar and light soy sauce which I'd brought from D.C. along with experimental packs of *kombu* and *katsuobushi* (dried kelp and bonito, respectively) from a Japanese grocery on upper Wisconsin. That was the first course.

To go with the second, I put large bowls of steamed rice at each end of the table and a round loaf of bread in the middle. (I hesitate to call my loaf "crusty," a term found on menus in second-rate restaurants, but thanks to a tray of ice on the oven's bottom rack, chips of the bread's crust scattered when you broke into it.) The Japanese, who were appreciative of French cuisine, preferred their lamb *à point,* and the differing thicknesses of butterflied meat were able to provide rare meat as well as well done (Dave's and Trudi's preference). Inspired by Trudi's grandmother's hand-me-down Basque recipes, I served the lamb on a bed of lima beans, the traditional Basque accompaniment. Only I cooked the beans in a sake-seasoned broth. Trudi's face was a study when she tasted them.

I don't know if lima beans are available in Japan, but in my mind they were as Japanese as sushi. When I was sixteen, my father took me along on a visit to a noted Japanese potter. The man lived out in Virginia, up against the Blue Ridge Mountains in a house hand-built by his students. We arrived at eleven o'clock on a summer morning and sat outside on his deck in the shade of a timbered overhang. A bent-over Japanese woman served us ice-cold gin and a flat basket of freshly picked, steamed lima beans. We ate these by squeezing the pale green pulp into our mouths, then depositing the hulls in neat piles on the table. The contrast between the soft, warm, pasty vegetable and the sharp frigid gin was a revelation. The visit seemed out of time. I was in a foreign, lushly green place where normal rules did not apply—where my father allowed me gin, and where neither man acknowledged the woman who served us. On the drive home, I asked, "Who was she?" and his answer shocked me.

"His wife," he said.

"Was she sick?" I wondered. "Why did she go around holding her stomach like that?"

"She was bowing," he said.

I served the J-E's guests with a straight spine, but was almost as invisible to them as the potter's wife. This was rather a relief. I was used to working for parties of jolly campers who expected the cook to engage in ongoing repartee, the more sarcastic the better.

The Japanese did not comment as I set the food before them, but their faces were interested, and as they ate their bodies relaxed. As a group, they were less fussy than some I'd cooked for. That morning up on the ridge, for example, I'd served Mr. Yamaguchi the first wedge of egg pie, and it tore as I coaxed it out of the pan. He waved away a better-looking piece and rattled something staccato. His colleagues laughed approvingly. Sam translated. Later I got him to teach me the words: *Hana yori dango.* Which is to say, "Dumplings are better than flowers when you are hungry."

Hil had resurrected, and he ate his dinner silently and hungrily in the breakfast pantry. After dinner, while he ran the dishwasher, I worked on my knives. A knife only obeys its owner, and I'd packed a favorite foursome. There is something highly satisfying about the rhythmic silken swishing noise of sharpening a blade, and I was happily whipping my eleven-inch chopper across a steel when Mac strolled in the back door.

"Danger," he quipped. "Chef at work."

"Cook," I corrected.

He settled his hip against the side of the counter to watch. I put the knife down. The best way to have an accident with a knife is to show off with it. "So what brings you into Dodge, stranger?" I asked.

The bags under his eyes seemed to have gotten darker, and his weather-tanned face looked strained, but the white Western shirt he wore open at the neck gave him a rakish air, as if he could jump right into an Errol Flynn stunt—without spraining his back. If middle age had thickened his brother, Dave, Mac still projected an elastic leanness. Under the pearl snaps of his slim-cut white shirt, his torso was as straight as a column. There were no small bulges at the sides of his belt and no slackness in the seat of his jeans. He had the body of a man used to walking briskly all day in the tracks of a grizzly, a man who could pop up the side of a tree, if necessary. Would I be able to keep up with him now any better than I had at twelve?

"I've got a present for you," Mac announced.

"Oh?" I said. I met his eyes. They were slightly bloodshot. Wind or whiskey, I wondered.

He held out a slim book bound in dark cloth. I put down my knife, wiped my hands on my apron, and turned it over in my hands. There was no title stamped on the spine. "What's this?"

"Dad's poems. You said you wanted them."

"Oh, yes, I did. I mean, I do." I opened the book. It was brand-new. "Poems," the first page said simply. And below the title: Olwyn MacDonald Fife.

"You're giving this to me?" I asked Mac. "To keep?"

"If you want it. There's still a whole carton of them."

"Mac, thank you," I said sincerely.

He smiled as if he'd just indulged a child. "You're welcome. I'll be interested to hear what you think."

"Of course." He made no move to go. I tested the edge of my chopper with my thumb.

"If I can do anything else for you . . ." He left the sentence open. A small smile teased the side of his mouth. His eyes were kind and full of humor.

I felt something sinking inside me. Maybe it was my willpower. "I'll let you know," I said.

He grinned.

When I finished in the kitchen at ten-thirty, I had a new batch of dough rising in the refrigerator, a bowl of duck stock cooling in the pantry, and a pot of oatmeal and milk on the back of the stove slow-cooking for Mr. Yamaguchi's breakfast. Sounds of general hilarity drifted out of the Big Room into the main hall, along with the reek of cigarette smoke. Trudi had set up a poker table by the fire, and even Dave, who was dealing, was smoking along with his guests. Monica, who was wearing enough red lipstick to pass for Miss Kitty, moved from the back of one chair to the next, whispering in ears and pouring shots from a bottle of hundred-proof Old Montana Red Eye bourbon. I brought them in a plate of deviled ham sandwiches, declined an invitation from Kaz to "loose" my shirt, and went to bed with Olwyn Fife's slender volume and a couple fingers of my own bourbon in a glass clinking pleasantly with ice.

* * *

If, as Wallace Stegner maintains, no place is a place till it has had a poet, Olwyn had made the J-E a real place. His sonnets were conventional (they catalogued the cruelties of an adored blonde called Ella) and in places they were forced, but he was clearly devoted to the antique discipline of the sonnet form and occasionally transcended it. However, it was one of his "modern" poems that moved me most. I've forgotten its title—I now wish I had kept the book, but at the time, leaving it behind seemed the best thing to do. Anyway, the poem opened with the simple statement "The West is not a place to satisfy desire." It was a place, Olwyn wrote, to plumb desire's dry wells, to trace the courses of its erosion down the walls of one's own heart.

What was it that Olwyn wanted? I doubted very much it was simply a woman named Ella. I lay there with the sharp, sweet taste of bourbon in my mouth and tried to sort out my own wants. Yes, I wanted to make love with Mac. And I wanted my mother to approve of me. And I wanted Rachel back, her blue eyes shining with health, and my father back as well, and more. Suddenly I felt subsumed by an oceanic wanting. I simply wanted. Every leaf, each touch.

Then, bingo, a soft knock at my door. I held my breath. Monica wouldn't knock. Would Mac? I felt terrified. So much for oceanic appetites.

Another knock, this time firmer. "Lee?" Trudi called through the door.

I started breathing again and sat up. "Yeah, come in," I told her.

Trudi was in her bathrobe, obviously without a bra underneath, so her torso was no longer battleship-firm but softly sloppy, like a cherished fuzzy pink pillow. Her face was pink too, flushed with excitement. "I saw your light on," she said.

"What's up?" I asked.

"I just talked to Sheriff Becker. Everything's okay, thank the good Lord! I just thought you'd want to know."

"What's okay?"

"The body you found?"

"Yes?"

"It wasn't human."

I stared at her. "What?"

"They x-rayed it at St. Patrick's, bag and all, to check for broken bones and bullets. Sheriff says it's the first thing they do when they bring in a body that's all decomposed like that. Anyway, the radiologist says it's a bear. A grizzly."

Chapter Eleven

The next morning, Easter Monday, my mother called at six. Trudi was giving orders to Hil in the kitchen, so I took the call on the extension in her office. I flicked on her halogen light and sat down in her ergonomic chair. I felt like Goldilocks trying out Mama Bear's desk.

"I'm sorry I didn't get back to you yesterday," my mother apologized.

"That's all right. How was your hors d'oeuvre party?"

"It was really very nice. It kept on going. That's why I didn't call." She sounded guilty.

"Don't worry, everything's okay now. I almost called you, but it would have been about one-thirty in the morning for you." The window in front of the desk reflected the white square of my apron's bib and, less distinctly, the pale ellipse of my face. I told my mother that the body I had found in the woods belonged to a grizzly.

"So now it's 'okay'?" She posed the question carefully, her voice in neutral.

"Mom, you know what I mean. I'm not for killing bears any

more than you are. But at least we don't have some Jeffrey Dahmer in chaps out on the loose. It was a poacher."

She digested the information. Then she objected, "But why kill the creature and leave it there?"

"Well, why not? It was pretty big. Too heavy for one person to move. What else was he going to do with it?" I picked a ballpoint out of a mug and started doodling a spiral on a pink Post-it pad. The ink in the ballpoint was red.

"He could have field-dressed it," she said angrily.

"Oh." I saw what was bothering her. "He wasn't after the meat," I explained. "Trudi says no one eats bear. It's full of trichinosis. She thinks they were after the skin. A bearskin rug with head and claws attached will go for two, three thousand dollars. Which explains the mystery of the missing extremities," I added with a Nancy Drew flourish.

"Dreadful," my mother muttered. I had the feeling she was directing some portion of her dismay at my flippancy.

"Yes," I agreed more soberly. I retraced my spiral. "There'll be an investigation. It's a federal offense to kill a grizzly. Maybe they'll get the guy."

She let out a sigh. I thought of Walt Surrey. "The wildlife people out here seem on the ball," I offered.

"That's good."

"What's the matter?"

"I just hope you know what you're doing," she worried.

"Mom, what I'm doing at the moment is sitting here talking to you, doodling on one of Trudi's Post-its. And when we finish this conversation, I'm going to go into the kitchen and cook breakfast. That's why I'm here. To cook. I assure you no one is going to ask me to go poacher hunting."

"What are you doodling?"

"A spiral. I'm doodling a spiral."

The line was quiet. I could almost hear my mother's antennae unfolding, stiffening, quivering slightly. "What does your spiral make you think of?" Her voice was charming, genuinely curious. Patients found her degree of interest irresistible.

I sidestepped. "What is this? A Rorschach test?" I said lightly.

Silence. I studied the red spiral I'd drawn. It was lopsided. What the hell, I thought. "It looks like the inside of a clock," I told her. "Like a spring unwinding," I added generously.

"A spring," she repeated.

I waited.

"Anything else?" she inquired.

"Not the right answer, huh? Okay, how about a shell? A many-chambered nautilus. Build thee more stately mansions, O my soul. Oliver Wendell Holmes. Eugene O'Neill. Drug addict mothers. Am I getting warmer?"

"Lee, for heaven's sake," she scolded. "Don't you know the spiral is a prehistoric symbol for bear?"

I looked at the ballpoint in my right hand. Slowly, carefully as if it held nitro instead of ink, I put it down on the desk.

"You *are* involved. I just want you to be careful," she said briskly. "Are you still smelling your smell? I haven't been able to reach my friend yet."

"That's okay. It's gone." This wasn't exactly true. Half an hour earlier, as I stepped out of my shower, I'd caught another nasty whiff. I sniffed myself, my towel, and the drains and decided that a plumber would help more than a psychiatrist. I asked my mother if she'd heard from my brother, John, and she was diverted. Yes, she chirped happily, he'd called from Aspen—as if Aspen were in China and he'd swum the Yangtze River to find a phone. I listened to news of my nieces' accomplishments. They were skiing down double black diamonds where Daddy feared to follow. They had U.S. Ski Team potential. "They look absolutely gorgeous," my mother reported, as if they were standing right there in their parkas shaking snow on the foot of her bed.

"They *are* gorgeous," I said sincerely.

We hung up. I pulled my doodle off the pad, folded it over a couple of times, and dropped it into the wastebasket. I put the ballpoint back into Trudi's mug, pushed in her ergonomic chair, and snapped off her halogen light. The sky outside the window had turned a paler shade of charcoal.

The early-morning kitchen was bright and warm and steamy. On the radio, the latest news from Waco, Texas, was that the FBI was blaring Tibetan chants instead of ammo into the besieged compound of Christian cultist David Koresh and his followers. Hil listened without comment, sipping coffee as he waited for his pancakes. He was looking greasier than usual. I could see the path of his comb through his black hair, which was collar-length and hung rather stiffly, like feathers. I could also see the pattern of broken capillaries in his eyes. But his mood was less grumpy than on previous mornings.

"Did Trudi tell you?" I asked.

"Tell me what?"

"That they x-rayed the body we found and it turned out to be a bear."

"Yep, she told me." His thin mouth didn't crack into a grin. But I had the feeling he was going to enjoy telling the story of how a griz played Gotcha with the cook, the sheriff, and the boss lady.

Then he surprised me. "Feel better?" he asked. It was the first time he'd asked me a direct question.

"Yes. I do. Thanks," I added. I poured four plate-sized pools of beige batter on the griddle. I remembered making free-form pancakes for Rachel: swans that looked like upside-down elephant heads; misshapen rabbits that ended up as tigers. Had I ever made bears? I flipped the pancakes and cracked Hil's eggs onto the griddle. The whites sputtered and bubbled festively. "You think they'll get whoever did it?" I wondered.

Hil shrugged. His eyes were on his eggs. He liked them runny. While the whites were still skim-milk blue, I slid them onto a plate with the pancakes. "Here," I said. "Syrup's in the dining room." He ambled in that direction. "Hil?" I asked. "When you have time, would you mind checking out the drains in my bathroom? There's a stink that seems to come and go."

The back of his head, dark as a falcon's, made a slight movement. I took it as an assent.

I couldn't sell my oatmeal. I took Mr. Yamaguchi's order first. "I have oatmeal for you," I told him. He smiled. Like a bronze buddha, his broad face was impenetrably benign. "Tomorrow, please," he requested. Today he wanted an omelet, a Western omelet. "Of course," I said, smiling back. He was making more of an effort with his English, but I still felt as if we were sailing past each other, calling out and catching only stray syllables.

Monica arrived at the table late, ordering nothing more than black coffee and a piece of dry whole-wheat toast. Last night, when she came in from her poker game, I had told her Trudi's news and her plucked eyebrows had shot halfway up her forehead. "No shit?" she had exclaimed. Her surprise was genuine. So whatever her anonymous source had provided, it wasn't a scoop on the x-ray.

Trudi and Dave had decided there was no point in trying to keep the Japanese in the dark, especially since, as the news spread, it was bound to cause a commotion. So over orange juice, Dave explained what had happened. His delivery was so laconic that the men were done with their Cheerios before they realized (with Sam's help) that a man-sized grizzly had been killed back in the woods behind the lodge. When Lynn and I brought in the omelets, the guests were talking animatedly in Japanese. Trudi, pleased by their appreciation of the drama, called their attention to me. "She's the one who found it," Trudi said. Suddenly I became visible. They regarded me with interest. I gave them a small nod, like a musician acknowledging applause in the middle of a set, and retreated back to the kitchen.

A few moments later, Lynn bounced in with the announcement: "Mr. Tanaka wants more toast. White. And they all want you to show them where you found the bear."

"Great," I said.

"It was Monica's idea. She wants to come along."

"Monica can—" I shut my mouth.

Lynn raised a knowing eyebrow. "Yes?" she dared.

"Go jump in the swamp," I said dryly.

"That not what you were going to say."

"No."

She grinned. This morning she was wearing an oversized navy-blue sweatshirt that hung like a tunic down to the knees of her jeans. Her sleeves were rolled up into doughnuts around her elbows, and her fine light brown hair was pulled back through another doughnut that looked like a ring of rumpled Kleenexes but was in fact ruffled white organdy. The navy and white, schoolgirl colors to my mind, set off Lynn's golden skin, which was perfect, even under the fluorescent kitchen light. Lynn may have been plumper than current fashion dictates, but she had a Juliet/ripe-apricot sort of beauty that more stylish girls lack.

The toast popped up. She buttered it. "Were you a virgin at my age?" she asked.

The question sideswiped me. "How old are you?" I asked, regaining my balance.

"Thirteen."

"Yes, I was." For a moment my answer seemed to satisfy her. Then she asked, "How old were you when you . . ." She hesitated.

"Nineteen."

She considered it. "That's old."

"I thought it was pretty old, too, back in the heyday of love and peace. I wanted to prove to myself that I wasn't an ice maiden. But that's not something you can find out in a one-shot deal. As it were." I gave her a rueful smile. "What I found out was that I didn't really like the guy very much."

Her frank hazel eyes were still curious, but there was uncertainty in them, too, as if she could not decide which door to open next. She seemed extraordinarily vulnerable. All of a sudden the notion of locking up one's nubile daughter in a tower struck me as eminently sensible. "What about your mom?" I asked. "You ask her about this?"

"Oh," Lynn said dismissively, "she never dated anyone except Dad."

"That doesn't count?"

She took out Mr. Tanaka's toast. When she came back, her manner was sassy again. "So are you frigid?" she demanded.

"Nope," I said. "Now, would you like to hear my lecture on birth control and safe sex?"

"Nope," she mimicked.

By nine o'clock the phone was ringing off the hook with calls about the dead grizzly. Neighbors were concerned and curious, reporters wanted statements, the sheriff's department was trying to reach Walt Surrey and so was a federal wildlife agent. To escape, Trudi went along with Dave and the Japanese on their morning ride. Monica snapped new batteries into her tape recorder, revved up the engine of her red rental, and in a flamboyant spray of gravel, peeled off for the institute. Lynn, on her way out the back door with her arms full of clean towels for the cabins, watched Monica's exit and shook her head disapprovingly. From the back, she could have passed for Trudi. But when she turned, her eyes sparkled with thirteen-year-old glee. "She's going to get her head chewed off," Lynn predicted happily. "Dad says Uncle Mac's gone ballistic."

By ten-thirty, I'd finished the lunch prep. Corn chowder was on the menu (corn, I'd read, was the foreign veg of choice in Japan—they even sprinkled it on top of pizzas). I also did Butte pasties, which are not made of sequins but of meat and potatoes baked in dough. The copper miners' wives used to pack them in their husbands' lunch pails. I took off my apron, put a corduroy shirt on over my T-shirt, my green vest over that, and went out for a walk.

There was no sign of the sun that had shone so thinly the day before; and no drama in the cloud cover. The sky was flat and dingy, but the bite seemed to have gone from the wind. I walked briskly past the guest cabins. Lynn's cleaning cart was parked under the pines outside Cabin Two, and the carpenters' pickup was back outside Cabin Five. Between the long whines of their saws, I could hear Garth Brooks wailing from the boom box Lynn carried on her rounds. I headed up the canyon road. A truck coming down the road, then a station wagon, slowed courteously as they passed. We peered at each other and smiled and waved. I recognized neither driver.

I was not squeamish about going back to the clearing. I simply had not wanted to play tour guide for Monica and the Japanese. (Dave was sympathetic and told the men he would take them himself after "things quieted down." Monica he referred to Mac.) I wanted to go back there on my own, to straighten things out in my mind. There was a disturbing *Through the Looking Glass* quality about the whole thing. I kept going back to my mother's implied question. Why was the death of a grizzly "okay" when compared to the death of a man? Did the degree of evil depend on who the victim was? Most people would agree that it was "worse" to kill a nun than a drug dealer.

But why does our judgment pivot around the victim instead of the killer? The mind of the poacher operates inside our model of reality; as in Cora's linen closet, we can place his need, his greed, on labeled shelves. But the psychopath's compulsions come from another closet, a closet where the shelves may be vertical arcs, where the light switch is hidden somewhere under the floorboards. In terms of safeguarding society, a psychopath is more of a threat than a poacher.

So why do our laws find an "insane" killing more forgivable than a "rational" one?

I felt my mind looping sloppily, like the spiral I'd drawn that morning. I focused on the straight line of the road, on the straight trunks of the pines on either side. Poacher or psychopath, a grizzly, not a man, was dead. Up ahead, a deputy's car and three trucks were parked alongside the road. Mac was getting into one of them. He started it up and accelerated past me. The windshield was opaque with ocher dust, but behind the half-moons cleared by the wipers, I caught a glimpse of his set jaw, his unseeing eyes. His handsome face looked pinched, as if his anger were imploding, pulling tissue and tendon toward an interior black hole.

Up ahead, the deputy recognized me. He had been one of the searchers when the bear was still a man. Now he was acting as traffic director. Half the county had driven out for a look-see, he said, but Walt wanted to keep the place secure till the feds showed up. He shrugged. "Ain't nothing changed since Saturday except the corpse." He waved me on into the woods.

The yellow tape and blue tarp were still there. And Walt was there with a game warden, an older man wearing a badge and holstered gun. The two of them were picking up scattered Polaroid wrappers. They seemed to find my questions a welcome diversion. I learned that the bear's remains would be transferred from Missoula to the wildlife lab in Bozeman for forensic analysis. The necropsy report would not only tell the bear's age and weight and general condition (information useful to Mac's census). It would trace the path of the bullet (or bullets) and establish whether the cartridge casing Walt had found belonged to one of them.

Walt and the game warden agreed that there was "not a whole lot" of bear poaching in the area, though there was "some" to the north on the Blackfeet reservation.

"They're after the skin?" I asked.

"Maybe," Walt said noncommittally. Then he added, "There's a big demand in the Orient for bear gallbladders and the male's reproductive organs. The Asians use them for medicine. A single gallbladder can bring up to five thousand dollars on the black market."

"Really?" I said.

"Of course, the poacher doesn't get that much," Walt went on. "He's got to go through a bunch of middlemen. Ideally, we'd like to nail the whole network, but some of these international rings are better-equipped than we are. They've got automatic weapons and state-of-the-art electronic tracking gear. In Appalachia, they locate radio-collared black bears and kill them while they're hibernating. It's big business."

"So how do you stop them?" I protested.

He gave me a level look. "Mostly we don't." He glanced at the blue tarp. "If it had been human, there'd be more to go on. With a bear, you can't go out and interview the guy he was drinking with the night before. Whoever killed this one did it weeks ago and took his beer cans with him."

For a moment we were quiet. The game warden's walkie-talkie squawked softly under his jacket. "Mac looked pretty upset," I said.

The older man spoke. "Sometimes it's hard not to think of them as 'yours.' "

"Mac's offering a ten-thousand-dollar reward," Walt told me. "Maybe it'll shake loose a lead." He didn't sound hopeful.

I saw Mac that afternoon when I drove Kaz over to the Sacred Paw Institute. Kaz wanted to borrow one of the institute's black boxes. The grizzly's death had excited his interest in a way that Mac's slide show had not, and he wanted to take home snaps of a grizzly dining on a cow. He arrived for lunch with a large aluminum suitcase that cushioned his camera gear in black foam. He showed Dave and Trudi a new remote device. It triggered the shutter by sensing motion. It was, Kaz explained happily, more reliable than the institute's heat sensor. He used it to stake out birds' nests.

Dave called the institute. Mac was taking no calls. He was working on "the Book" with Monica. But Clare said she saw no problem in setting up a second camera on one of the cows. She thought it might be interesting to compare results of the two types of sensors. She'd get one of the interns to work with Kaz on rigging another box. So while Dave took Mr. Yamaguchi on a tour of fishing holes along Givens Creek, I drove Kaz and his camera case to the Sacred Paw in my rental.

There was an assortment of pickups and cars outside, none of them new and shiny. There were Sacred Paw bumper stickers, black on white with the logo of a bear print, elegantly elongated in the style of Native American artists. There were also "Love Your Mother" stickers showing the green-and-blue sphere of Earth. Had the death of the grizzly mobilized Mac's troops? Then I remembered it was a Monday, the first day in the work week. The world of work weeks seemed very distant.

Inside the log building, the open space hummed with activity. Phones rang, granola types in Birkenstock sandals conferred around a copier, pecked away at keyboards. A young man wearing granny glasses, his hair in a ponytail, carried in an armful of stove wood. Again, I had the feeling of having stepped into a time warp. There were the same molecules of pure passion in the air as there had been at Students for a Democratic Society headquarters back in the sixties. But there were differences—improvements, actually. No one smoked. Men were typing as well as women. No one had purple mimeograph ink on his or her fingers. Everyone looked as if he or she used a lot of aloe soap.

The kid in the ponytail took Kaz off to a lab on the other side of the open work space. Clare went back to her office. I was helping myself to coffee from the communal urn when Mac came out of his office with Monica. Mac was looking better. Evidently, talking about himself into Monica's tape recorder for a couple of hours was a balm for his anger. For her part, Monica looked wilted. Her head sagged a little, like a fuzzy bloom past its prime, and her eyes were bleary.

"How's the book coming along?" I asked them.

"Great," Mac answered absently. He strode over to the threshold of Clare's office and called through the open doorway, "We need some food."

"There's some leftover pasties back at the J-E," I said. The words popped out of my mouth, involuntary as a knee jerk, but Mac waved them away.

Clare emerged from her office, face calm as a nun's emerging from prayer. "There's tuna fish at the trailer," she informed him.

Mac turned to the room at large. "We need some food," he announced again. Young faces swiveled around from blue screens. A pretty, obese girl whose bulges were barely contained in an India-print cotton tunic and knit slacks stood up and volunteered to go and make sandwiches with Clare's tuna.

"Ellie, you're an angel!" Mac exclaimed. He put an arm around her shoulders and gave her an affectionate squeeze.

"Only when you're hungry," Ellie cracked, but she was pleased.

Clare shook her head. "When are you going to learn how to open a can?" she asked Mac.

His dark eyes glinted mischievously. "Why should I?" He opened his hands and held them out like a triumphant magician. Mac the Magnificent.

There was no applause. Mac adjusted, shifting from comic to earnest in the space of a breath. "I know this isn't part of your job description," he said to Ellie with boyish sincerity.

"Just call me Angel," she quipped as she lumbered toward the door. Her dangling brass earrings swayed like the fringe on a circus elephant. I felt a sudden sympathy with her, as if I were a sister elephant and the name of our act was "The Way to a Man's Heart."

I thought of Mexican writer Laura Esquivel's thesis that for women, food is a sexual weapon, a way to penetrate the body of a man. I tried to imagine the effect of my meat pasties on Mac. The filling was seasoned with the sweetness of cooked onions and the summery tang of rosemary. How much of me would my pasties carry into the secret fibers of Mac's being?

"Lee?" He was peering at me. "Where are you?"

"Oh. Out to lunch, I guess." I could feel my face turning red.

"You're blushing," Monica accused. She and Clare looked curiously at me. Mac was amused, as if he'd read my thoughts.

I changed the topic. "I understand you've offered a reward for information about the poacher."

Monica's face sharpened with attention.

"You did?" Clare said to Mac. "How much?"

"Ten thousand."

There was a silence. The clicking of keyboards and the whine of printers had stopped. The other two workers were actively listening.

"We don't have it." Clare's voice was ice-cold.

"So we'll get it," Mac said airily.

"From where?" she challenged. "Your bear-loving Japanese pals? Dream on."

Anger flushed back into Mac's face. "You've got a small mind, Clare. You'll never get anywhere unless you can learn to keep the big picture in focus."

"Okay," she said, unperturbed. "Here's a big picture for you. The Sacred Paw folds. And all our long-term research folds with it." With her chin, she gestured toward the two interns. "Do you know you haven't paid any staff for three weeks?"

Mac turned to the workers and read their faces. Instantly, he was contrite. "I didn't realize," he apologized. "We'll get right on it." He grinned engagingly at his staff. "I'll confer with my bean-counter immediately."

The pair of workers, both young men, grinned back. "No problem," one of them said loyally. "Fasting's a real high," the other cracked.

"You'll have a check tonight," Mac promised.

Clare closed her eyes, as if drawing a steel shade down over her frustration.

* * *

Mac and Clare and Monica all showed up at the J-E for dinner—another slice of Americana: absolutely beautiful steaks, which I cooked on the grill outside and served with twice-baked potatoes, wilted spinach salad, and sourdough bread. Mac and Monica were chummy. Clare was more aloof than usual. She was wearing a lavender wool turtleneck with her jeans and had pulled the glossy cascade of her hair back from her face and twisted it into a loose knot at the nape of her neck. The contrast between the softness of the sweater and starkly ethnic planes of her face was stunning. I wondered if her bound hair was a statement to Mac. If so, he was oblivious.

After cleanup, Hil lingered in the kitchen. On the radio, NPR was playing a Brandenburg concerto. I wanted my nightly shot of bourbon, but I didn't want to drink with him around. At eight-thirty, his habitually slow way of moving was sloppy at the edges. But even at midday, his conversation didn't sparkle. All I'd managed to squeeze out of him in the four days I'd been there was that his name was Hilaire with one *l*, not two as in Hillary Rodham Clinton, that his father had worked for Olwyn Fife, and that he'd seen " 'Nam." I made myself a steak sandwich for my supper, slicing the rare meat thinly onto a chewy slab of sourdough. "You hungry?" I asked him.

Apparently not. He didn't answer. Finally he said, "I fixed your can."

It took me a minute to realize he was talking about my bathroom. I thanked him. He didn't leave. I thanked him again. He still didn't leave. I took my sandwich, a glass of ice water, and an old copy of *Montana* magazine into the staff dining room. On the cover, it had a picture of elk backlit in autumnal light.

He followed me, stopping at the threshold. "Trudi didn't tell you?" he asked.

"Tell me what?"

His lanky frame wavered slightly. "Don't put any more tampons down the toilet," he said bluntly.

Oh God, I thought. Talk about shit jobs.

"Tell her, too."

"Who?"

"Lois Lane," he said sarcastically.

"You mean Monica?" I was interested. "She play girl reporter with you?"

He thought about it, then nodded. "She wrote it down."

"What did she ask you?"

"She said she wanted to talk to a real live Indian. She wanted to know what it was like being 'Native American.' " He let out a derisive bark.

I was curious. "So what did you say?"

"I told her dogs had it better." His voice was thick with self-pity, but his eyes were dry and vacant.

Chapter Twelve

Dave and Trudi and their foreman were up that night with a bunch of two-week-old calves down with a viral diarrhea called scours. The week before my arrival, after a three-inch snowfall, the disease had run rampant through the youngest calves. Dave and Trudi had cut out the sick ones and forced syringefuls of antibiotics down their throats—a slippery, smelly business that didn't always work wonders. "If you think catching a greased pig is bad . . ." Trudi commented wryly.

I stumbled into them in the kitchen at five-thirty. Dave was unshaven and had the flat, tired look of a gambler who'd spent all night at the tables and lost. Six of the calves they had carried inside to nurse had died, and more deaths were likely. Like a mother quizzed on her children's sickness, Trudi was defensive. When I asked about calling the vet, she retorted sharply, "There's nothing he can do except bill us. The only control is to inoculate all the cows before calving, and the shots cost an arm and a leg. We've already fed one leg to the insurance company," she added angrily.

Dave was more resigned. He blamed the outbreak of scours on the cold weather.

At breakfast, Mr. Yamaguchi again postponed the pleasure of my oatmeal until "tomorrow." Dave told his guests that today they'd take an evening ride, since all hands were needed for the risky job of milking the sick calves' mothers. He also told them that I would drive them into Choteau for a tour of the combination gift shop and museum there. Then, after breakfast, Dave drove the men down to see his calves. He exuded a sort of grim satisfaction, as if fate had arranged an object lesson on "real ranching" for his potential investors.

Around ten-thirty, they were back, ready for the excursion to Choteau, loaded with enough camera equipment to make *Star Wars.* I asked Kaz if he had managed to get his camera set up for a grizzly.

"Okay, okay," he said enthusiastically. "We went to same place before."

"The swamp?"

"Yes, I arranged it on other side. There is little house, a cabin, very small."

"You mounted the camera on the cabin?"

"No, we put it on tree close by. Safely high up. The kid brought the ladder."

"Was there any sign of grizzly?" I wondered.

"No. But he will come to cow soon." Kaz held his nose, miming a monumental stink.

Monica, who said she had "some things to do," declined to join us. The men piled into the van, as exuberant as boys playing hooky. They were still in the cowboy suits they'd worn to breakfast, and the motley of their shirts—fuchsia and orange, black and turquoise—lent our excursion a carnival brightness. The mood was enhanced by the sun, which, if not exactly out, flooded the blond landscape with thin spring light. The van's shadow, rolling along beside us, was almost transparent. Through the windshield, the expanse of sky was white.

After we hit paved highway, the rolling landscape flattened out and the barbed-wire fence lines ran straight for miles. The ground looked barren except for tangles of stunted trees along creek beds. I had to wonder at the fences. Could all those enclosed acres of wispy grass support even one cow? We stopped and got out of the car at a historical marker commemorating the area as a former buffalo range. Buffalo, the sign declared, had sustained the Blackfeet Nation by providing meat, moccasins, robes, and tepees. According to Indian legend, the first buffalo had come from a hole in the ground. When the unimaginable happened and the buffalo were exterminated, some Indians claimed that the whites had found the hole, herded the buffalo back down it, and plugged it up.

Sam translated. Mr. Yamaguchi said something that sounded derisive, and the men all laughed. They photographed the sign and each other standing beside it.

The Front's rain-shadow stops short of Choteau, a small tree-lined grid set just inside the western leg of a vast fertile triangle of dryland wheat farms. The town has gray concrete grain elevators by the railroad tracks, a towering quasi-Romanesque courthouse erected of rough-cut gray stone, and quiet blocks of modest houses with wide aluminum siding and tidy front yards. The gift shop/museum at one end of the main street looked like a storefront built for an episode of *Gunsmoke,* only along with a hitching rail, there was a fifteen-foot-high dinosaur out front. Inside you could buy pocket-size quartz dinosaurs made in Mexico. There were also dusty displays of melon-size eggs. These had been laid by a recently discovered dinosaur that paleontologists had named Maiasaura. According to the exhibit labels (typed on an old manual typewriter), herds of these "mother lizards" had once nested at a site a couple of miles outside town.

The Japanese, however, crowded around more recent artifacts: a skeleton with Hudson's Bay Company arrowheads imbedded in the bones and two bullet holes through its crushed skull; a Victorian memorial wreath whose elaborate dark flowers were made of braided human hair; a fat piece of yellow rope used to hang a local murderer; a thinner piece of rope used to tie his hands behind his back. Beside these exhibits, the stuffed grizzly rearing up in a dim corner seemed tame, dowdy even.

The men were fascinated by the pieces of rope. They kept

touching them and spent a long time deciphering the accompanying exhibit of brittle newspaper clippings, black-and-white glossies of a gallows imported from another county and erected in a machine shed, and a printed card, formal as a wedding announcement, which "respectfully invited" witnesses to attend the execution on August 29, 1933, "between four and eight in the morning." The visitors were even more impressed when I told them that Montana still hangs people.

So the visit was a great success, even though the polyester T-shirts and pastel Indian-style clay pots did not tempt them. Photographs were not permitted inside, but they made up for it outside, posing with the dinosaur and against the hitching rail. Then we piled back into the van and drove slowly down the main street, peering at the bars. There were three, all with small, old electric signs. It was unclear whether they were open. They had a shuttered look, as if Jack Palance were inside, drinking alone and nursing a grudge. I wasn't sure I wanted to drop in, never mind with four foreigners.

Driving around the courthouse, I noticed a red Escort parked under the tall pines at the edge of the courthouse lawn. Then I saw a woman trotting toward it. It was Monica. There could be no mistake. Her trench coat flapped around her, a silver earring glinted in the pale sunlight, her red mouth was slightly open. I tooted at her and pulled over beside her car. We rolled down the windows. "Monica!" we chorused.

She recognized us and laughed. "Hey! How's it going?"

"Come have lunch with us," Sam said, leaning over me.

"Here?" she demanded, as if he'd proposed an outrageous act.

Sam laughed.

"Monica!" Mr. Tanaka waved from the backseat.

"Hey, sweetie," she acknowledged.

"Why don't you join us?" I asked as nicely as I could. I liked the idea of two hostesses a lot better than one, especially when the one was me.

"Not this time. I've got to get moving." There was a jag of excitement in her voice. "See you guys later!" She blew them extravagant kisses, the car keys in her hand jingling an accompaniment. "You're fabulous!" she told them through the open windows. She was flying high on something.

"Monica," I said. "What's going on?"

She leaned closer to the van. Her eyes flashed. "I think I've found my Pulitzer."

"Really?"

She closed her eyes tight, then opened them. "Really." She was serious. "Ta," she said jauntily as she unlocked her car.

Choteau had no "Macudonarudosu," as they say in Japlish, or Kentucky Fried either (a popular favorite in Tokyo, according to Sam). But behind the courthouse we found a primitive prototype of fast-food restaurants, a fifties-style drive-in. It was constructed of logs painted bright red. The original carport was still attached to it, but the sassy teenaged carhops who hung trays of burgers on your car window were long gone. *"American Graffiti,"* Kaz commented appreciatively.

Inside, the decor was ski lodge circa 1960: shag carpet and a freestanding enameled fireplace where a wood fire burned. It was late for lunch, and the place was empty of customers. Grateful for the warmth (it had been colder inside the museum than it was outside), we took a table beside the fire. The men ordered "hotto doggus" and burgers. I ordered a turkey sandwich on whole wheat. "Scratch the fries," I told the waitress.

Mr. Tanaka said something to Sam. Sam laughed, answered in a staccato burst, then turned to me. "He wonders why the fries are itchy!"

"It's a problem," I admitted. We sipped iced water in plastic glasses. "So," I said brightly, plunging into my hostess role, "tell me about the guy who was hanged—what did he do?"

"He robbed a man and strangled him with a piece of wire," Sam said.

"He drank too much *uisuki,*" Kaz said.

I looked at Sam. "Whiskey," he said.

"Both are named George," offered Mr. Tanaka.

"The murderer and the victim were both George?"

"Exactly." Mr. Tanaka gave a small, elegant nod.

Mr. Yamaguchi spouted something guttural. It sounded like an order. Sam said to me, "George the Murderer's last message was in the newspaper. He said he was leaving 'this good old earth' in good spirits and blamed no one but himself for what he'd done. He said we all must go sometime but he didn't want to go this way."

I looked at Mr. Yamaguchi. He nodded a sage approval of the hanged man's statement.

"Do you execute people in Japan?" I asked him. He indicated yes. Another bond: Japan and the United States were the only industrialized nations on the planet that had not abolished the death penalty. I imagined the bright arc of a sword above a kneeling figure. "What's the killing method of choice?" I chattered merrily on. "A sword?"

Mr. Yamaguchi's face hardened as he sucked in air through clenched teeth. He loosened a statement from the back of his throat. Sam translated without meeting my eyes. "In Japan, criminals don't deserve to die by the sword. We hang them like you do."

Clearly I'd offended Mr. Yamaguchi. I cursed all the Kurosawa movies I'd seen. I cursed Trudi for pushing me into the role of international tour guide. "I'm sorry," I apologized. "Please forgive my stupidity."

The cloud cleared almost instantly. Mr. Yamaguchi let out a satisfied "Haa!" He smiled at me as if I were a pupil with the right answer. "You not American." ("Amelican," he said.)

I smiled back while Sam explained, "Americans never say they're sorry."

I wasn't complimented. Maybe Mr. Yamaguchi had never talked to an American woman before. We're great at apologies. At the merest twitch of disapproval we curl into our lowly worm postures and pipe up, "I'm sorry." Moreover, from what I'd seen of Mac in action, he was pretty decent at apologizing, too.

I smiled some more at Mr. Yamaguchi and quoted one of the most irritating lines ever penned: "Love is never having to say you're sorry." I hoped he'd find it inscrutable.

Kaz perked up. His eyes narrowed. He sucked his teeth. Then he exclaimed triumphantly, *"Love Story!"*

I had to laugh. "On the money," I congratulated him.

He looked puzzled. Again, Sam translated. They all repeated it: "On the money."

We moved from the death penalty to street crime. The conversation was uphill all the way. Actually, it was less a conversation than a lecture—given by the four of them to an audience of one: me. In Japan, the men declared proudly, street crime is so rare that there is no word in the language for "mugging." Ownership of guns, swords, and daggers is outlawed, so even mobsters' battles are usually fought with fists or kitchen knives. They were all still deeply shocked by the killing in Baton Rouge of a Japanese exchange student, who unknowingly went to the wrong house for a party and was shot to death because he didn't understand the meaning of "Freeze!"

"It is hard to believe," Mr. Tanaka observed, "you cannot walk in your cities without fear."

By the time the burgers came, I felt exhausted. It was almost two o'clock. I remember checking my watch.

We got back to the J-E about four-thirty. Monica's car wasn't in the lot. Or, as I told the sheriff later, there was only one red Escort in the lot. I didn't check the license plate. I went to my room and stopped short at the threshold. The room had been torn apart—or at least half of it. Monica's bedclothes were ripped open, as if she'd lost something in them. Her dresser drawers, even though she'd never bothered to use them, were crookedly open. Then I noticed that all her things were gone—plus an old bra of mine that I'd left over the back of the armchair. Obviously, she had moved on to new pastures.

I felt more annoyed than relieved. Not only was my curiosity about her "Pulitzer" unsatisfied. (Was it something to do with her "Ted and Jane" story?) But after helping herself to my quilt, my hand cream, even my tampons until I hid them, she had gone off with my most comfortable bra and without even bothering to say goodbye. She could have left a note, I thought angrily.

I bumped into Dave in the hallway. He was clean-shaven but scarcely less tired-looking.

"Monica's gone," I announced.

"Good riddance," he said. Under his denim jacket, he was wearing a gun in a black nylon holster.

"Where are you going with that?" I wondered.

"I'm taking our guests out for an evening ride."

In the kitchen, Trudi and Lynn had taken over. Trudi was presiding over a sage-stuffed turkey in the oven (I'd already done a red onion compote in lieu of cranberry sauce) and Lynn was squeezing fresh lemons for a lemon pie. They were singing along with Lynn's tape of—who else—Garth Brooks on my box.

"Monica's gone," I interrupted. "All her things are gone out of my room."

"Really?" Trudi said. "She didn't say anything." She turned to Lynn. "You can take away a place at the table."

"Rather rude," I commented.

"You're surprised?"

They went back to Garth Brooks. Their sopranos were pretty enough, but the Sensitive New Cowboy lyrics were making me cross, so I was more than willing to volunteer for the "cocktail drop." This entailed loading the bar and nibbles into a hamper and driving it out to a prearranged spot along the creek ("crick," Trudi said) where Dave and his guests would dismount for a preprandial libation. I warmed up a can of black olives in olive oil and crushed garlic, sprinkled them with oregano, and packed them into an insulated jar. As I was slicing up a venison salami, I asked Trudi, "What's the likelihood of bumping into a bear?"

"Zilch," she said.

"So why is Dave packing a gun?"

"Just don't wander off too far from the truck," she advised.

Lynn suggested, "If a grizzly comes along wanting a piece of that salami, don't make it say please."

"Thanks a lot, gang." I arranged my slices in a Tupperware container and hoped it was smellproof.

The cocktail spot offered a distant view of Ear Mountain, but it was not particularly scenic. Perhaps they had chosen it because it boasted the only landmark for miles along the creek banks, a large dead tree trunk twisted into a crooked omega and scoured silver by the wind. I set the hamper in a well-used hollow under the tree's exposed roots, then climbed down the eroded bank onto the wide stony beach left by floods. Now, however, the creek was running shallow and clear, and its noise was calming. Some sort of sandpiper (it had spots on its breast) was bobbing on the rocks, head down, tail always up like a misweighted mechanical toy. In the west, over the line of snowy mountains, wisps of pale blue sky appeared. The late light turned almost peachy. Nighthawks swooped and skittered high above the creek, then plummeted in suicidal-looking dives, braking and pulling out at the last minute. I kept hearing loud bullfrog-like belches. It took me a while to realize that it wasn't coming from frogs in the creek; the sounds were attached to the birds' stunts—the "belches" were made by braking feathers as the birds reversed their dives.

I climbed out of the riverbed and leaned against the pickup's fender. At my feet, whorls of soft gray leaves starred the arid ground. Before me stretched the empty, tawny plains where grizzlies, before the thrust of civilization drove them back into the mountains, used to roam with the buffalo. A hump of land to my left darkened. Although I wanted to be gone before the party rode up, I resisted looking at my watch.

Gradually the landscape around me became more animal than vegetable, as if the bones of a monumental grizzly slumbered beneath its shorn hide—here a jut of hip, there the lift of rib cage. I felt as if I were dreaming. Then suddenly, without warning, the dream turned nasty. There were bones at my feet, a perfect skeleton, and as I stood there gazing down at it, putrefied flesh began to rot back onto it. The decay grew backward into the corpse of a bear. I looked down on it from a height. The dead bear was furless, its dry hide as hard as a mummy's.

I gasped as if I'd been hit. It took me some moments to push the images aside.

On the drive back, the light was pearly. In the distance, the J-E's cows stood velvet-black on blond grass. I wanted to take comfort in the sight of them, in their solid domesticity, but my vision, my waking dream, whatever it was, interfered.

Dinner worked out fine. (The white meat was on the dry side, but that's nothing new with turkey.) There were more eaters at the table than usual. Besides the Japanese and the Fifes and Clare (her hair was down again), there was Roy, the farm manager, his wife, and a visiting young farrier. With her freckles and single blond braid, she looked as wholesome as a Norman Rockwell model.

When Kaz commented on Monica's absence, Mac said she'd called his office early in the afternoon and canceled their taping session. "She said something had come up and she'd see us tonight," he said.

After cleanup, I went to my room, closed the skewed dresser drawers, and stripped Monica's bed. As I was balling up her sheets into the pillowcase, something fell and clunked on the floor. I picked it up. It was a root of some kind, dried and twisted, about three inches long. Bound to it with black thread was a bunch of broken stems. It looked as sinister as a witch's *bouquet garni*. What on earth was it doing in Monica's bed? Was she a member of a New Age coven? Or was the bundle some sort of experiment in aromatherapy? I sniffed at it. A faint dusty odor, nothing more. Exasperated, I tossed her charm into the wastebasket and her dirty sheets into the hallway. Then I tackled the bathroom. I wiped her hairs out of the tub and scrubbed the porous old porcelain with too much pale green cleanser. I had to admit that the bra she'd gone off with was shot. Its lace was ratty and its elastic held only the memory of stretch. I wondered if the manufacturer still made the same style. I stood up and inhaled the chlorinated scent of Comet. I thought about a hot bath and a big whiskey and rejected both.

I didn't need to mellow out. I needed to tighten my grip. The twilight dream images of the dead grizzly still tugged uncomfortably at the edges of my consciousness. I wrote the images down in my notebook, clustered key words in free-associative bubbles, analyzed the results. The horror of the vision, I decided, resided in the backward unrolling of decay. The death I saw made no fatter worms, no richer soil, no greener grass, no sleeker animals. The rot was reversed, perverted into a redeath.

The insight pleased me. I wrote it down for future reference. Still, the ballpoint didn't tame the images. I carried my notebook into Trudi's office and plunked myself down in her Mama Bear chair. Even if it had been earlier, I doubt I would have dialed my mother's number. I didn't really want to Process My Feelings with her. (I envisioned hunks of processed cheese, hygienically wrapped in supermarket cellophane. This was probably unfair.) I wanted a distraction. A nice, upbeat one. I opened my notebook and dialed the number I'd scribbled on the inside cover before I left Washington. It belonged to a friend named Luke who lived outside Helena. We had made plans to spend a couple of days together at the end of my "vacation" at the J-E.

Luke Donner is a state homicide investigator. We'd met the previous year while untangling the murders on my Bob Marshall Wilderness trip. Afterward, in the space of eleven hours, we had gotten tangled up in each other. When I thought of him, and it was often enough, I felt a little spring of hope. I don't know what he felt. Our Christmas cards crossed in the mail. Never mind what mine said. I borrowed some of it for a love poem that is now working on its fifth rejection. Luke's card had a Charlie Russell cartoon on the outside. Inside, under the printed Christmas message, he had written: "Hi, there. All the best, Luke." I studied the card, inside and out, like a Zen koan.

When I called him at the end of January to say I was going to be out his way in April, his voice seemed to expand with happiness. We talked about driving over to Big Mountain to catch the tail end of spring skiing. We talked again the week before I left, so I knew he was spending Easter weekend with his parents and his six-year-old son, but now it was Tuesday night. Unless he was working late, he should be home.

His phone rang three times. I was gearing up to leave a cheery message on his machine (lift the chest, brighten the voice) when a woman answered. "Hello?" she said.

"Hello?" I echoed stupidly.

"Yes?" she said.

"Uh, yes. Is Luke Donner there, please?" Maybe I'd dialed the wrong number.

But I hadn't. "No, he isn't," the woman answered. "He's working late tonight. This is Barb. Can I take a message?"

Barb. The name did more than ring a bell. It set off a screaming alarm. *What was his wife doing there?* He had told me they were separated. He had spent maybe two hours out of our eleven talking about her. I took a breath. "This is Lee Squires," I told her.

"Oh hi," she said pleasantly. "I've heard so much about you."

I didn't know how to answer. I resorted to apology. "I'm sorry to call so late."

"No problem. I'm looking forward to meeting you," she said graciously.

"Same here," I heard myself say. "Maybe you could have him give me a call?" I gave her the number, even though I'd already given it to Luke. I thanked her and hung up.

As a distraction from dead bears, the conversation worked just fine.

CHAPTER THIRTEEN

Wednesday morning I ate a big steaming bowl of my creamy overnight oatmeal. I didn't offer any to Mr. Yamaguchi, and he didn't ask for it either. A glimmer of light began to penetrate my brain. Later I asked Sam, "Do Japanese people like oatmeal?"

"Sure," Sam said. "It's like *okayu*—rice congee."

"But Mr. Yamaguchi doesn't want it."

"Maybe he prefers omelets," Sam said tactfully.

"So why did he say he wanted oatmeal?"

Sam looked puzzled. "He told you he wanted it?"

I let it go. Clearly, any kind of a deal between NVI and the J-E was going to encompass a lot more time and work than a single week. In the interest of preserving the *wa* (a.k.a. group harmony), the Japanese would say yes to oatmeal and then postpone eating it forever. What would their "yes" to Mac's Sacred Paw mean? How were we unsubtle barbarians supposed to distinguish between a real yes and a fake yes?

By eight o'clock the sky had scarcely lightened. Big leaden clouds banked over the wall of the Front and spat occasional puffs of icy rain, fine as a mist. The guests went off to the corral for their ride in crackling new yellow riding slickers that trailed on the ground as they walked. From my kitchen window, the men looked like a group of orphans lost in man-sized hand-me-downs. The sight triggered my PTA-mom mode. I sent Hil after them with a thermos of hot chocolate and a stack of paper cups for Dave's and Trudi's saddlebags. Then I mixed up a batch of cookies. They were oatmeal. For some reason, I seemed determined to get oatmeal into the Japanese. Call it an exercise in Perseverance Furthers. I slid the trays into the oven, set the timer, and trotted out to my car to get my Montana highway map.

Maybe Barbara Donner had only stopped off to snitch CDs while Luke was out of their house. (She was the one who had left—without her stuff but with a boyfriend.) However, if she was *chez eux* again, I needed to plot a new itinerary. Getting to know Luke was definitely Worth a Detour, as they say in the Michelin green guides. On the other hand, in my own book, couples in marital difficulty were worth avoiding altogether.

I opened the passenger side of my car and saw a crumpled M&M's wrapper on the floor and a foam cup lying on the dash. Milky coffee had trickled through the hole in the lid and dried on the dark red vinyl. I stared. I had not eaten M&M's lately, nor did I take milk in my coffee. I noticed red lipstick along the brim of the cup. *Monica,* I fumed. What had she being doing with my car? Had she driven it to Choteau yesterday by mistake? Not, I had to admit, a totally ditzy mistake. Both red rentals were two-door Ford Escorts, and Trudi had asked us to leave our keys in the cars in case they had to be moved out of the way.

I remembered my oatmeal cookies. Hurriedly, I scooped up Monica's trash, opened the glove compartment, and found—no map. I slid my hand under the passenger seat, then trotted around to the driver's side and fished around under that seat. I checked the backseat, the door pockets. Then a horrid suspicion made me stop. I reached over to the glove compartment and pulled out the contract. The yellow-and-black Hertz logo was printed on the outside.

But inside, it was made out to Monica Leeds. She had rented it six days ago at the Bozeman, Montana, airport for thirty-nine dollars a day less than I had rented the same car at the Great Falls airport. But last night, she had driven off in *my* Escort.

I sat behind the steering wheel going nowhere fast. Mileage figures, drop charges, and the fragile balance on my credit card danced in my head like rotten sugar plums. Gradually, a distant shrill note penetrated my mathematical efforts. I listened. A second later I shot out of the car and sprinted across the courtyard and up the kitchen steps. It was the kitchen's smoke alarm. Smoke poured from the oven, curled densely around the light fixtures, and seeped out under the kitchen doorways into the rest of the house. I could barely see to turn off the oven. I grabbed a towel, took the burning cookies out of the oven, and heaved them out the door toward Monica's car. Of course, they didn't make it that far. They dotted the cold white gravel like so many steaming little black turds.

I didn't rush to pick them up. When I did, after the kitchen was restored, I found a perverse satisfaction in the job, as if I were gathering the burned fruits of my anger. I played with the idea of mailing them to Monica. According to the address on her car rental contract, she lived in New York. Uptown New York. The East Seventies. Freelancing wouldn't begin to cover the rent. She had either an independent income or a rich roommate.

Back in the kitchen, I dialed information, then her number. The answering machine picked up. It mentioned no roommate. I left a—shall we say—assertive message about the car mix-up. The rest of the morning I chopped, stirred, and kneaded with the kitchen's cordless phone cradled first between my left ear and shoulder, then between my right ear and shoulder. Sartre maintained that hell is other people, but hold buttons and Muzak had not yet been invented. I don't know how many times in the course of the morning I told the sad tale of the switched cars, but by lunchtime I'd despaired of a cost-free happy ending. The only thing I knew for certain was that no one named Monica Leeds had turned in my car at the Bozeman airport.

Trudi came in from the ride, shivering. Her hair was damp and deflated. "They're taking hot showers," she said. "I told them not to hurry, we'd wait lunch." She sniffed the kitchen air, then lifted up the lid on my pot of chili. "Hmm. What'd you put in it?"

"A jar of salsa and black olives left over from cocktails last night."

She replaced the lid and sniffed some more. "You burn something?"

"Cookies," I said acidly. I told her about the cars. She was sympathetic for about thirty seconds. "Send her the bill," she suggested. She went upstairs for her shower.

Send her the bill. Simple. But what about getting her to pay it? I finally turned around and faced the fear that had been tapping me on the shoulder all morning. What if she damaged the car? In order to save $12.99 per day times ten days, I had not signed up for collision insurance. Now I was kicking myself for penny pinching. Since I owned no car, only a bike, I had no insurance. If Monica totaled my rental, I owed Hertz a new Escort. I went into my bedroom, pulled my flask out of my duffel, and tested it with a shake. There was still lots. In the kitchen, I poured a fat lady's finger into a stubby glass and felt better even before the first neat sip.

Nothing out of the ordinary happened in the next twenty-four hours. I spent a lot of it on the phone. None of the airlines I contacted would tell me whether Monica Leeds had been or would be a passenger on any of their "scheduled flights" out of Bozeman, Billings, Missoula, or Great Falls, Montana. "What about your nonscheduled flights?" I snapped at one voice.

It drawled back, "I'm sorry, ma'am, we don't have nonscheduled flights."

"Exactly!"

"Excuse me?"

My conversations with the Hertz Company's offices in Bozeman, Billings, Missoula, and Great Falls were no more satisfactory. I was responsible for everything that happened to their Escort except accidental fire or an act of nature. Nonetheless, I reported my car stolen to Sheriff Becker, who, once he understood the misunderstanding, was amiable and helpful. He turned me over to a deputy who was only slightly less amiable, probably on account of the paperwork generated by my report.

I did not hear from Luke. Of course, I'd been tying up the phone for hours at a stretch. But I had to wonder if old Thorn-in-the-Side Barb had given him my message. And what if she'd moved back in with him? Would Luke return my call and say, "Maybe next time, hon"? Or, like most men faced with an emotionally sticky situation, would he elect a course of no action at all? Perhaps he would simply not call. Did I want to try again? To call or not to call. Meanwhile, I tried to psych myself up for a solo tour of the Rockies, to see it as an adventure, as a freedom, as an opportunity for interior growth. But mostly I saw myself in a budget motel having a hard time getting out of bed.

The Japanese planned to leave early Saturday morning to catch a flight to San Francisco. From Trudi and Lynn, I gathered the visit had raised the family's hopes. There had been two more formal business meetings, one with a lawyer from the Nature Conservancy, and another at which Sam presented a video introducing their company, Nippon Vacuum Instruments. "Workers sign on with the company *for life,*" Trudi said, shaking her head. "They actually take vows—they hold this big ceremony and all the new workers swear to honor and obey NVI. It's like one of those mass Moonie marriages!"

"Didn't you sign up here for life?" I asked her.

"That's different," she said.

I liked to think my food was helping. Along with the usual lunch stews and soups, one night I did trout (from the ranch's freezer) with a smoked ham stuffing, and another night chicken-fried steaks, a Western standard in which round steak (I used sirloin) is dredged in seasoned flour like chicken, then fried in hot fat and served with pan gravy. This proved a big hit with the Japanese. "Like the Colonel's," Mr. Yamaguchi complimented. Trudi had venison in the freezer, but I could not persuade her that game was "guest food." "They're here for beef," she reminded me. For their final feast on Friday night, she had saved a pair of beef tenderloins.

There was only one discordant note. Dave, on the advice of his contact at the state chamber of commerce, was content to see the Japanese off without "wrapping things up." Mac, on the other hand, was pushing hard for some up-front money. He wanted to hammer out a preliminary agreement or the first draft of a contract. The brothers argued over this for two days. We all heard snatches of it, Dave angrily discussing Mac with Trudi, or Mac buttonholing Dave by the ice machine before dinner.

"Christ, let them shit or get off the pot!" Mac declared. "They've been here freeloading for a week!"

"It not the way they do business," Dave retorted stonily. "What's your hurry?"

Thursday afternoon, Trudi asked me to drive Kaz out to the swamp to check out his camera. "The little guy's got ants in his pants about it," she said. "I tried Clare, but she says the kid who helped him set it up is out sick and she can't spare anyone else—she's trying to get their newsletter out."

Of all the visitors, I was beginning to like Kaz the best. Sam, whose English was fluent, was easier to talk to, but Kaz was more fun. His delight in the artifacts of American culture was spontaneous and infectious. "No problem," I told Trudi.

But it was.

The first hitch was Monica's car. The plan was to drive over to the institute in it and borrow its pickup and extension ladder. But the keys to Monica's rental were not to be found. Kaz and I searched under the seats, flapped the visors up and down, opened the ashtray, slid our hands in the door pockets. I found a narrow reporter's notebook in one of them, but no keys. Somehow Monica Leeds had managed to drive off with both sets of keys. I was beyond surprise at this point, although I had to marvel at how someone with enough smarts to sell stories to *The New York Times* could be such a mush-brain when it came to living. Did she leave the same great, messy wake everywhere she went?

Since Trudi and Dave had gone off in their vehicles, I borrowed Hil's matte-pink truck. It was parked in its usual spot beside an equipment shed behind the kitchen. The truck was empty of garbage, and the keys were in the ignition. Hil was nowhere in sight. I rolled back the door of the shed. It was barn-dark inside and smelled of machine oil and cold metal. A huge old wooden sleigh dwarfed a lawn tractor and Lynn's ATV. On one wall, above rolls of fence wire, hung a rusty pair of crosscut saws that looked as if they belonged in a logging museum. An antique dealer would have a heyday in here, I thought. But there was not really enough time to explore. It was already two-thirty, and I wanted to be back in the kitchen by four. In the interest of saving time, we decided to bypass the institute and go directly to the swamp in Hil's chariot. "We might have to walk home," I teased Kaz.

"Okay, okay, let's go." His black eyes flashed with excitement. He liked the "hillybilly" truck.

"Okay," I said. I carried an extension ladder out of the shed and slid it into the bed of the pickup, and off we jolted, aluminum crashing against rusty steel.

There had been "activity" on the carcass of the cow. We stared at it a moment through the windshield. Then Kaz expelled a satisfied "Haa!" and we climbed out of the cab.

It was cold and depressing as February. Dirty banks of clouds withholding their rain moved slowly overhead. A sharp, damp breeze blew across the swamp. I snapped up my vest, swung the ladder out of the back of the pickup, and almost brained Kaz, who was anxiously dancing in to help. He ducked, then did a Charlie Chaplin eyeball-roll and swagger. We laughed. We approached the tree where he'd set up his camera.

Kaz frowned. "It should make flashes," he said.

I set the ladder against Kaz's tree and steadied it as he rattled up the rungs to the black box holding his camera.

On the far side of the carcass, maybe fifty yards away, the institute's camera was mounted on a cottonwood tree. To my left, above the shrubbery, I saw the roof of the little cabin Clare and I had explored. Off to one side, I caught a flash of bright red through the bushes. It was too big for a pileated woodpecker, even if they existed in Montana. I looked again. It wasn't moving.

"You okay?" I called up to Kaz. "I'll be right back."

He was preoccupied with his black box. "I'll be back in a minute," I repeated. I strolled over toward the red patch. It got bigger and bigger. I walked faster, tripped in a boggy rut, and landed on my knees. Cold water seeped through my jeans. I got up and walked over to my missing Ford Escort. Both doors were flung open like a set of vestigial wings. Monica's laptop was on the back-seat. And so was her silver nylon flight bag, her calfskin briefcase, and her purse.

I found Monica lying facedown in the grass halfway between the car and the cabin. The upper back of her trench coat was spotted with small holes. Half of the bubble of her hair was matted to her skull with blood. Her ear looked small as a child's. I caught the faintest breath of movement. I stared. Was I imagining it? I reached down toward her and a cloud of flies flew up in my face. I jerked away. The movement I'd seen was not the movement of life. It was the movement of death. There were insects stirring in her hair.

"Lee, Lee, Lee!" Kaz shouted. I heard the aluminum rattling of the ladder. "Lee, where you are?" I realized he was calling my name. Unable to call back, I walked toward him. He saw me emerging from the shrubbery and came in my direction, gesturing at the camera he'd mounted up in the tree. I couldn't understand what he was saying, but his face was flushed and he sounded angry.

"We have to go back," I said.

He didn't budge. He kept rattling away in Japanese, pointing insistently at his camera.

"Kaz, we have to go." Something in my voice made him look up at me. Then he looked behind me and saw the red car and the cabin. He marched past me. "No!" I shouted.

But he didn't stop. He walked right up to her. When I got to him, two seconds later, he had already turned away. He let out a shrill, shocked giggle. His face went gray. "Monica," he said. His eyes were unfocused. He staggered a little.

"Kaz," I said sharply. "Don't faint on me."

But he did. He dropped forward onto his knees, hands clutched together against his abdomen, his fuzzy black head flopping sideways as he fell into the brittle blond grasses.

CHAPTER FOURTEEN

In times of big trouble, it is often surprising to discover that little things still work. It struck me as close to miraculous, for example, that when I turned the key in Hil's truck and goosed the accelerator, the engine actually started. I shoved it into gear and plowed through the shrubbery over to where Kaz lay in the trampled marsh grasses. He moaned and tried to life his head. He refused to stay put till the color came back into his face, so I helped him up into the truck, an awkward maneuver that embarrassed him and pulled a muscle in one side of my back. He was much heavier and more muscular than his slight, wiry frame suggested. Once in the truck, he refused to keep his head down between his legs. He did accept a dose of Hil's glove-compartment cache of Tanqueray—even if it wasn't what the doctor ordered. Then we bounced back to the ranch, not saying anything, each tightly wrapped in our own private spaces like a pair of teenagers recovering from a bout of intimacy.

Within a couple of hours, the J-E was swarming with officials wearing patches and badges and guns. This time, of course, there was no way to hide death from the guests. Even if Kaz had not been along with me, they had all known and liked Monica, and the sheriff had indicated that he wanted to question them along with the family after he finished up down at the swamp.

Meanwhile, Dave and Trudi shepherded the men together into the Big Room, where we served tea and whiskey and guess what kind of cookies by the fire. The farm manager's apple-cheeked wife and teenaged daughter came up with an orange-glazed sponge cake and stayed to help Lynn distract the guests with a game of

Monopoly. Trudi was occupied answering the phone. I set up a coffee urn in the hallway for the troops who came and went, then one of Choteau's four police officers showed up to drive me back to the scene.

The wind rippling the swamp was colder, and the light was going, taking with it the slight colors of the place. A red bubble on the roof of a station wagon blinked like a warning light. Yards of sagging orange survey tape cordoned off the area around the cabin and Monica's body. Evidently the sheriff had used up his department's supply of yellow "crime scene" tape. But there were more officials tromping around inside the tape than outside. Someone had even driven a 4×4 over it. The truck's rack of spotlights illuminated my red rental as if it were in a commercial. A deputy in a backward baseball cap moved slowly around it with a videocam. Other men in uniform jackets and muddy boots walked around with Polaroids and measuring tapes. The game wardens wore their guns in brown holsters. Law enforcement wore theirs in black holsters. Fish and Wildlife wore only patches. I recognized Walt Surrey. Mac was there with two of his interns, both male. Clare wasn't. If death in bed was generally the province of women, death outdoors was the business of men.

A trooper escorted me past a local TV camera and under the tape. I retraced Kaz's and my steps for Sheriff Becker. We strolled from the tree where Kaz had mounted his camera through the screen of shrubbery to the Escort. "At least you've recovered your vehicle," Becker commented. No one had closed the doors. Twenty feet away, Monica's body still lay crumpled in the grass. Seeing her there again was another shock. Perhaps I'd expected that by this time she would have gotten up and walked away.

"This the way you found her?" the sheriff asked.

"Yes," I told him. "I didn't disturb anything." I noticed she was wearing bright pink socks with her combat boots. One black knit pant leg was scrunched up, exposing the back of her calf. The skin was purple.

Becker nodded gravely. "Pretty clear what happened," he said, as much to himself as to me. Becker, along with everyone else on the scene, was convinced that Monica had been killed by a grizzly. I don't know who first suggested this. But I remember driving back to the ranch with Kaz thinking that the wounds in her back were bullet holes. I told Dave and Trudi that she'd been bashed in the head and shot in the back. I thought she'd been murdered. I didn't say anything about the phone tip that had excited her so. I wanted to tell the sheriff first.

Then, maybe an hour later, everyone was talking about her death as a terrible accident. She had wanted to see a grizzly. She had bugged everyone at the institute about it. She had been warned how dangerous it was. Mac had assigned an intern to take her to several of the feeding sites to show her fresh prints and spoor, but she was not thrilled. It was generally presumed that after she packed up and left the ranch Tuesday afternoon, she had decided to try the swamp on her own.

I took a deep breath. "She was on the trail of some story," I told Becker. "She was all excited about it."

"Hmm," he said.

"I didn't have the feeling it was about bears," I insisted. "It was as though she had an exposé up her sleeve." I hesitated, then jumped in. "What if it wasn't a grizzly? What if someone wanted to shut her up?"

Sheriff Becker looked at me as if I'd been watching too much TV. "There'll be an autopsy," he said flatly. "The doc's on his way from Great Falls."

"The doc?"

"The medical examiner. The Nip, he touch her?"

"We didn't touch anything, Sheriff," I said firmly.

We moved away to a more decent distance. Mac and Walt Surrey joined us with a third man whose slight limp didn't slow him down. He was square-shaped and shorter than the other two. Under the jaunty brim of his canvas Aussie bush hat, he sported an aggressive black beard and a black eye patch. He looked like a pirate from the outback.

"So what was this big scoop she was after?" Becker wondered. But he was just curious, making conversation.

"She didn't say," I said lamely.

Walt Surrey introduced the pirate to us. His name was

Richard Zwart. He was a fed, a special agent with U.S. Fish and Wildlife. We acknowledged each other without smiling.

I was glad to see Mac. His dark eyes looked me over sympathetically. "Poor Lee," he said.

Perhaps there was something patronizing in his voice. Or perhaps I was simply unable to bear any show of kindness. In any case, I felt a squirt of anger. "Poor Monica," I snapped.

The men exchanged glances, as if I'd broken some rule.

Walt said hurriedly, "Yep, it's a real shame all right."

Sheriff Becker turned to Richard Zwart. "This young lady here," he said, indicating me, "is the one who reported it as a homicide."

The federal agent looked at me with his single blue eye.

"Those little holes in her back," I said defensively. "They look like bullet holes."

Zwart gave a slight nod. "Back in the late seventies, I spent a summer down in Yellowstone." His voice was higher than I'd expected, and milder than his beard, which was shot with white bristles and scraggly on one side. It looked as if a drunken barber had cut chunks out of it. "I had a job with a research crew who were collaring grizzlies," Richard Zwart went on, speaking more to the sheriff than me. "We used a dart gun to get the animals down. We'd underdose them rather than risk killing them with an overdose, and sometimes they'd come out of it before we were finished. One time we were taking a jaw imprint of this bear we called Ivan the Terrible—a real mean-tempered griz—and he started to get up. There was no way we were going to keep him on the ground, so we let him go and ran like hell back to the truck, leaving all our gear behind us on the ground. Well, luckily, Ivan took it out on the gear. We had this heavy metal equipment box, and you could have used it for a colander after he got through with it. Looked like a target on a rifle range."

He opened his mouth, curled back his upper lip at me, and tapped his canines with two fingers in a vee. His lips and gums looked more red than pink. "The grizzly's primary weapon is its canines, not its claws," Zwart instructed.

"You're saying the puncture wounds in her neck and shoulders are teeth marks, not bullet holes?"

"You got it."

Walt enlarged on it for me. "When they fight each other in the wild, they go for the face and head. They try to grab and break each other's jaws. In attacks on humans, they do the same thing—especially in sudden encounters." He glanced at Zwart. The man said nothing. Above his unruly beard, his face was impassive.

"Sudden encounter? You mean she surprised it?" I asked.

"Grizzlies don't have great eyesight—nor hearing, for that matter," Walt said. "Smell is their strongest sense. If the bear had its nose in the cow, then all of a sudden got wind of, uh, her"—he nodded in Monica's direction—"well, that's a sudden encounter."

Mac said blandly, "Which is how Rich lost his eye."

"And a chunk of my jaw," Zwart said. His one eye moved from my face to the sheriff's, gauging the impact of his statement.

"Christ," Becker swore softly.

I said nothing. There was something I didn't like about Richard Zwart. I suspected he was into head games, that he took some pleasure in dropping the bomb of his personal catastrophe on unsuspecting bystanders, that he enjoyed watching the way horror gave way to awe. For like him or not, the fact he had survived a grizzly's jaws increased the aura of his authority. Richard Zwart had the special status of one favored by fate.

"What happened?" the sheriff asked.

"Same thing as happened to her," Zwart said bluntly. "Only I was luckier. Same time of year, too. I came around a bend in the trail and there was this sow and her cub, not fifty yards away. I was well inside the critical distance. I saw her ears go back, and she charged. Came at me like a bullet. I didn't make it up the nearest tree. For some reason, I never lost consciousness. I lay there playing dead and she kept coming back to check on me. Turns out there was an elk carcass just off the trail."

"How'd you get out?" Becker wondered.

"Crawled."

"She get your leg too?"

Zwart shook his head. "That happened in the Mekong Delta."

Becker let out a respectful grunt.

"What's a 'critical distance'?" I asked.

"For a bear attack? Anything inside a hundred yards."

"So what do you think happened here?"

There was a cool silence. Maybe I was supposed to ask more questions about his own "sudden encounter." Zwart looked at me.

"If I may ask."

"You can ask." He wasn't warming to me, either. Looking back, I can see that for each of us, Monica's death had resurrected old losses. Zwart had lost his eye and part of his face. He needed to talk about it. I had lost my daughter, and there was no point in talking about it anymore. As my ex-husband and I learned the hard way, when it comes to bonding, sorrow—even the same sorrow—makes rotten cement.

Zwart lifted his chest, beefing up the authority in his voice. "She drove in, parked over here, and waited in her car for a bear to show. You can't see the cow real well from here on account of those bushes, so when the camera started flashing, she got out of the car for a better look." He looked at Mac and Walt. Mac nodded. Walt didn't.

"And the bear got a whiff of her and charged," concluded Becker.

"Yeah," Zwart said. "Looks like she ran for the car and got the nearest door open, the passenger-side door, before it hit her. You've got blood smeared on the outside of the door, and there's some on the seat as well, so she may have been trying to crawl inside. At some point, the bear took a swipe at her head with its paw—you can see where her skull's caved in. Then it must have dragged her to where she is now." He paused. His jaw tightened under his beard. "From the looks of those punctures, it kept going at her head and shoulders with its teeth—grab, release, grab, release. Like what happened to me—that bear wanted to make sure there was no more threat."

"She provoked it, Rich," Mac declared with some feeling.

"Obviously. But that's not going to satisfy your neighbors. You know as well as I do, that bear's got to be destroyed."

"We can relocate it, dammit!"

"And have it back next month looking for dessert? Mac," Zwart reasoned, "we're not talking about a griz knocking someone's garbage cans around."

"Don't give me that 'taste of manmeat' crap!" Mac countered. "There's absolutely no data that once a grizzly's killed a human, it's more likely to attack again."

Walt, siding with Mac, said, "The bear that killed that nature photographer—Chuck Gibbs? You let it go. The evidence showed he was crowding the bear."

Zwart was losing patience. "That was up in Glacier. Park Service was calling the shots. Teton County's under the sheriff here's jurisdiction, and wishful thinking on the part of the Nature Conservancy and the Sacred Paw ain't gonna turn it into a national park. You've got ranches all the way from here to Choteau. And every time a griz gets into someone's beehives or eats the dog food off his porch, people lock up their children and start screaming. Ask Walt here. It gets so bad you'd think we were asking them to integrate grizzlies into their school system."

"Rich," Mac said levelly, "there's no reason to kill a bear for doing what's natural. The bear was provoked, just like at Glacier. It was Monica's *own fault!*"

Zwart shook his head. "I know where you're coming from, Mac, believe me. But it's not going to wash."

I'd had enough. I left them arguing and walked over to my car. The cameraman was gone, but the spotlights were still on it. The dried smears on the door looked as if a child had tried finger painting with thin mud. The bear had left a five-pronged swipe across the fender. The scratch had gone all the way through the red paint to steel. Numbly, I wondered how much Hertz would charge me for it. The automatic seat belt hung across the doorway like a ribbon waiting to be cut. The bloodstains on it were surface smears. Inside, similar stains on the red tweed upholstery were almost invisible, but the velour on the upper part of the passenger seat was stiff, as if she'd bled against it for a long time. Had she, like Zwart, remained conscious throughout the attack? Had she smelled the animal's breath, heard its teeth crunching on her neck? I could not imagine her terror.

I spotted the key on the floor and walked around to the driver's side. The seat there was clean. How long had she waited for the bear? I leaned into the car and checked the ashtray. There was a Doublemint wrapper I'd put there after leaving the airport, but nothing from Monica. Nor were there any wrappers on the floor—a more likely place, given her habits. She had not eaten or smoked while she waited, and it looked as if she hadn't been working either. Her laptop in the backseat was zipped into its case. Her purse sat on top of it.

Had she listened to the radio while she sat there? I hesitated before picking up the car keys on the floor. I didn't want to mess anything up with my fingerprints. Then it clicked in: bears don't have fingerprints. I fished my K-Mart magnifiers out of my pocket and peered at the radio. If Monica had been listening to the radio, wouldn't it have scared off the bear? I slid into the driver's seat, put the key in the ignition and turned it. The radio didn't come on. I tried to start the car. Nothing. The battery, I concluded. The doors had been left open for two days, and the courtesy light must have run it down.

I walked back to the sheriff. Mac and Richard Zwart were still going strong, but the argument had shifted. It was no longer a matter of whether the grizzly that had killed Monica should be destroyed. It was a matter of when and how. Sheriff Becker wanted a couple of wardens to stake out the cow tonight. Mac objected that it was not unusual for carcass sites to be frequented by more than one grizzly. "At least make an effort to get the right animal," he declared angrily. "We've got the film out of our camera. It should show which bear—or bears—were feeding here Tuesday night. I'll develop it myself in the morning."

Zwart rocked back and forth on his heels, studying the ground.

Walt said, "We ought to move that cow. No point in complicating things by drawing in more bears."

"Okay," Zwart agreed. "We can set snares tomorrow. See if we get a griz that matches your film. That's fair."

Sheriff Becker gave a reluctant nod.

"And if there's more than one bear on the film?" Walt posed.

"Flip a coin," Mac retorted bitterly. "It won't be the first time."

"What about Kaz's film?" I interrupted.

"What?" said Mac. He seemed surprised to see I was still there.

I pointed to the tree where Kaz had mounted his camera. "He was trying out a new remote device. It was supposed to be triggered by motion. When the bear charged Monica, it would have come at her toward Kaz's camera."

"Right," Mac said impatiently. "Clare told us. But it so happens he didn't put *film* in the camera. We already checked it."

"What?"

"He forgot the fucking film."

Walt raised his eyebrows. "That's too bad," he commented.

I shook my head in disbelief. "After all the effort he went to—I mean, the guy is practically a professional."

"Pros never mess up?" Zwart asked ironically.

Sheriff Becker rubbed the back of his neck and moved off from the group. I followed him. "Sheriff?" I asked. "Is it okay if I look through her stuff for the keys to *her* car—the other one back at the ranch?"

He reflected a moment. "Might as well have a look," he said.

He walked me over to the Escort. I took her purse, a large sack of soft black kidskin, out of the backseat and laid out its contents on the hood of the car: a worn navy-blue leather wallet, a miniature bottle of hand cream labeled in gold script "Le Grand Hôtel de l'Opéra, Toulouse," a purse-sized checkbook in a Mark Cross cover, a pack of tissues, a plane ticket, a tin of Tylenol, two tubes of Estée Lauder lipstick, three Trojans, an airline towelette, a purple plastic wide-toothed comb, two tampons, a man's Zippo lighter with the chrome plate worn off at the corners, a set of keys attached to a green rubber frog, and bingo, Hertz keys on a plastic tag. I dangled them between us.

"Leave them here for now," Becker decided. "I'll have one of the boys inventory her effects."

"What about my car? The battery's dead. If you can give me a jump, I'll drive it back now. I need to get cooking."

"Better wait till the doc signs off on the scene. Tell you what. I'll have one of the boys drive you back, then after we finish up with your car, we'll drop it off at the lodge for you."

"Tonight?"

"I surely hope so."

His deadpan sincerity made me laugh. "I guess I was worried you'd impound it."

"For what?"

"I don't know. Evidence?"

He shook his head. "Ma'am, we've got enough pictures to convince a jury of twelve blind men."

"Sheriff?" A trooper trotted over. "Cheryl's on the radio. The computer's down again. And the TV people want to know when we can release the victim's name."

"As soon as we notify the next of kin." His voice was weary, as if he'd already said it a hundred times.

"Maybe you better talk to them, Sheriff."

"Excuse me," he said to me. They walked over to a van. Curious, I took out my K-Mart specs again and opened Monica's checkbook. The last two pages had not been balanced, but at the beginning of March, she had had just over two thousand in the Chase Manhattan Bank. I picked up the plane ticket. She was scheduled to fly back to New York on Friday night—tomorrow. In her wallet she had a New York State driver's license which put her weight at 110 and her age at twenty-nine. She also had $160 in cash and cards from Visa, MasterCard, Exxon, and Bloomingdale's. Along with her change, there was a silver St. Christopher medal. I fingered the demoted saint for moment, then dropped it back into the pennies and dimes and snapped the wallet shut.

Chapter Fifteen

Without his Hiyo Silver white hat on, Sheriff Ed Becker looked as if he'd stepped out of a movie about World War II. It wasn't simply that while the Fish and Wildlife men were hairy, Becker was shorn and clean-shaven, or that he wore a tan uniform while the younger men wore jeans. It went beyond exterior. Ed Becker reminded me of my father. Becker was probably not much over ten years older than I—in his early fifties, if I had to guess—but the revolutionary chaos of the New Age hadn't made a dent in his soul. Becker did not distrust Law and Order. It was his job.

I watched him in the Big Room as he questioned us after dinner and tried to decide if he was good at his job. He seemed relaxed, methodical, and honest. Did that make him good? I didn't know.

For dinner, the men from NVI had changed out of jeans into business suits and white shirts. Perhaps their formality was a gesture of respect for Monica's memory. Or perhaps donning their "salary-man" uniforms provided reassurance in the face of her death. In any case, the dark suits lent a funereal note to the sheriff's interview. When Dave introduced Becker, the executives bowed deeply. Embarrassed, Becker held up his hand as if to stay them, then executed an awkward series of jerks in return. He introduced a younger man in uniform who was setting up a tape recorder on a side table. Another round of bows. Everyone sat down, except Dave, who stood quietly at the back of the room. The guests looked interested. Trudi and Mac looked exhausted. Clare had not shown up.

It didn't take long. No one had much to offer. The Japanese men and I stated that we had seen Monica in Choteau around one-thirty Tuesday afternoon.

Mac said she had scheduled another taping session with him that afternoon, but had called the institute to say something else had come up. No, he was not sure what time she had called. Sometime after lunch. Perhaps Ellie, the office gofer, would remember. Ellie had taken the call and transferred it over to his private line.

Trudi and Lynn had met in the kitchen around four, and neither of them had seen Monica return from Choteau or leave the J-E. Lynn stated that she'd had the afternoon off and had fallen asleep in her room while plugged into her Walkman. She had heard nothing downstairs. But Trudi, who had gone out around three for a look at the calves, had seen two red Escorts in the lot. She remembered because at the time she thought I was back from town—then she realized that I'd taken the van.

Becker turned to me. "Do you recollect what time you returned from Choteau?"

"I think it was close to four-thirty. There was only one red car in the lot. She must have taken my car by mistake to Choteau, gotten back sometime before three, packed, and driven off an hour later."

"Looks like it," Becker said. "When she called you at the institute, did she say where she was going?" he asked Mac.

"Of course not," Mac answered. "She knew the swamp was off-limits."

The sheriff scanned the gathering. "I guess that's it for now," he said. The trooper turned off the tape recorder. Dave and Becker shook hands. "Thanks," the sheriff said.

"You bet," Dave answered.

So what it came down to was that between three and four in the afternoon, Monica had returned to the J-E, packed up her things in such a rush that she'd grabbed my bra by mistake, then driven off to the swamp to sit and wait God knew how long for a bear to come along.

It didn't compute.

On the other hand, if she'd met somebody at the swamp and had been shot, why were there so many entry wounds? I could believe three or four to make sure, even a whole barrel fired in anger. But there must have been a dozen or more holes in her neck and upper back. If they'd been made by a revolver, the shooter would have had to stop and reload.

In either case, there was nothing more to do about it. I'd told Becker about the story she was working on. If she had been shot, the ME would find out.

Dave escorted Becker and the trooper toward the door. "I'll be in touch," the sheriff said.

I felt restless and unsatisfied. I drifted over to the long Mission-style table behind the central sofa. A large arrangement of artificial peonies sat incongruously in the middle of the table. Light from a parchment-shaded lamp cast deep shadows between the silk petals. I straightened a fan of old magazines left by last summer's dudes: *The New Yorker, Forbes, Newsweek.*

Mac walked over. "Hello," he said.

"Hi," I said.

He grinned, and for a moment the strain in his face evaporated. "So, milady cruel and fair," he bantered, "did you get a chance to look over Dad's poems?"

"I did. And there was one I really liked." I looked at him. "But right now, I couldn't tell you which one to save my life. I feel as if this whole business has done something to my brain."

He laughed and gave me a comradely hug. "I can relate to that," he declared. I could smell the warm, damp sourness of his body. My deodorant wasn't working overtime either, but neither of us moved apart. I felt locked to his side like a magnet snapped onto metal. "We jumped your car," he said. "I drove it back. The keys are on the floor."

I thanked him. I don't remember what we talked about. I do remember experimentally inching away from him, testing his field of force. About twelve inches was the critical distance, to use a phrase I'd learned that afternoon. Any closer, I had to consciously resist latching on. The effect was so amazingly physical that if I'd known him better, I would have quizzed him about it. As it was, his bodily allure seemed as risky a topic as Monica's death.

Dave and Trudi joined us. "Well, that wasn't so bad," Trudi sighed.

"Becker's all right," Dave said. He turned to me. "I see they've returned your car."

"Mac drove it up. I guess they're done with it."

Mac shrugged apologetically. "It's a mess."

"I'm just glad I don't have to buy a new one," I said sincerely.

"Hil can clean it up for you in the morning," Trudi said.

"I'll do it," I protested.

"You stick to cooking," she ordered gruffly. It was as close as she would come to a compliment. I felt pleased. I followed Dave's gaze to his guests. They stood in a group by the fire, waiting for their host.

"I think a change of scenery is in order," Dave said.

"What do you mean?" Trudi sounded alarmed.

"I mean run our guests into Choteau. Show them a bit of cowtown color. Stop off at the Longhorn Inn for a couple."

"Or five," Trudi said sarcastically. "Don't you think it's a bit late?"

"It's only eight-thirty. Come along."

"Babe, I'm bushed. Really." She gave him a tired smile. "How come you're so full of beans?"

He turned to me. "Is that what that mashed stuff was tonight? Beans?" His blue eyes smiled mischievously.

"Purée of turnips and carrots," I told him.

"You said you liked it," Trudi accused.

He turned to his brother. "You up for the Longhorn?"

Mac shook his head. "Another time."

I pictured my empty bedroom, saw Monica's empty bed. "You want a designated driver?" I asked Dave.

"Atta girl," he approved.

Trudi gave me a grateful glance. "Let me change my shirt," I said. "I'll be ready in five minutes." I gave Trudi a quick hug. She smelled like roast turkey.

Maybe there were rooms somewhere at the back of the Longhorn Inn, but it wasn't the sort of place the *Mobil Guide* would recommend to Mom and Pop Tourist. The "inn" was, for all obvious intent, no more than a bar—a bar whose sheet-paneled walls boasted a black velvet painting of a chimp in a suit and a tapestry of a blue stallion against an orange sunset. More predictably, given the name of the place, the walls also displayed two stuffed longhorn cow heads—or perhaps they were bulls. One was white with black specks, the other brown. There were also deer and elk heads with impressive racks. In the place of honor, above the center of the back bar, the little head of a white rabbit sprouted a large pair of antlers. A jackalope, Dave said. The Japanese had to work at it.

Four men in billed caps sat at a table under a revolving

Miller Lite sign. They looked as if they'd gotten off a construction site at four and been there ever since. With a slow, stoned kind of curiosity, they watched us take a line of stools at the bar. The top of the bar was salmon-pink Formica; the rim of it was cushioned in brown vinyl—providing comfort for customers' forearms or foreheads, depending on the amount of booze consumed. The bartender wore a black Hawaiian shirt with pink and red orchids on it. The rim of one ear was studded with metal, and her hair looked like Kaz's—a fuzzy *en brosse*—but not as dark. She looked expectantly at Dave.

"What'll it be?" he said to me.

"Bourbon," I said to the bartender. "You got Old Forester?"

"Old Grand-Dad, Jack Daniel's black—"

"Jack Daniel's will be fine," I interrupted. "Rocks, please. No water."

She nodded and looked at Dave.

"Bud," he said. He encompassed his visitors with a gesture. "Put it all on one tab," he instructed. "Gentlemen?" he asked them. "What is your pleasure?"

Mr. Yamaguchi ordered scotch. Mr. Tanaka and Sam followed suit. Kaz, however, hesitated, then said, "Gimme a shot of red-eye." He said it almost without an accent, as if he'd been practicing.

Deadpan, the bartender slapped a shot glass down in front of Kaz, moved over to the back bar, and took down a red-labeled bottle. Expertly, she slid it down the bar to Kaz, *slap,* right into his hand.

Kaz was ecstatic. Triumphantly he waved the bottle in the air and crowed in Japanese. The men laughed and broke into rapid chatter. Obligingly, the bartender repeated the trick three more times, once for each of them. The mood was fun time. Dave took the first sip of his beer and raised his glass to the bartender. "Thanks," he said.

She shrugged. "They all want to pretend they're the tough guy walking into a Tombstone saloon."

"Cheers," I said. I shook the ice in my drink and took a long sip. It tasted wonderful. I rattled the ice again and inspected the glass. A short drink. What I really wanted was a double. "You get a lot of Japanese visitors here?" I asked the bartender.

"Japanese, Germans, last week it was a group of Russians looking at wheat."

A man in a black cowboy hat and muttonchop sideburns strolled up from the far end of the bar carrying his drink. The glass was three-quarters full, but all the ice had melted. He'd been nursing it for some time. "Hey, sport," he said to Dave.

"Maynard," Dave acknowledged.

Maynard indicated the Japanese with his chin. "You want to show 'em cowboys and Indians, take 'em across the street to the knife and gun club." The bartender watched him as he took the empty stool on the other side of Dave. Maynard met her gaze. "Whaddya think, Doris?"

"I'm not paid to think."

He leered at her. "I forgot."

"Knife and gun club?" I asked Dave.

"The Roundup," Dave explained. "It's a bar."

Muttonchops took a sip of his watery drink through a bent inch of a tiny striped straw. "Ye ol' Injun watering hole," he said. "Right, Doris?" He leaned across Dave and said to me, "Her old man used to be a regular over there." He thought about it, then confided, "Here you get the upper echelon."

I looked him over. "I can see that."

The bartender almost smiled. After four beats, it registered somewhere in Maynard's brain. "Well, excuse me for breathing, girlie." He looked at me and he looked at Dave. Then, with careful dignity, he picked up his melted drink and moved back down to the lonely end of the bar.

Dave drained his beer, set the glass down on the countertop, and gave it a little shove toward Doris. She picked it up. "You?" she asked me.

Oh yes, I wanted to say. Instead I asked, "You got Perrier?"

"With lime?"

I raised my eyebrows. "Like the man says, a classy place."

She grinned. Her teeth were crooked, but it was worth the price of admission.

"What's your pal Maynard do?" I asked Dave.

"Sells real estate." After a moment, he added, "Family used to have a big spread up on the Teton River. Then the old man committed suicide and they lost it. Now he's selling off pieces of it for the bank."

Judge not. "Oh dear," I said contritely.

"The place had been in the family for three generations. The economics of ranching can get pretty depressing. Last recession we had, back in the early eighties, the suicide rate out here was epidemic. Over a three-year period, something like nine hundred ranchers in our tristate region blew their brains out."

A warning bell dinged faintly inside my head. "Dave?"

"What?"

"Am I hearing what's called a cry for help?"

It took him by surprise. "Me?"

"You. Are you okay?"

"Yeah." He meant it. He smiled and nodded toward the men from NVI. "Besides, we're still in the game. I ain't heard the fat lady sing yet. But thanks anyway." He slid off his stool and held out his hand to me. "Come on. Time to beat our heads against the language barrier."

Successive rounds of red-eye and a pair of pinball machines kept the Japanese well entertained. By eleven o'clock, their hand-eye coordination, if not their hilarity, was seriously impaired. The pinball contest had degenerated into a game called Who Can Feed a Quarter into the Slot? Dave was mellow on Budweiser and I was bored and sloshing with too many Perriers and Diet Pepsis. I went to the "Fillies" and took my time rebraiding my hair and reading the graffiti.

When I came out, Dave said, "What's so funny?"

"The writing on the condom vendor. 'This gum tastes like rubber.' "

Dave pondered it a moment, then smiled wryly. "How much are they?" he asked.

"The condoms? Fifty cents each. A rip."

"They're only a quarter in the men's."

"What?"

Dave shrugged. "Stallions get half price."

"Who's the owner of this dump?" I demanded.

He grinned. "Take it easy. I was just testing your feminist knee jerk." The flash of humor lightened him. For a moment, he was uncannily like Mac.

"Wait a sec. How much are condoms in the men's room?"

Dave sipped his beer. "I have no idea," he confessed happily.

"I need a drink."

"Take a rain check. You're driving, remember? We'll go as soon as I finish this one."

We stood together against the bar in companionable silence watching the Japanese men giggling and clowning at the pinball machines. Boss man Yamaguchi was as wrecked as his subordinates. All the men's ties were askew. They hung on to each other a fair amount, as if communal unsteadiness were shared comfort. Their voices, unabashedly loud, shot up and down a harsh, grating scale.

We were the only customers left. Maynard had gone home half an hour before and the quartet of construction workers before that. (When they paid their tab at the bar, I noticed that if you added up their missing finger joints, they'd lost at least two whole digits among them.) Doris was down at the street end of the bar, plugged into a Walkman, staring out the window at the lit doorway of the Roundup Bar and Café across the way.

Bears were back on my mind. "Dave?" I asked.

"Yes, ma'am?"

Maybe the "ma'am" was an adaptive tic, something picked up along the way, maybe at stock sales. I couldn't imagine Cora drilling "ma'am" into her boys. I pushed it out of the way. "Could the bear tracks I saw back up the canyon belong to the same one that got Monica down at the swamp?"

"It's possible. They've got a big range. It takes about a hundred square miles to support one bear."

"They don't stick to one carcass? This horse is mine, that cow is yours?"

"From what Mac and Clare say, grizzlies are more into social hierarchy than territory. Studies show their ranges overlap. So you may get three or four animals feeding on the same carcass, but in some order of rank. As I understand it, as long as the hierarchy is respected, there's no aggression." He paused, then reflected, "Maybe there's a lesson there for UN peacekeeping."

"So who gets higher rank? The Bosnians or the Serbs? The Israelis or the Palestinians? The Japanese or the Chinese?"

Dave polished off his beer and moved back to firmer ground. "Mac says it was either a sow or a subadult male back in the canyon. They got it and a black bear on the film. Along with the big male the poacher got and some coyotes."

"Grand Central Station."

"In living color." There was a sarcastic edge to his voice.

"They use color film?"

"Oh yeah. Mac bought a state-of-the-art color developer for the project. The famous Evan Fife risk the sacred film at Rexall? Guess again." Evidently, without Trudi around, he was free to disapprove. He did not sound particularly bitter. More like disgusted. "My brother the techno-junkie. He's seduced by equipment. You wouldn't believe the money he sinks into his toys."

We studied our empty glasses. When I looked up, Kaz was standing beside us, steadier than the last time I looked. He ran a hand through the soft brush of his hair. In the revolving light of the beer sign, his skin had a damp, golden glow. He might have been an athlete at the end of his game.

"Hey, Kaz," Dave greeted. "'Bout ready to go home?"

"Film," he said.

"Yeah?" Dave said.

"I put film in my camera. You tell sheriff, please."

Dave frowned. "Tell the sheriff what?"

"I put film in my camera. For sure."

"Sure," Dave humored him. He looked at me.

I asked Kaz, "You talking about the camera you set up down at the swamp?"

"I put film in." Kaz's voice was getting belligerent.

I explained the business of the empty camera to Dave, then turned back to Kaz. "When did you load it?"

"The kid was on the ladder."

"You put the film in down at the swamp?"

"Yes. I put film in."

"Did the boy see you load?"

He swayed slightly. "The kid was on the ladder," he insisted.

"What kind of film did you use?"

"Kodak. I use Kodak Gold. Two hundred ASA."

"Not Fuji?" I teased, trying to lighten it up.

"Fuji good for scenery," he maintained stolidly. "For blue and green. Kodak better for leads."

I shook my head. "Sorry. Leads?"

"Lead, lead. Lead blood. Kodak better for blood."

Then it dawned. "Oh. Red."

Dave and I looked at each other. Dave inquired, "You were expecting blood?"

Kaz stood his ground. "Cow is not blue inside. I put film in," Kaz repeated loudly to us both. His colleagues turned to listen.

"So what do you think happened to it, Kaz?" I asked.

"Someone took it out. Maybe Monica."

The accusation stunned both of us.

"Monica wants bear picture for her magazine," Kaz said. He turned to his audience of colleagues and addressed them in an angry spate of Japanese. I saw the contents of Monica's purse laid out on the hood of the car. There had been no film. I interrupted Kaz and told him. It didn't seem to register.

"Kaz, listen. How would she have gotten it?" I argued. "There was no ladder. You and I had to bring one along with us, remember?"

He ignored me. To Dave he said, "My pictures are stolen. You tell sheriff, please."

Dave let out a sigh. "Okay, Kaz. I'll tell him. First thing in the morning."

"You tell Mr. Sheriff Becker. Okay?"

"Okay," Dave said firmly, putting the lid on it. "Thank you," he added, nailing it down. He turned to the rest of his guests. "Bottoms up, everyone," he announced. "Time to roll."

CHAPTER SIXTEEN

Before noon the next day, Friday—the visitors' last full day—Sheriff Becker had a preliminary report from the state medical examiner. The promptness may have been due to the fact that Columbus Hospital in Great Falls simply did not have to cope with the sheer number of bodies, both living and dead, as did the hospitals of our nation's capital. In terms of geographic density, eastern Montana averages about four souls per square mile; in the District of Columbia, it's ten thousand per square mile. On the other hand, Monica had turned out to *be somebody,* as the young Brando put it so poignantly in *On the Waterfront,* and that may have helped speed up postmortem procedures as well.

The name Leeds rang no bell for Sheriff Ed Becker. But when he said "big cheese New York family," I went, "Oh, *that* Leeds." Leeds was a name that went all the way back to the original Dutch families who settled New Amsterdam, and their ancestral tree had borne a distinguished share of diplomats, historians, and newspaper columnists. (In the brief back-page article my mother clipped from the *Post,* a connection with Washington Irving was mentioned.) The family's means had been comparatively modest until the last century, when a maverick brother named Archibald joined a railroad partnership and made an immodest fortune. Monica had been an offshoot of Archibald's branch. If nothing else, the family name would have given her entrée to the editors of New York's glossies. But perhaps her background was also a chip on her shoulder that fueled her fierce ambition. A Pulitzer would prove she was more than a privileged dilettante with good connections.

"There's a Leeds wing in the Metropolitan Museum of Art," I told the sheriff. He let out a be-that-as-it-may grunt. We were talking on the phone. Both Trudi and Dave were out with the Japanese on their last ride; they'd gone up the canyon trail with binoculars and cameras hoping to spot elk. When the phone rang, I'd pounced on the kitchen extension, thinking it might be Luke. But it was Becker on the other end, and he was surprisingly chatty about the case. I grabbed the lined yellow pad I used for working out menus and took notes.

No bullets had passed through Monica's body, he reassured me. The holes in her neck and shoulders were puncture wounds, and the lack of blood around the wounds suggested she'd been dead when they were made. Cause of death was hemorrhaging from a single blow to her head. Her cheekbone and skull were fractured, and her scalp was torn. "The doc says the injuries are consistent with a mauling," Becker said. "There was some lividity in her lower legs—"

"What's lividity?" I interrupted, remembering the sight of her scrunched-up black pant leg, her dark purple calf.

"Blood settling. After death, the blood tends to pool at the lowest points. In this case, her calves and feet. Which suggests she died sitting up. I talked to Zwart. He thinks she made it back to the car and lost consciousness in the passenger seat."

"So how'd she get to where we found her?"

"Bear came back later and dragged her out. From the lividity in her legs and the lack of blood around the puncture wounds, the doc says she'd probably been dead at least six hours before she was moved."

"But why did the bear come back and drag her out of the car?"

"Maybe it was hungry."

"Oh," I said. I saw Monica's mauled body lying in the grass. "She wasn't *eaten,*" I observed.

"There's no predicting a griz," Becker said. "Something probably scared it off—maybe another bear. That's what Zwart thinks. He's out at Mac's now, going over the pictures. See what they got."

"Did you, uh, talk with Monica's family?"

"And just about everyone else, from the family lawyer in New York City to Senator Baucus's top aide in Washington. Seems like the old man's best fishing buddies with half the state house. He was pretty upset, talking about suing, Mac and Dave both."

"For what, in God's name?" I exclaimed.

"Didn't say." Becker's voice was laconic. "But I'll bet you lunch that his lawyer can come up with something."

"That's appalling!" I felt outraged and helpless on Trudi and Dave's behalf. First a spoiled trophy wife brings the J-E to the brink of ruin, and now Monica's grief-angered father stood poised to kick it over the edge. But I knew Becker was right. Anyone can sue for any wrong, real or imagined. It's the modern equivalent of a duel at dawn. Only the satisfaction is money instead of blood.

"Do Dave and Trudi know?" I asked.

"Reckon there's no need to mention it." There was a warning in his voice. "Like my daddy used say, 'Don't worry about tomorrow's bread today.' The poor guy might just need to rattle a few cages. It all may blow over if we get the griz. Zwart's been taking as much heat as I have."

"So what happened last night?"

"Nothing. They got rid of the cow, that's all. Zwart's out there now setting snares with Walt and the wardens. I can tell you one thing. Given the autopsy on the girl, if there's a griz on Mac's film, I ain't fooling around none with fecal samples."

"What do you mean?"

"You get a griz in a snare, it'll shit its insides out trying to get loose, if you'll pardon my French. Walt and Mac and the Nature Conservancy are pushing for scat tests. They say if the Bozeman lab finds any human hair or skin, they'll agree to putting the animal down, even if it's a female." He paused, as if lining up his ducks. "But then we're sitting on a pissed-off griz while we wait half a day or more on the Bozeman microscopes. You think that ain't gonna draw a crowd? We'd be lucky if we only got half the state out to see it."

I had the feeling Becker was arguing to himself as much as me. "One way or another," he went on, "someone's likely to get hurt.

Besides, the doc can't say that the griz *ingested* any of the girl. So if Mac's film's got anything on it, that's good enough for me. The sooner we move on this, the better. The lawyer's flying out from New York this afternoon."

"For what?"

"Make arrangements," he said. "I'm guessing look around a bit."

"Will he come out here?"

"Can't stop him. But we've got all her effects here in the office. If he wants to check out the scene, he can view the tapes."

"Well, be sure to tell him that her rental's sitting out here." Let someone else have a turn on the phone with Hertz, I thought.

Becker asked, "You got a fax there?"

"Nope. Trudi's the last holdout. But Dave might have one down at the farm office."

"You got a number?"

"You want me to look?"

"No. Just tell them if they want to see the autopsy report, I'm faxing a copy over to the institute. The lab work won't be in for a couple of weeks, but Dave might want a look at what they got."

After we hung up, I realized I'd said nothing to Becker about Kaz's film. Let Dave handle it, I decided. Nonetheless, Kaz's angry certainty nagged at me.

The oven timer dinged. I took out my batch of hamburger rolls, set them on a rack to cool, and stepped out the back door to test the air. It was mild. The morning sky was pale blue streaked with milky patches of clouds. On the far side of the service yard, the bare upper branches of a big cottonwood scraped in a dry breeze. I'd planned to grill burgers outside for lunch, but it was warm enough to eat them outside as well. I wondered what April was like in Japan.

I went looking for Hil and found him and my car out by the machine shed. The Escort's engine was running. Hil was charging up the battery while he worked on the interior. The doors were open, and the radio was on loud. A rock voice rasped to a thumping bass, almost drowning out the whine of the "doors open" signal. I yelled over the music, "Hil!"

He backed out of the passenger side and squeezed his sponge out over a plastic bucket. The water in it was bright red. The upper half of the velour seat was wet and dark. "A bitch," he grumbled.

The word grated. "Leave it," I said. "You won't get it all out. The medical examiner says she bled to death sitting up."

Ignoring me, Hil picked up his hose, wet down the sponge, and turned back to the car's interior. The outside of the car gleamed in the thin sunlight. The cleaning revealed another set of claw scratched on the door. I drew my fingers along them. I recognized the next song on the radio: Eric Clapton's "Tears from Heaven", a Grammy winner. Clapton was singing to his son—a four-year-old who fell to his death out of a skyscraper's window. I thought of all the poems I'd written about Rachel and wondered, not for the first time, what prompts us to make music out of pain.

"Hil," I called over the lyrics. "Can you set up the picnic tables on the front lawn and get the grill going over there for burgers? I'll want the fire ready to go about twelve-thirty." His back didn't acknowledge me, but I was pretty sure he'd heard. "Thanks," I said, making an effort not to sound sarcastic.

He unfolded himself from the car. "They going after Honey Paws?" He looked me up and down with a smirk.

I squared my shoulders. "You mean the grizzly? It looks like it."

He gave a satisfied grunt, then bent over the bucket and twisted more blood out of his sponge.

The riders were late getting back, but the morning's excursion had been a great success. They had toured (and filmed) the clearing where I'd found the mutilated grizzly, then bushwhacked through the forest up to seven thousand feet. They had found no elk, but had scared up several deer, and Trudi had spotted mountain goats on an opposite cliff face. Kaz came over to tell me as I flipped burgers on the grill. He was pleased and excited. The goats had been too far away for pictures, but the party had watched the animals through binoculars for a long time. "They are like white butterflies," Kaz said. "Always moving." He made poetic motions with his hand, alighting, leaping, alighting again. He made no reference to the night before and no apology for his belligerent manner. Had he forgotten about his missing film? Amazingly, at breakfast, Kaz had seemed no worse for wear. None of them did. Somewhere I'd read that Japanese drinkers nibbled ginkgo nuts to ward off hangovers. Maybe the men from NVI had brought along a secret supply.

There wasn't much cleanup after lunch, thanks to the grill and the paper plates, so during naptime I rolled down all the windows of my sodden Escort and took it out for a spin to charge up its battery. Monica was a presence in the wet passenger seat beside me, but an expected one, and along with the rush of air through the open windows, I felt an unexpected rush of invincibility, as if I were borrowing power from the claw marks on the fender, as if I could blow a semi off the road like dry straw. It was like holding a loaded gun. There was the same shift in the perception of personal power. A pretty good feeling, as much as I hate to say it.

Of course, I ended up out at the swamp. The expanse of water lay under the sky in irregular shapes, linked by channels and outlined by borders of willow and aspen. Across the rumpled brown plain, Ear Mountain rose out of the blue-gray mountains like a grizzly's snow-dusted hump. I drove slowly along the track, inhaling the scent of rotting reeds and new grasses along with the Detroit smell of wet velour. Just past the cabin, a group of game wardens and deputies were working with brush and logs. I spotted Walt's truck next to the grove of cottonwoods on the far side of the carcass site. The cow, as the sheriff had said, was no longer there, only a bare circle of dirt. Walt stood at the back of his truck, threading steel cable through an angle iron. I pulled up beside him and got out of the car, leaving the engine running.

"Lee," he warned, "don't walk around none. We're working on six different snares. You probably shouldn't even be here."

"Sorry." But I made no move to go. "What's that?" I asked.

"Aircraft cable, quarter-inch steel. For a trail set." He held up a six-foot loop. "This gets clamped to a swivel, then a tailpiece gets anchored to one of these cottonwoods."

"Where do you put your noose?"

"It lies on the bear's path. You've got to conceal it. And the spring as well," he explained. "That's what takes so long setting these things up. You've got to make it look natural. We sift a layer of fine dirt over it, put back the grass, match everything up. Then we lay down obstacles to direct the bear's step. You put a rock or some sticks in the bear's way and it'll tend to avoid them, step on your spring instead. But you got to be careful. It's got to look right or the bear won't go for it."

I watched him test the snare's slide lock. "Found out anything from Mac's film?" I asked.

"Yeah. They only got one bear at the carcass the night your friend was killed."

"A grizzly was feeding on cow?"

"Yes," he said.

"So it probably wasn't hungry for Monica," I said.

"Well, we don't know the sequence. The bear might have been planning to make a meal out of her, then gotten scared off and decided the cow was a better bet."

"What's on the film?" I asked.

"Either a female or a subadult male. You can't really tell from the pictures. You can identify individuals by their color and markings, but not the sex. We'll have to wait and see what the snares turn up."

"And what if it doesn't match the bear on camera?"

"We let it go. The snare don't hurt it. It just gets real agitated."

"I can imagine."

Zwart emerged from a swale of aspen. Under the brim of his Aussie hat, his eye patch was askew, his face sweaty and smeared with dirt. "What's she doing here?" he demanded.

I met his single blue eye. "She's leaving," I said pleasantly.

Back at the J-E, there was no time for my afternoon run, but after twenty minutes of yoga in my room, I felt up to my culinary home stretch: a departure "banquet" in the lodge's summer dining room. Hil had had a fire going since early morning to take the chill out of the cavernous log space, and had moved the several tables to make one long one by the hearth. Lynn had vacuumed and dusted and set the table with overlapping green-checked bistro cloths. The farm manager's wife had sent up two baskets of pansies for centerpieces. She and her husband were expected for dinner, along with a Nature Conservancy administrator, a lawyer friend who worked *pro bono* for the Sacred Paw, and Mac and Clare. Including the guests of honor and Trudi and Dave, there were twelve for dinner. Lynn and the farm manager's daughter, Heather, rather than join the party, had elected to wait table.

Most of the menu was not demanding. I had the tenderloins marinating in red wine and crushed peppercorns and had already made a Cumberland-type sauce—using Trudi's huckleberries instead of currant jelly. We would also serve a horseradish-and-whipped-cream sauce, separate dishes of wild rice and steamed white rice, an endive-and-spinach salad, and for dessert a black cherry cobbler. (Along with her huckleberries, Trudi had frozen quarts of last summer's cherries from Flathead Lake.)

But I had wanted a show-off first course—something that bore out the East-meets-West motif of the week. Eventually I decided on ravioli/wontons masked in a light ginger-flavored broth. I planned two stuffings: one made with dried shitake mushrooms, which I'd brought with me, the other made with J-E smoked trout. My chief difficulty was that Trudi had not been able to find ready-made wonton wrappers at her supermarket. Homemade pasta would serve the same purpose, but I'd made it only twice before, fresh pasta being the yuppy carb of choice in D.C. and thus readily available in the upscale neighborhoods where I ended up house-sitting. Still, rather than abandon my oriental ravioli, I decided to try mixing up a dough. Eggs and flour we could afford to waste.

In the pastry pantry, I kneaded up two batches, the second in case I tore too many of the first. I used a bit more flour than noodle dough calls for, and the result proved workable. I found a large round cookie cutter with scalloped edges and decided to use it, on the theory that round wontons would have handmade cachet. I was about to start rolling and cutting when someone banged at the back door. I covered the dough with a damp towel, ineffectually wiped my floury hands on my apron, and went to see who it was.

It was Luke. He stood there lean and lanky and grinning. "Oh," I said. I was grinning too. We hugged and kissed like old friends. I felt an unbraiding sensation, a release within. "I thought maybe I wouldn't see you," I said.

"Not a chance," he said.

Another hug, quick and hard. I pulled back for a look. He looked the same. Same brown hair, shaggy at the edges as if he'd been out of reach of a barber, but receding prematurely. (I was more comfortable with his hairline than he was. Maybe because it made him look closer to my age than his own—which was thirty-three.) His mouth was the same, professionally deadpan, and his eyes still full of humor and kindness. With some people, it's hard to recall the color of their eyes. But Luke's were olive brown flecked with light. When we met, the color had reminded me of a stream bottom in summer. I'd wanted to dive in. I found I still wanted to. He was not a conventionally handsome man, not in the movie-star way of Mac Fife. Luke's features were not symmetrical enough. His jaw was slightly crooked (as a child, there'd been no money for an orthodontist), and his nose, big enough for a Roman emperor, had a dent in it (a souvenir from his college days on the rodeo circuit.) *Beau laid,* the French would call him. Beautifully ugly. With Luke in the kitchen, I felt as if I'd just floated out of choppy water into the calm of a natural harbor.

I washed the flour off my hands at the sink. "You want something?" I asked. "Coffee? A beer? If you give me a minute, I'll wrap up my dough."

He shook his head. "I can't stay."

I suppressed a pang. "You here on business?"

He smiled. "No. I wanted to see you."

"But you know about Monica Leeds—the reporter who was killed?"

"By a grizzly, I hear. Not my department." He sounded relieved.

"No."

He considered me. "You think it is?"

I winced. "I don't know."

"So that's why you're glad to see me," he teased.

I met his eyes. "No, it's not," I said seriously.

"Lee—"

I interrupted him, afraid of what he was going to say. "But as long as you're here, you might as well be useful."

He laughed. "Okay, okay. What's the story?" He settled back against the counter, crossing his right boot over his left at the ankles. There was no pull in his jeans—the legs were loose as extra-long sleeves. The length of him was relaxed, attentive. I told him about Monica, sketching in her stay at the J-E and her sudden departure, going into more detail when I got to the autopsy report.

Luke uncrossed his legs and stood up. "I'll take you up on that coffee."

I poured us two mugs from the machine in Trudi's office. We carried them into the staff dining room and sat down across from each other at the sunny end of the table. Luke's eyebrows shot up when he tasted the coffee. "You want milk?" I offered. "I can make a new pot."

He shook his head. "Go on."

"I don't know. It's just a whole bunch of little things that don't add up."

"Like?" His face was serious, like that of a doctor probing for symptoms.

"Like her pulling out without saying anything to anyone. Like packing my bra."

"You said she was in a rush when you saw her in Choteau."

"Yes, but Mac was her *subject.* She was working up a book proposal on him. All the writers I know *woo* their subjects. They don't suddenly run away from them. At least not until *after* the book's out. And my bra was pink."

"Pink?" A smile played across his mouth.

"Oh, stop it," I said. I could feel a flush rising up my neck. "All her underwear was black. She was into black and purple and olive. Bruise colors. Besides, it wasn't her size. I just don't think she would have made that mistake. I mean, it would be like you picking up an oversized pink jock in the locker room."

Luke looked disconcerted. It was my turn to smile. "And then there's the business of her purse. She had the keys to her car in it, but it was in the backseat, along with her laptop and her bag."

"So?"

"So when a women drives alone, she drives with her purse in the front seat."

"That's weak. You just told me she took the wrong car and the keys were in it. She doesn't need to fish around for them in her purse. She just dumps everything in the backseat and drives off." He studied his coffee without taking a sip, then looked up. "Anything else?"

I let out a sigh. "There's the business of Kaz's film disappearing. Also, I don't understand why she was in such an enormous rush to go sit for maybe hours waiting for a bear to show up. And if she really wanted to see a bear, why did she park where she couldn't see the dead cow? There's a clear sightline from the little cabin—I was out there poking around when they were setting up the institute's camera. And you can also get a clear shot from the tree where Kaz set up his camera. But she parked behind a line of bushes between the cabin and Kaz's tree."

"Maybe she thought the car would scare off the wildlife."

"Maybe. But maybe someone brained her and left her to the bears."

"Look, Lee." He leaned toward me across the table. "Nothing you've told me is solid. You've got nothing that's going to stand up in court. It sounds to me like you've gotten lost in the loose ends. Every case has them. Even when the perp's caught with the gun still warm, some of the victim's actions are inexplicable." He paused. His face was concerned. "Did you like her?"

"No. Not really. She was pretty abrasive." I thought of the witchy root that had fallen from her sheets. We sat in silence a minute. I added, "I liked her drive, her nerve. At least in retrospect."

"It's not like what happened last year," he pointed out. "Up in the Bob, we had the murder weapons. And a confession. Thanks to you," he conceded with an ironical smile.

"Such is the stuff cases are made of," I said sourly.

"I'm not saying you're wrong, Lee. I'm saying there's nothing you or I or Sheriff Becker or anyone else can do about it unless there's probable cause. Investigations take time and money. You've got to have something more than maybes to go on."

"Such as?"

"Weapons are always nice."

I thought of a grizzly's pointed teeth. Then flash, I was back in a twilight landscape. I caught the edge of my vision of flesh rotting backward onto bones and quickly shook it away, like a swimmer with water in the ears.

"I've got to go," Luke announced. I looked at him. He was wearing a gray woolen tweed shirt over a white T-shirt that sagged at the neck. I could see the taut jut of his collarbones. I remembered the feel of the small of his back under my hands. Did the man have a clue what was running through my head, yanking at my heart?

He pushed back his chair and stood up. Reluctantly, I followed suit. "Tell me," I said. "Does Becker know what he's doing?"

"To be honest, I don't know the guy. I hear he's playing it by the book."

I didn't say anything.

"Sometimes," he tried to reassure me, "you're better off with a guy like Becker, someone who doesn't deal routinely with murder. It can make a guy more careful."

"Than you?" I challenged.

Luke smiled a cocky little smile. Then he looked down at his boots. They were black. Deep wrinkles in the worn leather made triangles out of the pointed toes. "I'm getting back together with Barb," he said, looking up and searching my face.

Thud. I made my voice casual. "So Big Mountain's out. You're standing me up." I tried to smile and didn't do so well. Luke stood there looking miserable. I took a breath. "Look, I'm just feeling sorry for myself. I hope it works out for you." I found that I really meant it. "I know what you're going through. And you're braver than I was. Clint—my husband—wanted to try again and I wouldn't. Part of me has always been sorry."

We picked up the coffee cups, carried them into the kitchen, and set them down on the counter. Luke's was untouched. "The man can't even get a decent cup of coffee," I said.

"Lee," he said, pulling me toward him. We kissed, this time

like lovers. We moved apart. His off-kilter face was shining. He reached out and with great tenderness brushed a stray piece of hair off my forehead. At that moment, standing together with Luke in the kitchen of the J-E, I felt whole and light and entirely happy.

Since then, I've spent a fair amount of time inventing different endings—all of them considerably steamier than what happened. Like the other single women I know, I've adapted to celibacy like a desert nomad. The long dry stretches—years at a time—present no discernible obstacle to the movement of my life. Even so, when I allow myself to think about the trip Luke and I never took, I want to bang my head against the wall.

"This girl's death," he said as he left, "I know you're not going to let it go. I want you to call me if you turn something up."

"How about a baseball bat covered with bloody prints? Would that do?"

"I'm serious. Don't get in over your head."

"Like last time?"

"Promise," he insisted.

"I'll call you," I promised. I raised an eyebrow. "Any excuse." He turned to go. On the back of his shirt there were blurred floury marks. My handprints. "Wait a sec," I said. I brushed them off.

Chapter Seventeen

Trudi was right, I had to admit. The J-E's tenderloins made a memorable farewell feast. Although my laborious ravioli came out well enough to please a foodie, it was the butter-soft beef full of animal richness that drew growls of pleasure from the guests. Venison, though more exotic, would not have punctuated the purpose of their visit nearly as well. After Lynn and her friend Heather brought back the empty *primi* plates into the kitchen, I took off my bandanna and put on a clean white apron. While the girls distributed warm plates and brought in the accompaniments, I carved the meat at a side table in the dining room. Cutting from both the "mignon" and the "Chateaubriand" ends, I filled a platter with slices ranging from barely pink in the center to darkest crimson. Lynn passed it around, starting with Mr. Yamaguchi, who was sitting on Trudi's right.

Trudi looked pretty in a turquoise blouse with ruffles down the front and buffalo-head-nickel buttons. Clare somehow managed to look severe in a feminine floral print dress. Maybe it was the plain white collar, which gave her a starched look. She sat down at Dave's end of the table. Mac was up at Trudi's end talking over Mr. Tanaka to the Nature Conservancy rep, a younger man with a pale, earnest face and a preppy haircut, short in back, long and floppy in front. He was the only man in a button-down shirt and jacket. The shirt was blue oxford cloth and the jacket was tan Harris tweed. Both said "Easterner." He was listening somewhat uncomfortably to Mac, whose voice rose passionately above the general conversation.

"Ursus arctos," he declaimed, "has got the lowest reproductive rate of any mammal in North America, and they're ready to kill a healthy female! They won't even *consider* the possibility of reconditioning."

The Nature Conservancy man soothed, "Hey, we're on the same team. But it's just not practical. Even if it works—and there's no guarantee—you're talking maybe ten grand."

Mac sneered. "Look at what we've spent on whooping cranes, on condors. It's not money. It's a mind-set. The bureaucrats are going to look bad if they don't 'punish' a bear for killing that idiot woman."

"Mac," Trudi said. She nodded at the platter of meat Lynn was offering. He helped himself to five pieces. Mr. Tanaka smiled broadly and also took five. Trudi had also been right about needing two of the tenderloins. I concentrated on carving.

* * *

Back in the kitchen, I asked Lynn, "What did Mac mean, 'recondition' the bear?"

"Oh, he's got some scientist friend who teaches bears to run away from people. He sprays them with Tabasco."

"Tabasco?"

"Yeah, and mustard oil and ammonia. And if that doesn't work, he shoots them in the butt with rubber bullets."

Lynn's companion Heather giggled. Lynn looked pleased. "It's true!" she insisted. "I did a science paper on it last year. It takes about five days to recondition a grizzly. Uncle Mac says they're very adaptable. He took me over to see the lab, but they didn't have any bears when we were there." She stopped and sniffed the air. Cigarette smoke. It was unmistakable. "Hil!" Lynn accused.

He was standing half in shadow just inside the back door. I'd left it open to let out some of the heat in the kitchen. I hadn't heard him come in through the screen door, but he'd been there listening. "Tabasco," he said, shaking his head in disgust. "Lot less trouble to shoot and shovel." He raised his cigarette to his mouth and took a drag.

"You aren't supposed to smoke in here," Lynn scolded. She sounded exactly like Trudi.

Slowly and defiantly, he blew a stream of blue smoke in her direction. He stared at her, then turned, opened the screen door, flicked the butt into the night, and followed it out.

"Creep," Lynn muttered.

I had to agree. My liberal bleeding heart was inclined to make large allowances for the dispossessed—if not embrace them. But poor Indian or no, there was something creepy about the man, and it wasn't simply that he liked his eggs runny.

I yawned my way through dessert, which, thanks to champagne and exchanges of long speeches and only slightly shorter toasts, dragged on till almost nine o'clock. I dismissed the girls, who went upstairs to watch TV. While Hil ran the washer in the dish pantry, I mixed up a pancake batter. Only breakfast left, I comforted myself. I wasn't sure what I was going to do after the Japanese departed. I'd been counting on several days with Luke before flying back. I was, however, ready to get out of the kitchen. Suddenly, red-penciling comp papers looked pretty good. Washington's soft springtime looked even better. The hosts of golden daffodils along the parkways would be finished, but the azaleas and dogwood in the gardens of Georgetown would be in full bloom.

I fell into bed before ten, too exhausted even for a nightcap. At three, I woke up sharply, like a diver surfacing from cold water. If it was a dream, I don't remember it. But as I waited to sink back into the warmth of sleep, all the "maybes" of Monica's death woke up and started to worm around in my brain. It was as if they had hoarded their strength for darkness.

I turned over. The bedsprings let out a rusty squeal. I thought of steel snares artfully woven into the bear's footpath. Had a grizzly been caught yet? I turned over again, *sprong,* and the phrase "darkling plain" came to mind, compliments of Matthew Arnold. The poet's despair-ridden image seemed apt. But on the J-E's stretch of open plain, it wasn't ignorant armies clashing by night. It had been one brash freelancer and one wild bear.

Or had it? I tried to picture Monica parked behind the screen of stunted aspen and red osier, waiting—for what? Then suddenly I remembered the notebook I'd found in *her* rental—the one she hadn't driven to the swamp. I'd come across it hunting for my highway map, but at the time I had been too upset by the car mix-up to wonder why she'd gone off without her notebook. Maybe it was only an extra one. I sat up, turned on the light, pulled a heavy sweater over my nightgown, and trotted barefoot down the corridor, through the dark kitchen, out to Monica's car. Her notebook, a narrow spiral-bound reporter's pad, was still there in the door pocket. I took it back to my room. My feet were freezing. I poured yesterday's allowance of bourbon into my tooth mug, sat cross-legged under the bed covers, and opened the note pad.

At the top of the first page, Monica had written "Turner/ Fonda" and the date. Her interview had taken place on the Thursday before the Easter weekend when she'd appeared at the J-E. Below that were several phone numbers and directions from the Bozeman airport to the Turner/Fonda ranch, the Flying D. Monica had underscored the name, then underscored "130,000 acres" twice. Her handwriting, in fine ballpoint, was compact and businesslike. There were no flamboyant loops or slashes. The rest of the notebook was three-quarters full of ballpoint hieroglyphics which ran down the left-hand side of the red center line.

About half the squiggles were recognizable letters. Evidently, Monica had used a form of speedwriting rather than shorthand, but it might as well have been Russian as far as I was concerned. All I could read was the arabic numbers, and only a few of them made sense. "J = $60 mil. T, 1.4 bil." (Had they *told* her their worth?) On the blank side of one page she had penciled in the word "buffalo" opposite "2,000 hd."

I sipped at my bourbon and tried to think of a good reason why she would leave without her notes for a story assigned by a top-of-the-heap glossy. Even if she'd taped the interview as a backup (and she had been taping Mac), her notes would be handier than untranscribed voices. Or had she already written up Ted and Jane on her laptop? When was her deadline? Had she sent off a disk to *Vanity Fair* the day we bumped into her in Choteau? That had been a Tuesday, the day she disappeared.

I turned the notebook over in my hands. What I was looking at was another "maybe," another stray tile from the mosaic of Monica's death. I wanted all the maybes to belong to the same picture. I wanted an entire mosaic, even if it didn't have saints with golden halos and lambs of redemption. Perhaps it was a childish want. Luke had insisted that sudden deaths are seldom tidy. For all I knew, the scattered pieces I was turning over in my hand might have come from three or four unrelated sites. Perhaps I should leave my fragments to the experts and go home.

On the other hand. Suppose someone had bashed her over the head and left her to bleed to death in the car, and a bear had gotten at her body *after* she had died. Suppose it could be proved that she was killed chasing down a story instead of running from a grizzly. Would the force of Big Daddy Leeds's anger be diverted away from the J-E?

At breakfast the next morning I cut myself. I was dicing more peppers at the last minute (inconveniently, *all* the visitors had decided on Western omelets), and in my haste I took off a slice of fingernail and skin on my left forefinger. It bled profusely all over the peppers and hurt all the way up to my elbow. It wasn't the first time I'd shaved that finger—the one that feeds food to the knife. A good quarter of the tip was already gone. But as I stanched the blood with ice and a succession of Band-Aids, I could hear my mother trilling: "Your body is trying to tell you something." Like, don't nip whiskey at three in the morning and chop peppers at seven?

Trudi had to finish up the omelets. Guiltily, I sat on a stool by the sink and watched. I held my throbbing forefinger up in the air as if testing the weather and entertained thoughts of alcoholism. On the radio, the news from Waco, Texas, was that the FBI was trying out a new sound track. They were assaulting Ranch Apocalypse with the shrieks of rabbits being slaughtered. You had to wonder how they'd gotten the tape.

The phone rang as Trudi was flipping the omelets. I picked it up. It was Mac. His voice was dry, his message short. A grizzly had been trapped in one of the snares. It matched the photo and the game wardens had shot it. "A lactating female," he added acidly.

"Oh, Mac," I said in sympathy. But he had already hung up.

The guests did not have to leave for their plane till eleven, so after breakfast Dave and Trudi drove them out to the swamp for a look at the kill. "They got themselves one *big* mother," Hil volunteered. He had already been out there. I left the kitchen to him and followed the van's cloud of dust in my Escort. I rolled up the windows as we sped along the J-E's fence lines, but nonetheless, fine gray dust puffed through the vents, settling like talc on the still-damp passenger seat.

At the swamp, the cordons of survey tape were gone. Now the area around the cabin was defined by a rough semicircle of parked station wagons and trucks. The morning sun whitened the windshields and, beyond them, the wind-ruffled surface of the swamp. Several dozen spectators in bright parkas and worn denim jackets made a ring inside the vehicles. They welcomed Dave and Trudi, joshing and shaking hands with them, nodding and smiling at their Japanese guests. The group mood was festive, as if school had unexpectedly been let out for the morning.

A good half of the people there had cameras or videocams and were milling around trying out angles, looking for openings in the inner circle of uniforms around the dead grizzly. The men from NVI, back in regulation pinstripe but wearing their new cowboy hats, removed their lens caps. As they stepped forward to photograph the bear, their silk ties and Italian shoes gleamed softly in the sunlight.

Death had not diminished the grizzly. Stretched out on the trampled grass, she was enormous, jet black, with a cape of silver-tipped guard hairs over her hump. She had been brought down with a shoulder shot to the heart from a .338. There was little blood. In front, her fur was lighter-colored and fluffy-looking; long black nipples protruded. Her eyes were open. They were small and brown. Her muzzle was narrow, like an intelligent dog's.

Clare was kneeling on the feces-covered ground, examining one of the huge paws. The claws were maybe three inches long and whitish at the tips. Richard Zwart was hunkering beside Clare. I looked around for Mac. He was standing off to one side with a small group of men, three or four of them, beside a battered gray pickup with one bright green door. The men's faces were strong-boned and weathered like those of migrant workers. One of them had a long ponytail down the back of his Norwegian-patterned brown-and-gray cardigan. Another, with tarnished silver hair and a sunken jaw, might have been Mr. Yamaguchi's toothless brother. They stood erect, eyes closed, mouths moving slightly as if praying, heads nodding in silent rhythm. Mac's mouth, however, was clenched shut, his eyes open, and even at the distance I stood, the hardness in them was clearly readable.

Walt Surrey wandered up to me, as aimless as a man after a funeral. "Who's with Mac?" I asked him.

"His friends off the reservation."

"Blackfeet?"

"Yeah. The old guy's a traditional medicine man. He's pretty famous."

Walt looked as if he could have used a cure. His face had a pinched look, as if he'd swallowed something he couldn't quite get down. There were dark circles of fatigue under his eyes, but his heavy beard looked recently shaven. "Were you out here last night?" I asked.

He shook his auburn locks. "Nope. But I might as well have been for all the sleep I got. That boy of mine's got a set of lungs, I can tell you. At one point, we let him go for a twenty-minute stretch. I timed it. He won. When I picked him up, he was still going strong."

We stood there, our eyes on the bear. It was hard to look elsewhere. It was as if the creature's life had not entirely fled. The inert mass of black fur still had an aura of power, a numinousness to use one of my mother's words. "So what's wrong?" I asked Walt.

"What do you mean?" His tone, normally genial, had an edge to it.

"Well, I don't want to be cynical, but my ex-husband was a New Age dad, and he had no problem whatsoever snoring right through our daughter's screams. I just wondered if something besides your baby was keeping you up."

He said nothing.

"You think they got the right bear?" I pushed.

"Kinda late if it wasn't."

"You don't want to talk about it."

He gave me a grim little smile. "I like my job. Most of the time."

I met his eyes. "I'm just passing through," I said.

We looked back at the bear. The patches and badges around it seemed to be waiting for something. Walt said slowly, "You know those puzzles, what's wrong with this picture?"

"Yeah?"

"Well, there's nothing upside down or backward about the picture Zwart put together. But there's something missing. He's being sitting behind his desk too long."

I waited.

"In a livestock depredation, a grizzly leaves a lot of signs. You gain an eye for it, after a while. Nothing real obvious, like tracks or scat. But there'll be pad impressions in the grass. You can see where it went, how it moved, where it dragged the animal. 'Course, everyone tramping around the girl's body, you can understand there not being much to find. But if the bear charged through that line of brush like they think, there oughta be broken twigs and bits of fur caught on the briers. You've got wild rose all through there. I can see where you drove the truck clear enough. But there's no black fur. Not a hair." He sounded as if he'd checked every twig.

"So how do you explain that?"

"I can't."

"You tell Zwart?"

"Yep. And Becker." End of conversation.

I opened a new one. "So where's her cub?"

He shook his head. "It wasn't in the photo. Cub mortality rate's pretty high. About forty percent of all grizzly deaths occur between birth and age one and a half. She must have lost it. Recently. Because she still had her milk. Might have made her touchy."

"More likely to charge?"

"Maybe. Hard to say."

One of the wardens worked the snare loose from the bear's right wrist and began coiling up the cable.

"I can't believe Monica got out of the car to look at a mother grizzly," I said, as much to myself as to Walt.

"Oh," he answered, his voice cheerful again, "I don't have a problem with that. It's people who are hard to explain, not grizzlies. There's no accounting what people will do. My dad showed me this old clipping about a couple of tourists down in Yellowstone. This was back when the place was crawling with road beggars and—"

"Road beggars?"

"Black bears looking for handouts. So this couple wants a home movie of a bear licking their toddler. They paint honey on the kid's face and stand him outside the car, and you can guess what happened."

"Jesus," I said, shocked. "He died?"

"You bet. Critter ate his face off. The dad had it on Super Eight."

"They sue the Park Service?" I said acidly.

Walt's dark eyebrows scrunched together in a frown. "What?"

I waved it away. "Nothing. I'm just feeling dyspeptic." I

noticed Clare. She was talking to a warden. Dave was talking to Zwart. Zwart nodded, then, importantly as a traffic cop, waved the Japanese in for close-ups.

The Japanese, laughing and joking in their own language, improvised sight gags for their cameras. Sam shook the dead bear's giant paw. Mr. Yamaguchi straddled it and squatted down on its back, as if ready for a ride. The crowd laughed appreciatively. A six-year-old boy with a face determined as a bulldog's strode forward, stopped three feet short of the grizzly's head, and hurled a stone at it. One of the game wardens shooed him back.

"You don't need to do that, Jason," his mother said in a loud stagy drawl. "That's a *good* bear." More laughter.

Off to the side, the Blackfeet men stood with their eyes closed, seeming not to hear.

I thought of the skinned bear back in the canyon. That carcass had no ceremony. I asked Walt, "You any closer to finding your poacher?"

Walt shrugged. "The forensic vets say there was only the one bullet. Whoever did it was a crack shot. That gives us maybe half the men in the county."

A warden held up the coiled snare cable and called to Walt, "Where do you want this?"

"Excuse me," he said.

I watched Clare approach the grizzly with a tool kit. She knelt, opened the bear's mouth, and examined its teeth. The crowd edged closer. The Japanese men peered over her shoulder. I glanced over at Mac. He and the old man had moved off a distance from their companions. The old man stood against the open sky like a boulder. Mac was quick-stepping, like an impatient boxer confined to his corner. Then abruptly he turned and strode toward the crowd, pushing his way through. "What do you think you're doing?" he asked Clare.

She looked up, surprised. "I'm going to take a premolar."

"No, you're not."

Embarrassed, the Japanese men stepped back. Mac's anger, already bursting at the seams, ripped loose. "I'm telling you to leave it alone! This is a farce," he yelled, pacing the ground. "A fucking farce! Get up. Get up this minute!"

Clare didn't move. "Information is information," she said evenly.

"Christ!" he exclaimed. He wheeled away and in the next step wheeled back. "What the hell difference does it make how old she is? She's dead!"

She took out a pair of pliers from her kit.

"Put that back," he ordered, his voice more under control. "Goddamn it, Clare, the grizzly doesn't need more studying. It needs more space. I'm telling you, we are not going to touch this animal!"

Clare studied him for a moment. Then, with the precision of a dentist's assistant, she replaced the pliers in the tray of her kit. She stood up, eyes on Mac, then stooped to pick up her tools. Her long hair slid over her shoulders, hiding her face, but as she walked away, her back was straight, her head unbowed.

Trudi appeared beside me. "Honest to God," she sighed wearily, shaking her head at Mac's outburst. We watched Clare climb into the institute's truck. "I'll say this for her," Trudi commented with grudging admiration, "she's managed to outlast her predecessors. By some."

A large cumulus cloud moved across the swamp, casting its shadow like a giant sail. Sedately, the shadow engulfed us. The grizzly's fur lost its luster. Several onlookers zipped up their jackets. Walt backed up a dual pickup into the circle. There was a crane mounted on the corner of its flat bed. Zwart and the wardens roped the dead bear's four feet together. Walt lowered the crane's hook. There was a hydraulic whine and the bear's carcass swung off the ground like a sack of cargo.

"Well, that's that," Trudi said as the men maneuvered the dark bundle onto the truck's bed. "We've got to get moving. They've still got some packing before we leave."

I glanced at my watch. It was only nine-thirty. It felt much later. "You going to the airport with them?"

"Yes. But I want you there to wave them off—you, Lynn, Hil, everybody."

"You sure you haven't been watching too much *Masterpiece Theater?*"

"What do mean?"

"It just sounds rather feudal, the servants all lined up in the courtyard. Do we get to hold our hands out?"

Trudi looked at me.

I rephrased the question. "Have you instructed our guests about the time-honored American tradition of overtipping the help?"

"Oh sure," Trudi said. "I told them, 'And for the cook, five big ones should do it.' "

She bustled off to help Dave usher the Japanese back into the van. I walked over to the cottonwood where the snare had been anchored. The cable had bitten into its bark. I wondered how long the tree would live.

CHAPTER EIGHTEEN

So the Japanese flew off into the sunset trailing clouds of goodwill if not glory, and I stayed on at the J-E. Trudi didn't have to bend my arm at all. I told her about being stood up by Luke, and her sympathy felt just fine. "Men are such shits," she said. Of course, I defended Luke. But I had a discouraging sense of *déjà vu*. I'd had the conversation before. Maybe starting in sixth grade. Only the "he" in it changed. Or did he? A thought too deep for tears.

In any case, I let Trudi fuss over me in an apple-pie way that I never would have allowed my own mother. In our family, my mother the doctor, despite her steel-edged therapeutic insight (or perhaps because of it), was the fragile one, the one who needed protection and mothering. After the wars of my adolescence, my father and I ended up buddies in this regard.

After the great goodbye—a sincere surge of affection had

welled up between us all—I went back to my room to check out Sam's envelope and smelled a faint stink of cigarette smoke. Hil checking on my plumbing? I didn't think any more of it at the time. I was admiring the five crisp hundred-dollar bills in the envelope. Fair enough, I thought. I tucked the money into my duffel and considered the expanse of free time before me. I thought about a nice long hike. A chance to find the wildflowers along the way, if not smell them. I could pack a pair of beef tenderloin sandwiches and my wildflower book and head out into open space, maybe up the ridge where I'd seen the *Douglasia* growing on Easter Sunday morning. Without brunch to worry about, I might find other alpine bloomers as well. But first I wanted to get Monica's notebook off my chest. It was right where I'd left it on the bedside table under the volume of Olwyn Fife's poems. I took it into the Big Room along with my AT&T card and started dialing.

The editorial offices of *Vanity Fair* in New York were closed for the weekend. So there was no way to discover right then and there whether Monica had already turned in her tale of Ted and Jane among the buffalos. Next, I tried the sheriff's office in Choteau. Ed Becker was back from the swamp, but he didn't want the notebook. The Leeds's family lawyer had stopped by to pick up Monica's effects earlier that morning. He was staying in Great Falls, but was planning to be at the funeral parlor in Choteau this afternoon. He was going to fly back with Monica's body that night. I might catch him there. The lawyer's name was Putnam. The undertaker's name was Enders—you had to wonder which came first, the name or the trade. Becker gave me the number. Mrs. Enders answered. I explained about Monica's notebook. She said Putnam had just gone out for a bite to eat and to come on by.

"It'll take me about an hour," I told her. "I'm calling from the J-E."

"Oh," she said. She sounded impressed, as if the J-E were fancy. "Well, you take your time, honey. We'll keep him here for you." She gave me directions. My wildflower walk would have to wait.

* * *

The Enders Funeral Home was located on one of Choteau's tree-lined side streets. Like its neighbors on the block, it looked as plain as a child's drawing—small windows in aluminum-sided walls, asphalt shingles on a low-pitched roof, carefully spaced red tulips along the block foundation. The side of the house was more commercial-looking. The adjacent lot had been paved over for parking, and a striped aluminum awning sheltered double doors in the center of a long one-story addition. The entrance was flanked by square patches of lawn, which was not as green as the Astroturf covering the three steps. Under the doorbell, a notice engraved in wood-grained plastic said, "Please ring and walk in."

I rang and walked in. Inside, the carpet was Dusty Rose. I peered into the windowless chapel. Other than an organ and pair of standard lamps with frosted pink glass shades (they looked authentically Art Deco), the chapel was bare. Maybe all the folding chairs were out on loan. Mrs. Enders bounced out of the office with a boom box. She looked like an aerobics instructor, thirty-something, pretty and peppy in pink spandex under a cardigan and jeans. She was, in fact, on her way to teach a class in a church basement. I wondered if working with dead bodies made one more careful of one's own.

I found Mr. Enders in the office with the Leedses' lawyer. Enders wore dark slacks and a short-sleeved white shirt whose breast pocket sagged with gold ballpoints. Through the poly-cotton shirt, you could see his V-necked undershirt. He looked as if he might sell cars as well as coffins. "Tom Enders," he said.

"Lee Squires," I reciprocated. I looked at the lawyer. He was about sixty and tanned. "Mr. Putnam, I presume?"

"Jon," he corrected with a smile. I had expected him to be snootier, more patrician-looking. Jon Putnam had the right hair (Episcopalian silver), the right clothes (a Republican red power tie and a Brooks Brothers pinstriped suit), the right shoes (black wing tips with thin soles). But his face was as open as a Missouri cornfield, his manner upbeat. Behind his gold-rimmed glasses, his blue eyes were both as friendly and as sharp as Johnny Carson's.

We shook hands all around, then Enders withdrew. Putnam and I settled into chairs around a glass-and-brass coffee table that held several leatherette albums. Anyplace else I would have flipped through them.

"Mrs. Enders said you're with the J-E?" Jon Putnam prompted.

"Temporarily. I've been cooking for them over Easter week. Monica and I shared a room." I paused, then added, "I'm sorry."

He nodded in acknowledgment.

"Did you know her well?" I asked.

He thought about it, then smiled ruefully. "I was going to say yes. Over the years, Jack Leeds talked about her often. I feel as if she was one of my own daughters. But we seldom met except on matters of family business." He paused, then quietly pulled out his big credential. "I'm the executor of her estate."

"The game wardens destroyed the grizzly believed to have killed her," I said. "A female. Did the sheriff tell you?"

"Yes." The note of regret in his voice encouraged me. Maybe he contributed to the Sierra Club. I pulled out Monica's notebook from the day pack I was using as a purse and gave it to him. He took it, and without opening it, laid it in front of him on the glass table. A man of restraint. I launched into an explanation of where I'd found it and how it seemed strange that she'd left it behind. I also told him about the "hot tip" phone call I'd overheard from the Big Room's balcony.

"Exactly what are you suggesting?" the lawyer asked. Behind the friendliness, his eyes were noncommittal.

"Exactly? I don't know. I was the one who found her. When I saw her lying there, I thought she'd been murdered. By a human being. Sheriff Becker is satisfied that she was killed by a grizzly, but—" I stopped.

"You're not," Jon Putnam supplied. "Sheriff Becker told me."

I took a breath. "Maybe I'm just in an obsessive mode. But I'd like to check out her laptop, see if her *Vanity Fair* piece is on disk. If she'd already written it up, it's easier to see why she'd leave without the notes. I'd also like to look for a second notebook. When she took that call from her anonymous source, she was making notes. I could hear her flipping pages."

"Anything else?"

I hesitated. "No."

"Well, let's have a look. I've got her things out in my car." We stood up. Easier than expected, I thought. Then Putnam stated firmly, "If you don't find what you're looking for, I want your assurance that you'll drop it. The family's got enough grief as it is."

"And if we do find something?"

"Should further investigation be indicated, I'll handle it." His tone was pompous, but he seemed sincere.

"Fine," I said.

He looked surprised.

"This isn't my idea of fun," I pointed out.

He let out a little paternal cluck of protest. "Of course not." He relaxed. I was being reasonable.

His rented Buick was the only other car in the lot. Putnam opened the trunk for me. I unzipped the computer case. There were no disks in the case's pocket compartments. I unzipped her bag and started working through the tangle of her clothes, smoothing and folding them, laying them in piles on the trunk's gray carpet. Putnam's thin-soled shoes shuffled impatiently on the blacktop, but he said nothing. I found no disks, no notebooks, no tape recorder, no cassettes. Kaz's film was not among her things, and more surprisingly, neither was my missing bra. I repacked the bag. My neatness seemed to satisfy Putnam. Maybe he was thinking of Monica's mother opening the bag.

I peered at the computer in its case. "You know how to work this?" I asked him.

He stuck his head into the trunk for a closer look. He flipped up the screen and pressed a switch. The screen lit up.

"Can you see if there's anything on Fonda/Turner and the Flying D in there?"

Humoring me, laptop illiterate and possible crazy, he clicked several keys and read the screen. "Huh." He tapped more keys. He shook his head. "There are no files listed on the hard disk."

"You mean there's *nothing* in there?"

"Right." He flicked the computer off and zipped up the case.

"That's odd. She kept pounding away on it."

Putnam gave me a stern look. "Need I remind you—"

"Hey." I held up my empty hands in surrender. He shut the trunk with a hollow thud. "May I have your card?" I asked him.

"What for?" he countered.

"In case I need to drop something into your extremely capable and expensive hands."

His affable face wasn't lit by any smile. He pulled out a thin wallet from his suit coat and handed me his card. A narrow white rectangle with the impression of the copperplate on the back and thin block letters on the front: Jonathan A. Putnam, Esquire.

"Thanks," I said. "Don't forget to call Hertz about her rental," I reminded him.

By the time I got back to the J-E, I was obsessing full steam ahead over my missing bra. Where the hell was it? I tore my room apart looking for it. I'd expected to find it in with Monica's things. I felt sure that she had not packed them herself, that someone else had hurriedly stuffed everything in sight into her bag. If that someone was her killer, I could understand the missing notebooks and disks. They might contain damaging evidence. But a wornout bra? Had the hypothetical killer, thinking it was Monica's, kept it as a souvenir? I felt uneasy.

Keep moving, Squires. I remade my bed. In the middle of a hospital corner, I remembered the faint stink of cigarette smoke I'd smelled that morning in my room. I froze. Hil had been in my room that morning while I'd been down at the swamp looking at the dead bear. Were there other times? He'd fixed the plumbing earlier in the week. But what of the day Monica had disappeared? I'd come back from Choteau with the Japanese late that afternoon to find all her stuff gone. How had the room smelled then? I strained to remember, and suddenly caught a very real whiff of something more cloying than cigarettes. I wheeled around.

Hil was standing in the doorway, silent as a bad dream.

"What do you want?" I said sharply.

"You know what I want," he said.

"Fuck off," I said.

Poor word choice. He grinned. I might as well have said "Come and get it, big boy." He took a step into the room, stopped by the oversized armchair. Still grinning, he ran his hand along the stuffed curve of its back. "I know *you'd* like it."

I glanced around the room for escape. The window between the beds was open, but it was going to take some doing to dive through it. The sill was chest-high and the screen was taut in its frame. The only easy way out was right past Hil. I wondered where Trudi was. Probably not down the hall in her office—I doubted he would have intruded if she'd been there. Was she upstairs? If Hil came at me, would she hear the fight?

Fear, I told myself, is a negative image of the future. I lifted my chin and plowed right past him into the hallway. The alcohol fumes almost knocked me down. Every pore in his body must have been breathing gin. "Ain't you gonna finish making the bed?" he drawled after me.

I kept on going. I wheeled into the kitchen and grabbed the first pot off the rack.

Hil followed, in no hurry, amazingly steady. He settled into his corner against the counter, took a tobacco pouch out of his back pocket, and stuck a plug in his jaw. I filled the pot with hot water, put it on the stove, and turned the flame on high. Hil may have been drunk, but drunk didn't mean weak, and tossing a pot of boiling water was going to be a surer defense than fending him off with my big chopper. Pinpricks of air began multiplying in the water. I relaxed slightly. Hil tucked his pouch back into his pocket.

"Can't get enough of the stuff, huh?" I said.

"What?"

"You chew and you smoke."

"Double your pleasure," he said.

Several bubbles broke on the surface of the water. "There's some things missing, Hil," I said levelly. "Some of Monica's stuff. Like her notebooks. And some of my underwear."

A sly look came over his face. "I didn't take no notebooks." Coy emphasis on "notebooks."

I stared at him and saw again his hand moving across the stuffed curve of the chair in my room. I'd left my bra draped over its back. He'd taken it. And he knew I knew. He cocked an eyebrow and said appreciatively, "Thirty-six C."

I reached for the pot handle. "Hil, get out of here," I ordered angrily. He didn't move. "I mean it. Leave. Now!"

He lowered his eyelids to half-mast, as if the light were suddenly too bright, and walked to the back door. He opened the screen door, then turned back. "I seen you with your boyfriend." He made it sound dirty. I felt sick to my stomach. Contaminated. He waited.

Finally I said, "He's a cop, Hil. A homicide cop." Emphasis on "homicide."

He left. I made a cup of camomile tea with the hot water. It didn't help.

Back home, on a Saturday night after a week full of visitors, it would have been kick-back-and-send-out-for-pizza time. But since the nearest pizzeria was some fifty miles away, Trudi defrosted a block of spaghetti sauce in the microwave. The sauce, which had at least four pounds of hamburger in it as well as catsup and Worcestershire, was like nothing any self-respecting *mamma mia* ever put on pasta, but it tasted superb, especially since I hadn't lifted a finger to cook it.

There were just the four of us at the table, Trudi and Dave, Lynn and I. "I asked Mac to join us," Trudi said to Dave, "but he says he's fasting."

Dave gave her a neutral grunt.

"Fasting?" I wondered. "Why?"

Trudi sprinkled Parmesan out of a green foil cardboard cylinder onto her spaghetti. "I think he's having one of his Indian rituals over there. At least, that's what I gathered."

"Really?" I said, interested. "When?"

"He didn't say. Whenever his buddies show up with their tomtoms, I guess. Hard to pin them down. They run on Indian time."

"Pass the Parmesan," Lynn said.

"Please," corrected her mother.

"Okay, don't pass the Parmesan," Lynn said sarcastically.

Both parents looked up. I looked down at my plate. I heard Dave put his fork down. The silence was as thick as Trudi's sauce. I noticed that she'd put canned mushrooms in it.

"Please," Lynn capitulated.

We resumed eating. I pictured Mac in paint and breechclout. No doubt he'd look better than most. "The ritual," I persisted. "What's it for? Do you think I could watch?"

My interest amused them. Dave, his mouth half full of spaghetti, said, "Not much to see. Not like at a powwow."

"What's a powwow?"

Lynn offered, "Kind of like a Stampede or Rodeo Days, only Indians instead of cowboys."

I looked blank. "A festival," Trudi explained. "They sell fry bread and silver jewelry and Indians come from all over to compete in dance contests. The costumes are really something if you're into that kinda thing, but most of the dancing gets old pretty quick, everyone shuffling around in a long line."

"And Mac dances with them?" I asked.

"I don't really know what he does," Trudi said. "The only time we went to one of his things was right after he opened the institute. He had his shaman friend come out here, and the guy put on this moth-eaten bearskin, head and all, and stomped around going 'Huh, huh.' Like Dave says, not much to see, but then I'm not into it like Mac. I do my praying in church." She turned to me. "You want to come with us tomorrow?"

I shook my head. "Thanks anyway."

"Ask Mac, if you're interested," Dave suggested. "He'll talk your ear off about stuff like that." He spun the lazy Susan and spooned a quarter cup of blue cheese dressing onto the three small hunks of iceberg he'd picked out from the romaine. "Four, five years ago, Mac talked me into doing a sweat," he recounted. "The lodge was up on the reservation. We squeezed into a space smaller than this table with the medicine man and half a dozen naked hippies. Blacker than pitch, literally can't see your own hand in front of your face, then they bring in these hot rocks and throw water on them. I'm telling you, I could hardly breathe, it got so hot. My skin got burned by the steam, and my legs went completely numb from sitting cross-legged. I was pretty sure I was going to die."

"But he didn't crawl out," Trudi noted ironically.

"I figured if Mac could take it, so could I."

"Macho man," Trudi teased.

Lynn surfaced from her sulk. "You were naked?"

"He wore a bathing suit," Trudi reprimanded. She frowned. "Didn't you?"

Dave grinned at her.

"Oh for heaven's sake!" she exclaimed.

For the rest of the meal, we rehashed the Japanese visit. Along with the spaghetti, we shared a sense of relief, of celebration even. A week-long task had been accomplished. We'd all done our best. Dave seemed confident that the groundwork for negotiations had been firmly laid. "In a way, we lucked out," he said. "They won't forget about us soon. That dead grizzly sow capped off their visit. They talked about it all the way to the airport."

Lynn excused herself from the table. "You want help with the dishes?" she asked. A peace offering.

"Nope. I want a hug," Trudi said. She reached up and embraced her daughter. Lynn hugged her back awkwardly. "You were a great help, sweetheart," Trudi praised. "We couldn't have done it without you." She said to Dave, "Wasn't she great?"

"She did fine," Dave approved.

Lynn looked pleased. She bounced out of the kitchen. The three of us washed up. There was no sign of Hil. "Must be drinking up his tip," Trudi commented. She was sponging off the stainless-steel counter.

"You can say that again," I said acidly. "How safe is he?"

Her hand stopped. "What do you mean?"

At the sink, Dave turned off the water. I told them about my afternoon encounter with Hil and my missing bra. Their faces were grave.

Trudi said, "I don't think he took anything the other time."

"The *other* time?"

She ignored the question. "We'll get it back for you."

"You think I want it back?" I shivered. "What's going on here?" I demanded.

"He's a peeper," Dave said with disgust.

"And you keep him on?"

"It was just once," Trudi put in defensively.

"How do you know?" I accused. I looked at them in disbelief. "You've got a guest ranch and you keep a peeper on staff?"

Trudi looked at Dave.

"Where else was he going to go?" he burst out angrily. He slapped down his dishtowel and strode out of the kitchen.

"Talk about bleeding hearts," she muttered bitterly. She took a swipe across the countertop with her sponge, then looked up. "You okay? I mean, he didn't—"

"No."

We finished up in silence. Forget the dinner-table camaraderie. The evening was dead. Trudi, however, couldn't help giving it another stab. She shut the refrigerator a last time. Still holding on to the handle, she demanded, "Did you keep your curtains drawn?"

Chapter Nineteen

I spent the night cocooned in my extra blanket and quilt on the old sofa up on the balcony above the Big Room. The finger I'd cut that morning throbbed. Trudi's blue cheese dressing kept sending up sour reminders. I left the cork in my flask and chewed Tums instead. I kept envisioning Hil climbing like a commando up the outside log wall, pressing his beaked face against the gable window, and, with the help of a swift shove from me, falling and breaking his neck. When I wasn't replaying and fine-tuning this scenario, I was devising educational comebacks to Trudi's curtain accusation. I must have dozed some too, because I woke up a couple of times. About six, I woke up again and, still swaddled in my blanket, hopped over to a rocker by the window.

The view through the top branches of the pines was to the east. Under the predawn sky, the rolling grasslands below the lodge were indigo and had a liquid quality. Gradually, above a dune-like bench that blocked the prairie horizon, an opalescent glow stretched into a peach smear. The bench solidified. The cloud cover lightened to oyster gray. I watched shadows turn from navy blue to olive brown. A line of cottonwoods emerged along the base of the bench. Then their upper branches turned white, like trees in a negative, and I could pick out the galvanized metal roofs of Dave's cattle sheds and the road. But there was no sign of the sun.

It was Sunday morning. I was not scheduled to fly home until Tuesday evening. I had no Tuesday classes, and a colleague had agreed to sub for me on Monday. But the business with Hil, and Trudi and Dave's reaction to it, had killed whatever nostalgic affection for the J-E had survived my week in its kitchen. There was nothing to keep me. The job was over. As for the misgivings I had about Monica's death, they seemed remote, no longer relevant.

On the other hand, changing my super-saver ticket would require a cash penalty, and arriving home early would require explanations. I really didn't want to present Hil the Peeper to my mother or tell my obliging colleague that my tryst with Luke had gone down the tubes and she'd subbed in vain. I decided to head east toward Fort Benton and the Missouri River and spend a couple of days learning about Lewis and Clark, at least enough to know which was which. It didn't sound wonderful, but it beat staying put.

I packed up while Trudi and Dave and Lynn were at church and said a restrained goodbye when they returned, just before noon. By that time it had started to rain. "I hope everything works out for you," I told them.

"Say hi to your brother," Trudi said with forced cheerfulness.

Hil made no appearance, and none of us remarked on it. I

took Trudi's check, gave Lynn a quick second hug, and drove off wondering if I was overreacting. *Nope,* said a hard little voice inside me. I turned on the windshield wipers. At the Sacred Paw sign, I turned up the road to Mac's. At least I could leave him on better terms.

He wasn't at the institute, but I found Clare in her office. The room was remarkable in that, unlike the rest of the J-E, it displayed nothing Old Westish, no Navajo rugs, no Blackfeet artifacts, no bucking bronc bookends, no antler hat racks. The only decoration was a framed collection of bird prints and photographs—a meadowlark beside a purple thistle, bluebirds on a weathered fence post, iridescent green hummingbirds in red bee balm. The display of bright flowers and brilliant plumage gave the heavy log interior a feminine feeling—never mind the fact that the birds portrayed were mostly masculine. Clare sat behind a Scandinavian blond oak desk poring over a sheaf of faxes. Mac, she said, was somewhere around. Had I tried the trailer? Her eyes kept going back to her faxes.

"Is that the autopsy report?" I asked. "Becker said he was sending it over."

"Came yesterday. I was just going over it again."

"Does it say Monica was menstruating?"

"Yes." She looked up.

"Could that have been a trigger?"

Clare gave an impatient little shrug. "As I told you before, it's possible. I don't give it a lot of weight."

"I was just wondering. No one's mentioned it."

"Well, there was some noise when the National Park Service released that information after an attack up in Glacier. Zwart didn't want a bunch of feminists on his back." She raised an ironic eyebrow.

I smiled. "Bubble, bubble."

"Toil and trouble," she finished. She picked up a piece of graph paper. "Speaking of weirdness, have a look at this."

There were no lines on the graph, only a random pattern of penciled points. "Connect the dots and get a picture of what?" I asked.

She shook her head. "That's the question. I've been measuring these damn dots for the last hour. Look." She took the graph paper back, laid it on the desk, and picked up a metric-scale ruler. "None of these points are equidistant. There should be repeating pairs. But the sets I come up with are all off by a centimeter or so."

I felt a twinge of math anxiety. "Pairs of what?" I asked dubiously.

"Canines."

"Pairs of dogs?"

She gave me an incredulous look. "Teeth," she said impatiently. "The sow's teeth."

"Clare, I have no idea what you're talking about."

Her face remained expressionless for a moment. Then she backed up and tapped the graph paper. "These are the puncture wounds on Monica's back and neck. I took them off the autopsy's body chart. And they don't match up. The distance between the sow's canines was six point four centimeters—approximately two and a half inches. But no matter how you pair up the holes in the body, none are two and a half inches apart." To demonstrate, she moved the ruler around on the page. "I get five point six centimeters, seven point one centimeters, even seven point three centimeters."

"Are grizzly bites that precise? I mean, flesh gives, tears."

"That's the other thing," she said, exasperated. "There should be more tearing. In the photographs, the wounds look . . ." She hunted for the word. "Too discrete," she decided.

"What do you mean?"

"Well, the ME says she bled to death sitting up in the car and that the puncture wounds were made later, after death. So the bear killed her with a head blow, then came back later. It would have returned to feed on her. Its teeth would have pulled away her flesh, not punctured it. There shouldn't be distinct holes."

"Now that you mention it," I said slowly, "none of her clothing was ripped, either."

Clare shook her head. "Something's screwy here. Rick Zwart maintains the bear came back to feed, was spooked, and went into an attack frenzy, biting and releasing. I suppose that could account for the lack of tearing." She sounded dubious. "But it doesn't explain the chaotic distances between the canines. There should be a pattern. Even if I blew the measurement."

"What does Mac say?"

"He asked me if the sow had a loose tooth."

"And?"

"She didn't," she said firmly. The phone on her desk rang. "Excuse me," she said. She picked it up. "Sacred Paw Institute," she intoned. Then a smile lit her face. "Hey," she said happily. "We've been trying to get hold of you, too." I waved her a goodbye and left.

I found Mac in his trailer behind the institute. The trailer, a long, rectangular block, stood like a giant milk carton in a cluster of dwarf pines. The satellite dish beside it might have come off a broken toy. The two machine-made geometries lay sharp as insults against the undulating landscape.

There was no porch over the trailer's cinder-block steps, and I got wet standing in the rain, banging on the door at decent intervals, waiting for Mac to open up. When he did, he looked surprised. "It's you," he observed.

"You were expecting someone else?"

"No." He let me in. "Only bill collectors knock around here."

"I've already got my fistful of dollars. I just came to say goodbye," I said.

"Ah," he said. Then he smiled at me. He seemed more than mellow. Maybe it was his fast. Maybe it was grass.

I took my wet sneakers off on a clear plastic runner over the Harvest Gold shag. Though there were stacks of papers and magazines on every surface, the piles were neat. One of Clare's bird prints hung above the sofa, but the rest of the paneling was crowded with framed photos. Mac with white men in business suits. Mac with black men in safari shorts and ranger hats. Mac wearing a beard. Mac wearing a bear-claw necklace. Mac with schoolchildren. Mac in airports, in a Land Rover, on a raft.

Mac in person pointed out some of the biggies: Mac with Jane

Goodall holding one of her chimps on her hip; Mac with "Bob" Redford and Norman Maclean. I put my glasses on and peered closer. The snaps were recent. The celebrities' faces looked lined and worn. But the glare of flashbulbs had bleached years off Mac's face. He looked unfairly collegiate.

The framed trophies spilled over into the narrow hallway and erupted again in the trailer's cramped bedroom (queen-size bed, white chenille spread). "Lady Bird," he said proudly, indicating a frame over the bedside lamp.

I squeezed in for a look. Mac in a dinner jacket towering beside Mrs. Johnson. She looked about a hundred years old, but her hair and the teeth in her smile hadn't shrunk at all. "You clean up okay," I bantered. "I'm impressed."

But I was also disconcerted. It was as if I were moving around inside a private altar and the god himself were giving me the tour.

Back in the living area, I asked, "Trudi said you were fasting for some kind of Indian ceremony?"

He raised an eyebrow and declaimed, " 'How but in custom and ceremony are beauty and innocence born?' " There was a mocking edge to his voice that made me uncomfortable.

"Is it a dance?" I tried.

He sat down on the sofa, flopping back against it as if the tour of the trailer had tired him out. "More like a walk," he said. "A bearwalk, you could call it." He grinned.

"So tell me about it. What's it for?"

Mac's handsome face sobered. "I don't think so."

"What?"

"It's not really a good idea to talk about it."

His superiority irritated me. I felt ten years old again, with my brother still excluding me from his secret club. "Why not talk about it?" I demanded. "You know, I never bought that pearls-before-swine bit. If the pearl is real, a pig could gobble it up and it'd come out the other end still a pearl."

He didn't answer.

"Are your Blackfeet friends coming?"

"I don't know," he answered. "A couple might show up." He closed his eyes.

"You don't need them?"

He opened his eyes and looked at me intently. "No."

I considered flopping down beside him on the sofa, to see what happened. Instead I said, "I was just talking to Clare. She says there's something wrong with the tooth marks on Monica's body. She says they don't look as if the bear had come back to eat her."

Mac's handsome face sobered. "Right. Grizzlies protect their food by burying it. You would have found the body covered with dirt and brush."

"So what happened?"

"They got the wrong bear."

"How do you mean?"

"The sow Zwart killed took the rap for an older bear. One with a loose tooth." He sounded resigned—more discouraged than angry.

I changed the subject. "So when are you going to do it, your bearwalk?"

He thought about it. "Well, I'm not sure. Maybe tomorrow. Maybe the next day."

He was flying again. I lost patience, wished him good luck, and left. He didn't get up off the sofa. His Eminence. I trotted back to my car thinking of Clare in that bedroom full of pictures. I gave her a mental salute. All yours, darlin'.

I drove north on gravel toward Ear Mountain. The top of it was shrouded in a bruise-colored mist. I could find nothing but static on the radio, so I turned it off and drove to the metronomic thump of wipers. We were still experiencing some rain activity, as the weatherpeople say. The moist air felt good on my skin, but the wet shoulders of my shirt made me shiver. I turned on the heat. At the turnoff to the Pine Butte Preserve, I took the road toward Choteau, pulling over to read No Trespassing signs at Egg Mountain, where archaeologists were excavating dinosaur eggs. I stopped again at a chain-link-and-barbed wire enclosure where the Pentagon had planted one of its two hundred Minutemen. A bizarre combo buried under the Montana prairie: dead eggs and live missiles. Now that the Cold War was over, where were the Minutemen aimed?

The road dipped and rose like a sea stopped in midswell. Across the horizon ahead, scattered squalls of rain hung from the line of clouds like pieces of torn lining. Flying downhill in a spray of gravel, I spotted a tiny figure on the crest of the next rise. A man on my side of the road. His back was to me. He was walking toward Choteau. I slowed as I came closer. He was hatless, gray-haired, and wearing a rust-and-black-checked wool shirt. There was something familiar about him. I passed him, leaving him a polite amount of space, then glanced in the rearview mirror and recognized him. He was one of the Blackfeet men who had prayed over the dead grizzly. The older one who had reminded me of Mr. Yamaguchi. A shaman, Walt had said. I stepped on the brakes.

My wipers squeaked on the glass as I waited for him. I turned them off. This stretch of road was dry. I watched him approach in the mirror. He walked unhurriedly, with an easy stride that looked used to distance. He was younger than I thought, closer to sixty than eighty, and better-looking than I remembered, a strong, lined face with a serene, high forehead. I leaned across the passenger seat and opened the door for him.

"Hello," he said, sticking his head in. "Thanks for stopping."

"I saw you out at the J-E," I told him. "You know Mac Fife."

"Right. I was out there yesterday morning." He shook his head. "Shame about that bear."

"You want a ride? I'm headed toward Fort Benton," I offered.

"If you could let me off at Choteau, I'd sure appreciate it. I've got to pick up a part for my truck."

"Hop in," I told him.

He slipped in and shut the door. The automatic seat belt buzzed and slid across his chest. I pulled back out into the road and drove on.

"I'm afraid your seat might be a bit damp," I apologized. I wondered if he could tell Monica had died in it. Did medicine men have hindsight?

"I'm not going to complain after getting picked up by a

pretty lady," he said cheerfully. "I was getting worried about pushing my luck too far. The rain's been missing me since this morning." He chuckled. "Like the farmer and his dog. You know that one?"

"No," I said.

"I didn't think so. You're not from around here, are you?"

"Washington, D.C.," I said.

"Well," he said, settling back into his seat, "this farmer drives into town with his dog in the back of his pickup. Nice day, sun shining. He picks up a couple hundred pounds of fertilizer down at the co-op, and while he's shooting the breeze, he sees the sky start to darken up. Plop, the first drops of rain start to fall. So he hops into his truck, steps on the gas, races home just ahead of the storm all the way, and makes it. He gets out of his truck feeling pretty good that all those bags of fertilizer in back didn't get soaked, walks around to unload, and there's the mutt, floating like a drowned rat in the bed of his truck!" He laughed.

The story wasn't my brand of thigh-slapper, but his good humor was infectious. "Guess the fertilizer was wrecked as well," I said, smiling.

"You bet. And that's plains weather for you," he said, his black eyes mischievous. Then he said, "My name is Leonard, Leonard Thunder Moon."

"Lee Squires," I said.

"You a friend of Mac's?"

"Of the family," I said. I explained the connection. He listened carefully, with interest, without questions. I talked about the Japanese visit. I talked about my teenaged summers at the J-E. He fished out a blue bandanna from his pocket and brought it up to his mouth. Then he made an odd wet clicking sound, folded the bandanna around something, and slipped it into the large breast pocket of his wool shirt. I glanced over at him. The bottom half of his face had crumpled into a wrinkled wad. Suddenly he was ancient.

He winked at me and patted his pocket. "My choppers," he said. "I put them in when I'm looking for a ride, but I have to say, after a while, they hurt more than my feet."

"Pretty good disguise," I said.

He brightened. "I hadn't thought of it that way."

"They say age makes you invisible."

"Being Indian helps, too."

"I used to think it would be wonderful to have a cloak of invisibility," I mused. "Like the hero in 'The Twelve Dancing Princesses.' "

"I don't think I know that one," he said.

"Once upon a time," I started, "there was a poor soldier returning from the wars." I hesitated.

"Go on," he encouraged. He was an appreciative audience. It felt good to be driving down an open road telling a favorite fairy story. Rachel might have been sitting in his lap. The land flattened out. I finished, and he nodded thoughtfully at "happily ever after." We drove in companionable silence, disentangling ourselves from the tale. Then I said, "Walt Surrey told me you were a medicine man."

"Yes," he said.

"Were you the one who did a bear dance at the J-E?"

"That's right."

"What *is* a bear dance?"

For a minute I thought that, like Mac, he wasn't going to tell me. But he was hunting for the words. "I suppose you could say it's a way of honoring the bear. The grizzly is a sacred animal to the Blackfeet. In the old days, it was taboo to kill one—people would rather starve than eat its flesh. Only warriors were permitted to wear its claws. And only the medicine men were allowed to use its hide."

"How do you use it?"

He took the question literally. "I put it on." Obligingly, he described the straps, the fastenings. But it wasn't what I wanted to know. "Once you've got it on, what happens then?" I persisted.

"The bear takes over." By way of explanation, he added, "I have a bear inside me."

"I'm not sure I understand."

He chuckled. "That makes two of us."

I tried again. "What does the bear do?"

"Well, the dance we did out at your ranch was part of a healing ceremony. The bear is a very powerful healer."

"Who was sick? If it's okay to ask."

Leonard Thunder Moon smiled as if I'd said something funny. "Mac wanted it."

"What was wrong with him?"

"Gallbladder trouble, if I remember right."

"And did it work?"

He cocked his head, as if considering it for the first time. "You know, I never asked. I guess you'll have to ask him."

Ahead of us, the trees and grain elevators of Choteau rose out of the prairie. "Is Mac a shaman?" I asked.

"Huh," he said in surprise. "I never heard that."

"He was talking about doing a 'bearwalk.' "

Leonard Thunder Moon frowned. "I wouldn't know anything about that," he said gravely. He was pensive for the next couple of miles.

"Mac was pretty upset about the bear they killed at the swamp," I said.

"Oh, yeah," he agreed. "He was angry, okay." He added ruefully, "Might be a good idea to stay out of his way for a while." It was hard to tell whether he was talking to himself or me.

He got out at a gas station at the edge of town. I bought a Hershey bar and drove on, feasting on stale chocolate, sorry that Leonard Thunder Moon wasn't going farther.

Chapter Twenty

I took 89 south toward Great Falls. Now that I was alone in the car, the only distraction from the undulating miles of winter wheat and hay fields was occasional mailboxes at the end of farm roads—and I often clocked ten miles between mailboxes. The road was empty in both lanes. I flew along under the wide dome of spring sky, trying to focus on what lay ahead, but a couple of puzzles kept pulling me back to the J-E. One was the wounds on Monica's neck and shoulders. Out on the open road with nothing particular ahead of me, a new "maybe" light flashed on in my head: the "chaotic" puncture pattern that Clare had plotted on her graph paper might indicate not a loose-toothed bear, but a murderous human being.

Suppose Monica had been brained by a threatened human being, not a threatened bear. Suppose a human killer had knocked her unconscious, left her to bleed to death in my car, then returned some hours later to fake "attack" wounds. How would it be done? What kind of tool or instrument was the size of a bear's tooth? And was there a chance of finding it?

I thought of the equipment barn behind the lodge, with its big wooden sleigh and its haphazard collection of old tools. There were tools all over the ranch—a pretty big haystack for a needle that might or might not exist. I imagined a dark figure at the edge of the swamp, kneeling over Monica, pounding her over and over with some sort of spiked implement, then standing and hurling the thing into the water.

I put Hil's face on the figure and wiped it off. A peeper doesn't necessarily a killer make. And as satisfying as it was to imagine Luke Donner carting Hil off to the pen, Hil wasn't the only one with enough bear lore to fake an attack. There was Richard Zwart, for starters, and Walt Surrey, and Mac and his Sacred Paw workers, and no doubt dozens of others.

A human killer would explain not only "chaotic" puncture wounds but other mysteries—Monica's missing notebook, her blank computer files, and Kaz's missing film. But how did bears fit into the picture? Clearly, at some time or other, a grizzly had been on the scene. Both Monica's head and the fender of my car had been raked by its claws.

The other puzzle that kept nagging at me as I drove across the prairie was the twisted root I'd found in Monica's sheets. I wondered if it was still in the wastebasket where I'd dropped it. Was it connected to her death? Why had she hidden it in her bed? I saw myself sneaking back to the J-E for it, plucking it out of the wastebasket—and then what? Send it off to the FBI for analysis? Take it to a psychic?

I felt a peculiar urge to bury it. Not in any actual landscape but in the arid, twilight dreamscape of my "rotting backward" vision. I wanted to dump the root in a grave, a grave that held the peeled, desiccated carcass of my chimeric, larger-than-life grizzly. I wanted to fill in the hole with loose yellow earth and let it be, in the hope that, given time, the rectangle of earth would sink like a chest exhaling in relief. I wanted to believe that eventually the soil would turn black and potent, would nourish grass.

A root planted in the wrong kind of bed, tooth marks that didn't pair up. At a dot on the map called Vaughan, I got on Interstate 15 for three exits, then, zipping along under the green signs outside Great Falls, I rear-ended an idea. It occurred to me that the key to Monica's death was in Choteau. I got off at the airport, looped around, and headed back the way I'd come.

In Choteau, I checked into the Star Brite Motel at the edge of town. For twenty-five bucks on my Visa, I got a sagging double bed with a thin brown cotton spread, a Norman Bates memorial shower with a paper mat that said "For Your Convenience," and a bar of Ivory one inch by two. The sheets, however, were stiffly clean, and a small black-olive pizza from a storefront parlor on the main drag helped dispel the smell of stale smoke and mildew in the neatly vacuumed shag.

The next morning I drove over to the courthouse and parked under the tall old pines at the edge of the lawn. Large patches of clipped grass had turned brown under the drooping black boughs. I remembered Monica striding toward our van, her trench coat flapping like a triumphant flag. "I think I've found my Pulitzer," she'd said. She had almost danced off the sidewalk with excitement.

Inside the gray stone building, I found the clerk of court's office and talked to a statuesque woman behind a wooden counter. She was wearing red lipstick and lavender-rimmed glasses. Pallas Athena in disguise. Her champagne-colored hair shone like a polished helmet. Under the thin jersey of her classically draped blouse, her breasts pointed aggressively, as if armored in perfect steel cones. I was reminded of an obscure line from the *Chanson de Roland:* A man loves with his heart, a woman loves with the point of her breast. I'd never been able to figure out whether this enigmatic declaration was an ageless truth or an example of medieval sexism.

"Can I help you?" asked owl-eyed Athena.

"I hope so," I said humbly. "A young woman was in here last week. Skinny. Frizzy orange hair. Big silver earrings?"

"Oh yes, I remember her."

I felt a wash of relief. I'd counted on Monica's creating an impression; and on Choteau as being a place where strangers would be noticed. "Well"—I lowered my voice into a sad tone—"we were staying out at the J-E together."

The woman's interest sharpened. She leaned forward slightly. "At the Fifes'?"

"Yes," I said. Behind her, the noise of typing stopped. "She was the reporter who was killed by the bear."

Her eyes widened behind her glasses. *"She* was the one?"

"Yes," I said.

"Oh my goodness, I had no idea." She turned to the secretary at the desk behind her. "That girl with the orange Afro in here last week? She was the one killed by the Fifes' bear."

The secretary offered, "Paper said it weighed almost four hundred pounds."

"My cousin went out there to see it," Athena said to us both. "She said you've never seen such a big bear." She clucked indignantly. "You've got to wonder why Mac Fife wants to save them critters."

"Hmm," I said. A moment of respectful silence. Then I pulled myself up and announced, "I was wondering if she dropped one of her earrings in here. It hasn't turned up anywhere else. They were kind of like her trademark, and the funeral home in New York called. . . ." I let my voice trail off.

Athena frowned. "I don't think anyone's turned in an earring." She consulted with the typist, went off to check in other offices. When she came back, she said, "You'll want to check in Records. That's where she went." She folded back a section of counter and stepped through it.

Records was directly across the aisle, a gated area with beige vinyl floor tiles, a copier, and two scarred oak reading tables. Shelves between the high windows held boxes of documents and folio-size volumes bound in dark leather. The leather on the spines of the older volumes had cracked and peeled, leaving a soft brown suede. Bands of transparent tape held the covers together. The only reader in the room was a man with thinning yellow hair pulled back into a ponytail and fuzzy gray sideburns. He sat at a long oak table strewn with papers, yanking at a loose hank of hair.

He looked up as we approached, tucked the strand of hair behind his ear. The length of his rather narrow face was accentuated by a small goatee that might have been grown for an impersonation of Custer at his last stand. All he needed was a fringed jacket. He was wearing, however, a navy-blue windbreaker over a plaid shirt. "Rosalie," he greeted Athena in a world-weary baritone.

Rosalie? Rather a demotion, to my mind. She gave him a flirtatious smile and explained about the fictitious earring. He listened, welcoming the distraction with theatrically arched eyebrows. "Poor, unfortunate girl," he sighed, looking me over. "But no," he said, "I have found no earring." He opened his hands in a Shakespearean gesture. A diamond winked on his left pinkie.

A lawyer? I wondered. I asked him, "Did you see her? It was last Tuesday."

"Madam," he rebuked me, "I've been *dwelling* here for the past two weeks, literally tearing my hair out over these damnable documents. Of course I saw her. We conversed at some length."

Getting warmer.

Rosalie shot me a complicit look of amusement. Clearly she ranked the man as a Certified Colorful Character. "Cal's a landman," she said, as if that explained everything.

Cal's chair squealed on the tiles as he pushed it back and stood. He was a tall man, six two or three in his gray lizard-skin boots. An oversize scenic belt buckle bit into his soft belly. With a neat flourish that presented both his card and his diamond, he announced, "Cal Bentley. At your service."

I introduced myself and took his card. Like his belt buckle, it was oversize: a glossy black rectangle embossed with gold letters.

Under his name, the card read "Lease Broker." Running up the left margin was a gold oil rig.

"You're with an oil company?" I asked.

"I'm an independent agent," he corrected. "I deal my own book." He paused and smiled at me. "I also play the trumpet and own a piece of a ski resort."

"And enjoy Mozart and long walks on the beach?" It just popped out. A bit too sharply.

"Mozart?" He looked confused.

I tried a *Mona Lisa* sort of smile and hoped it was alluring, not asinine. "So what's a landman?"

"Ah!" he exclaimed in relief. "What is a landman? A landman is part geologist, part lawyer, part petroleum engineer, part peddler. Our business is the business of leasing oil and mineral rights. 'No lease, no grease,' as we say."

I looked at Rosalie. She translated, "Cal buys oil and gas rights from property owners, then sells them to the big drilling companies. He's been here working on a title search."

"I've lost the trail," he despaired grandly. "The property vanishes off the face of the Front in 1882."

"Don't worry. You'll find it," Rosalie chirped. "You always do." She turned to me. "Cal knows his way around this room better than any of us."

We chatted a bit more. Rosalie/Athena went back to her desk. Cal Bentley sat back down to his papers. I made a nose-to-the-floor tour of the room. He asked me where I was from. He seemed to welcome distraction. I asked him about his search, and he launched into it, in grandiloquent detail. I perched on a chair and listened. Or at least made noises in the openings. My eye kept going back to the shelves of documents. Talk about haystacks. "Hmm," I went. He was looking at me, curious. I realized he was finished. I decided to jump in with both feet. "What was Monica Leeds after in here?" I asked. "Do you know?"

He sat back in his chair. "You're employed at the J-E?" His question came out as casually as mine.

"Just the past week. I'm on my way home to D.C. I hired on as cook for some businessmen."

"Ah yes, Mac's Japanese scheme."

Mac's? I wondered. What about Dave and Trudi? "You known the Fifes long?" I asked.

He looked through me, all the way to some piece of the past. "Yeah," he said finally. "We go back." His voice was grim, no hint of the Bard.

I waited. He didn't elaborate. "Monica and I shared a room," I told him. "She said she'd found a Pulitzer here."

"So you're looking for that, too?"

"Excuse me?

"One silver earring, one Pulitzer prize."

I looked him in the eye. "I'm not a feature writer."

He tugged thoughtfully at his goatee. Then he shrugged, as if washing his hands of the matter. "It's public record." He pushed his chair back, stretching his back like a lioness, then abruptly stood up. He crossed the room, took down a deed book from one of the shelves, and placed it in front of me on the table. "Here you go." He flipped the heavy pages until he found the place.

I read. I reread. I looked up. My expression seemed to satisfy him. Cal Bentley, landman, smiled a bitter little smile. "Obviously, Mr. Ecology would prefer to keep this particular document out of the public eye," he observed pompously. "Your reporter friend's death was most fortuitous for him, now that I think of it."

I sat in my car out in front of the courthouse studying Jon Putnam's card. In the last hour, I'd learned some interesting facts. For instance, oil does not occur in underground lakes; it occurs in rock, which holds it like a sponge. By dynamiting the earth and "listening" with "geophones" to the shock waves passing through the pores of the rock, oilmen can predict how much oil or gas lies beneath the surface. I asked all the questions I could think of, and Cal Bentley kept on answering. But I didn't know what to do with his answers.

I slipped Putnam's card back into my wallet. I looked at my Timex. It was almost eleven. I got out of my Escort and walked to the red log restaurant where I'd taken the men from NVI. I missed them, especially Kaz. Our lunchtime communication difficulties now seemed like a take from Eden. I sat at the same table, ordered coffee and tuna on rye. I kept coming back to Trudi and Dave. Did they know?

After two cups of coffee, I signaled the waitress for my tab. She looked at my uneaten sandwich. "You want a doggie bag, hon?" she asked.

"That's okay," I said. I sounded like my nieces. The phrase "No thank you" was not a part of their vocabulary. I left a dollar under the plate and walked back to my car. Behind the courthouse, I noticed a white Mercedes parked in the lot. The plates said OYL. Guess whose.

On the drive back to the J-E, Leonard Thunder Moon's mild observation floated back to me: *Might be a good idea to stay out of his way for a while.* Amen. I drove under Olwyn Fife's sign gate and took the fork to the farm office, hoping to find Dave rather than Trudi and thus spare myself the awkwardness of having to ask to talk to Dave without her. No one was in the office, a one-room log square at the end of a row of equipment sheds, but the door was unlocked, and the concrete-block chimney running up the side of the building emitted a frail strand of wood smoke. Somewhere behind the sheds, a calf was bawling, raucous as a toddler screaming in the supermarket. I waited on the steps. The calf stopped abruptly, then Roy, the farm manager, appeared from behind the building, carrying a bucket and a cartoon-scale syringe. Judging from his coveralls, he'd just lost a wet-cow-pie war.

"Hi," I said. "Dave around?"

"Just missed him," Roy said. "He went up to the lodge to clean up and get a bite to eat."

"Thanks," I said.

Dave was in the kitchen, wet hair slicked back, skin pink from his shower, building himself a pair of baloney sandwiches. "Well, hello," he said, surprised to see me.

"I need to talk to you," I said.

He set his jaw. "It's over and done with." He picked up a plastic jar of yellow mustard and squirted doodles on the tops of white bread.

Wait a sec, I thought. "What's over and done with?"

Dave slapped his tops onto the pink baloney. "The show you girls put on for Hil. I talked to him. It was like Trudi suspected. You left your curtains wide open."

"You need to evolve, Dave," I snapped. "Look what happened to the dinosaurs. What I've got to say has nothing to do with Hil's sicko jollies. It's about your brother."

He closed his eyes in exasperation. "Lee," he warned, "please spare me the—"

"Listen to me," I interrupted angrily. "It's about the J-E. I'm talking about your *future*. Where's Trudi?"

The question threw him off balance. "In Helena. She and Lynn went to Helena." He plucked a knife off the magnetic rack on the wall behind him and slashed his sandwiches into uneven halves.

I could feel my heart thumping. Now or never, I thought. "Did you know Mac's sold the oil and gas rights to this place? That's all I want to know. Yes or no, and I'll go."

He didn't need to say anything. I could see it on his face. He hadn't a clue. "What are you talking about?" he demanded.

"I'm talking about a ten-year lease to the mineral rights under the land you rent from your brother. Seems like eight years ago, he sold them to an outfit called Front Resources. The price was rock-bottom—the few wells already sunk in the area hadn't exactly made anyone rich, so Front Resources was buying on pure speculation. Mac got five bucks per acre as a signing bonus, plus a dollar per acre for five years, renewable for five more. But multiply the lease money times your twenty thousand acres and it adds up to a decent piece of change—around a quarter of a million dollars so far."

Dave's face was closed tight. "Where'd you hear this?"

"From a landman named Cal Bentley."

He stared at his baloney sandwiches. After a minute he raised his blue eyes. They were sincere and pained. "Cal's wife left him for Mac. Did you know that?"

"No."

"It didn't even last a year. Bentley's got an ax to grind. Not that I'm excusing Mac's behavior in the whole mess," he added sternly. "But sounds to me like old Cal's spouting libel along with his usual quotient of hot air."

"Dave, I saw the contract. Bentley was the agent. Front Resources is his company. His signature was on it, and so was Mac's."

I could almost hear the slow, painful creak of wheels turning inside Dave's head. "When did Bentley's wife leave him?" I asked.

Dave frowned. "Must have been six, seven years ago," he said.

"After he bought the lease from Mac, then."

"If you say so."

"Well, Bentley seemed more set on making his fortune than on getting back at Mac, but either way, he's got your brother over a barrel—an oil barrel, to be precise. He says Exxon and Chevron are fighting to buy up private leases along the Front. The Department of the Interior has already approved FINA's permit to drill on public lands just north of you, so the other companies are scrambling. Apparently, new computerized readings of old seismic data have reawakened interest. And Bentley's had an offer for the J-E's rights that he can't refuse."

He perked up. "Exxon and Chevron want to drill here?"

"Bentley didn't say who made the bid. Only that he'd given Mac the opportunity to buy his rights back. 'For three mil, Mac can keep on playing Mr. Ecology' was the way he put it."

Dave stared at me. I kept on going. "Bentley gave him a month to come up with the money. Mac told him not to worry, that a group of Japanese greenies would advance it to him."

"Sweet Jesus," he swore softly.

I hadn't finished. "I think Mac killed Monica," I rushed on. "She found out about the lease and was planning to break the story. Monica Leeds, the nineties' answer to Woodward and Bernstein. Sacred-Paw-gate. That's not the kind of publicity that's going to attract yen from Japanese investors, never mind pennies from American schoolchildren."

Dave snorted contemptuously. "That's ridiculous. Mac wouldn't have—"

"Let me finish," I interrupted. "She checked a phone tip out in Choteau, at the county courthouse. It was the day you and Trudi were up to your neck in scours and I drove the Japanese into the little museum. We bumped into her as she was leaving, and she was high as a kite. Too excited to eat lunch with us. She got back here and called Mac over at the institute. I think she couldn't resist toying with him. But whatever was said, Mac couldn't afford to let her write her 'profile.' It would have ruined him. All the Sacred Paw's work would have gone straight down the tubes."

I took a big breath and plowed on. "So he drives up here, brains her, dumps her into the passenger seat of my car along with all her stuff, and drives her down to the swamp."

Dave looked incredulous.

"You remember the fuss Kaz made over his film when we went to the bar? Well, your brother didn't know about the second camera. He was busy taping with Monica when Kaz asked permission to set it up. It was Clare who arranged the whole thing. When he drove down to the swamp to dump Monica, he would have triggered Kaz's box. Flash, he's on candid camera. Kaz didn't forget to load his film. Mac took it out. He wouldn't have needed a ladder. He's used to shinning up trees—it's practically a job requirement."

Suddenly I felt exhausted, tired of my own argument. I was ready to go home. "He takes the film," I summed up, "leaves Monica sitting in the car, and hikes back here in time for supper. According to the autopsy, she was in a sitting position for at least six hours before she was moved. Maybe he went back later that night to see if there'd been any bear activity. Maybe he waited till the morning. But at some point, he decided to fake it. He must have used some sort of spike."

Dave was holding on to the kitchen counter. "Get out of here," he choked. Then his throat opened and it came out in a roar. "Get out! Goddammit, get out of here!" He let go of the counter and strode toward me, stopping short as I backed to the door.

I held up my hands. "I'm going, I'm going."

"How dare you!" he stormed. "Who the hell do you think

you are, calling my brother a murderer? That woman was killed by a grizzly."

I shook my head. "I don't think so." I turned and opened the back door.

"Wait," he ordered. "Why are you doing this? What did my brother do to you? Just tell me that. What have you got against Mac?"

"You don't want to hear it, Dave."

"Yes, I do."

We stared at each other, then, in an uneasy truce, moved back to the counter. I told him what Clare had said about the tooth patterns, what Walt Surrey had said about no grizzly fur in the bushes. I also told him about the phone call I'd overheard. "Monica had her own Deep Throat. Someone in the house picked up one of the extensions. She remarked on it. It could have been Mac. He could have known she was on his trail."

"This is unreal," he said. "You actually think Mac killed this girl, put her out for bear meat, and when the bear didn't oblige, went at her himself with hammer and nails?" His voice rose with disbelief.

"I didn't say hammer and nails. I said a spike. I don't know what he used. I do know that your brother's been living a lie. There's proof of that in the court records. As for Monica, he had both motive and opportunity. I thought you ought to know." I heard myself and inwardly cringed: I sounded prim as a playground tattletale.

Dave let out a bark of a laugh. "Oh, thanks very much. Just what I wanted to hear. My brother's a killer. Great."

"Maybe he had Hil do it," I said.

He waved the suggestion away in disgust. "Who else have you told—I mean about the lease?"

"No one."

We stood squared off on either side of a baloney sandwich, I precariously perched on a high horse, Dave low to the ground, immobile as a bull with locked knees. Finally Dave said, his voice calmer, "Was the three million a legitimate offer?"

"I don't know. You think Bentley's conning him?"

"I don't know."

"There must be a way to check," I told him. "Monica got her tip from somebody. I don't think it was a media chum. The caller didn't know what 'off the record' meant. I had the feeling it was a business person. Whoever it was needed coaxing."

"Doesn't sound like Bentley," Dave said tartly.

"She wasn't a dummy, Dave. She could have found the records in that courthouse without Bentley's help."

"And you saw the lease."

"Yes."

He rubbed the back of his neck, then observed wryly, "A couple oil wells wouldn't hurt none."

"Right. Killer makes a killing."

"What the hell's the matter with you?" he burst out. "How many times do I have to tell you? Mac didn't kill that little slut."

"You don't know that."

"Neither do you. Exactly what is your problem? Did Mac turn you down?"

"I don't believe this." I grabbed my head, lacing my fingers into my hair and pulling at the roots.

"Christ almighty, Lee, everyone could see you had hot pants for him."

I felt shame welling up, swamping my brain. I let go of my scalp, and what came ripping out through my mouth wasn't sugar and spice and everything nice. I don't remember—or more accurately, I don't want to remember—exactly what I said. Dave's sexist logic set me off, but I was more deeply wounded by Mac's betrayal. "Losing my temper" is too mild a phrase for what happened—something more than "temper" erupted. It was as if every old wound, every time-nursed scar, had burst wide open. My anger pulsed like a beast, spewed blame the way no animal ever blamed.

I think now of Leonard Thunder Moon and his matter-of-fact statement that he had a bear inside him. It had startled me at the time. But now I think perhaps we all have bears, or packs of wolves, or screaming eagles, inside us. Saints may know how to cage them, but only shamans know how to let them out for the commonweal.

Dave looked as if it were all he could do not to deck me. He strode out of the kitchen, slamming the back door hard enough to rattle the windows over the sink. I did not feel better for "letting it all hang out," to borrow a phrase from the feel-goods. I felt distinctly shaky. I paced guiltily around and around the stainless-steel counter. Then I stooped, tightened up the laces on my sneakers, and went out for a run up the now familiar canyon road. When I got back an hour later, Dave's baloney sandwiches were still untouched on the counter, their edges curling. I sealed the plate in plastic wrap and drove down to Dave's farm office. I was ready to apologize. I wanted to leave with a better ending. I was convinced I was right. I hoped that after cooling down, Dave might see things differently.

But Dave wasn't there. I began to worry. I walked through the Big Room, touching the backs of chairs, then wandered down the hallway, into the room where Monica and I had stayed. It looked the same, curtains open, quilts smooth on the beds. I peered into the wastebasket. The evil-looking root was still there. I retrieved it, put it in the front pocket of my sweatshirt. Then I picked up the extension in Trudi's office and dialed the farm office. No answer. It was four o'clock. I tried the institute. One of the interns told me Clare had gone to Missoula, and no, Mac hadn't been in all day, but Dave had come by looking for him. Had I tried the trailer?

I didn't want to try the trailer. I spent the next hour at Trudi's desk, writing and tearing up apologies. The phone rang. I picked it up.

"Lee?" said a man's voice.

"Yes?"

"It's Dave."

"Dave?" It didn't sound like Dave.

He cleared his throat. "We need to talk. Come over to Mac's place. The trailer." He sounded like a robot.

"Are you all right?" I asked.

"Yeah, I'm fine."

"You sound funny. Look, I'm really sorry. I didn't mean—"

"We need to talk," he repeated, this time sounding like himself. "The three of us." Abruptly he hung up.

At the J-E, there is a small, windowless outbuilding called the Tool Box. It stands under an old cottonwood at one corner of the kitchen courtyard and is convenient to both the equipment sheds and the lodge. When I was out at the ranch as a teenager, the Tool Box was Olwyn's province. It was a dark, mysteriously masculine place smelling of dry wood and tobacco and gun oil. One went there to "borrow" spools of fishing line or find a nail in the neat rows of baby-food jars. Olwyn had leather punches and pliers in there, mouse traps, old brass spray guns that had once held DDT, lumps of beeswax, cards of thumbtacks, and little tin oil cans that clicked when you pressed their bottoms. A bare light bulb hung from the low rafters over a workbench against one wall. Against the opposite wall, Olwyn had built a gun closet for the collection of shotguns and rifles and pistols lent to guests for target practice and skeet shooting. The cupboard's varnished doors were always padlocked, even when Olwyn was pottering around inside, and when he wasn't, the outside door was also kept padlocked. This had not changed. The Tool Box was still securely locked.

I rifled Trudi's desk looking for keys and found none. Then I went out to the equipment barn with the hope of finding a stray hacksaw and instead found Hil loading a wheel of barbed wire onto the back of his truck. The sight of him made me want to run away. Instead, I walked toward him. He shut the tailgate and watched me, one elbow propped up on the side of the truck.

I stopped five feet away, put my voice in neutral, and asked, "Do you have the keys to the Tool House?"

He shifted the chaw in his cheek.

"Because if you do, I'd like to borrow a gun."

There was a flicker of interest in his bloodshot eyes. "You goin' hunting?" His voice was amused, ironic.

"Let's just say I'm nervous about the bears."

He said nothing. I stood my ground. Then he pushed himself

off the truck and walked off in the direction of the Tool House. I followed. He took a ring of keys out of his jeans pocket and unlocked the outside door, stepped inside, and reached up to pull on the light cord. Then he opened the gun cupboard and stepped back. "Take your pick."

I pulled out a felt-lined drawer below the shotguns and rifles. The two single-action .22 handguns might have been the same ones we used to plink at rows of our parents' beer bottles. There was also a .38 Special, and for guests who wanted to play Dirty Harry, a monumentally macho .44 Magnum. I picked up one of the .22s and wondered if I could still hit anything with it. Then I put it back and took the .38. Whatever was left of my aim would be worse with it, but in terms of making an impression, the visuals were better, and even if I missed at close range, it beat relying on tooth and nail.

From a lower drawer, I took a handful of cartridges and loaded the revolver. I could feel Hil's eyes on my back. I put the extra cartridges back and closed up the cupboard. "Thanks," I said to Hil. "I'll bring it back."

He locked the outside door. "You only taking six rounds?" He sounded as if he were humoring a two-year-old.

"If I bump into a bear, I don't think I'm going to have time to reload." I paused. "Judging from what was left of Monica."

His eyes narrowed a millimeter at her name.

I turned to go, then turned back. With my left hand, I fished the root out of my pocket and held it out to him. He didn't take it. "Do you know what this is?"

"What is it?" he said cautiously.

"That's what I'm trying to find out, Hil."

He shrugged. "Looks like some kind of voodoo shit."

"Did you put it in Monica's bed? A token of your esteem, perhaps?"

Under the beak of his nose, his lips tightened into a narrow smile. "You mean like a love potion?"

"If you say so."

His black eyes flashed slyly. "I can put something better than that in your bed."

I kept my mouth shut. I'd already done enough damage with it for one day. I turned and walked back to the car, gun heavy in my right hand, root light as dust in my left.

Chapter Twenty-One

I wish I could say that I had overreacted, that the gun was an unnecessary, even foolish, precaution. I wish I could say that Monica had been mauled by a natural-acting grizzly and that Mac and Dave sat down together that afternoon in the trailer, resolved the J-E's land-use conflicts, and lived happily ever after. But the magic of wishing doesn't work backward.

There were no cars in the lot at the institute. I stopped briefly to pull off my sweatshirt and put on my down vest. It wasn't cold. In fact, the wind blowing in from the west was ominously warm. But the pineapple puffiness of my vest disguised the lopsided sag of the loaded gun in its right-hand pocket. I drove on up the track to the trailer. Dave's Bronco was the only vehicle outside. Clare must have taken the truck to Missoula.

I knocked on the trailer's flimsy door. Mac or Dave—I couldn't tell which—called, "come in." I opened the door, shoved both hands in my pockets, and stepped off the cinder blocks into the doorway. The first thing I saw was a broken table lamp, pieces of the base pottery scattered on the oak coffee table, the linen shade lying on the mustard-colored shag. Dave was sitting back on the tweed sofa, hands laced behind his head, ankle resting casually on an opposite knee. On the paneling behind him, Mac's trophy snaps were hanging askew, as if the trailer had suddenly been launched into a storm at sea and all the photos had slid off center. I half expected to find Mac lying dead on the floor, but he was standing, very much alive, against the dinette counter, pointing a revolver in my direction. It looked like my borrowed .38 Special, but heavier—it was probably a .357 Magnum. I decided not to show him my gun. The Magnum's cartridges could do a whole lot more damage than the Special's. Moreover, it looked dangerously comfortable in his hand.

"What's going on?" I said, as innocently as possible.

"Shut the door, please," Mac instructed.

I took my hand out of my gun pocket and shut the door.

"Take your other hand out of your pocket," he said.

I brought out the twisted root in my left hand and held it out toward him.

"Where'd you get that?" he said sharply.

"In Monica's bed."

A slow smile. "And now you have it." He laughed. "Works like a charm. As it were." He raised a mocking eyebrow.

"A charm. As in mandrake?"

"Lomatium cous, actually. Biscuit-root. The Indians called it *cous."*

"And what's charming about *cous,* pray tell?"

"It attracts bears."

A chill prickled along my spine. I saw Monica's body lying like a rag doll in the greening grass. "Really?" I said.

"Really." He slipped out of his sparring mode into World-Expert-Speaks. *"Lomatium* is what we call a high-preference food item. The grizzly locates it by smell—they go for the taste of it, even though it's mostly empty calories, the ursine equivalent of candy. For the same work, nuts and berries provide a lot more energy." He glanced at the root. "What happened to the rest of it? There was some *Vaccinium* with it."

"What's that?"

"Blueberry," he said impatiently.

I touched the stems under the black thread. "Looks like it broke off. It's probably in the laundry."

He nudged the Magnum's barrel in my direction. "Put it back in your pocket."

I did.

"You know," he marveled, "moving around on this plane is really incredibly poetic."

"Mac. What are you on?"

He mimicked, " 'What are you on?' You're every bit as bourgeois as Dad. You go around mewling after your dead daughter and call it poetry." He sneered. "Yes, I've seen your pathetic 'slender volume.' Don't look so surprised. Your brother was a real pain in the ass forcing it down everyone's throat last summer. Listen to me. You want to know what real poetry is? An ax. An ax that breaks the frozen sea within."

"Thank you, Franz Kafka," I said dryly. But inside, I felt shaken. His attack was a direct hit, right in the softest spot of my ego. *Mewling.*

Dave stood up. "Let's get on with it," he said grimly.

I began to worry about staying alive. "Which one of you called me over at the lodge?" I asked. I looked at Dave, hoping for reassurance. He wouldn't meet my eyes. Not a good sign.

Mac smiled. "Does it matter?"

I didn't answer.

"Okay, outside," he ordered. Without taking the gun off me, he stooped, picked up a day pack, and slung it over his shoulder.

"Where are we going?" I sounded shrill.

"On a little hike," he said pleasantly.

We walked single-file past a weather-beaten outhouse behind the trailer and randomly up through the pines. Dave led the way, eventually picking up a game trail. I followed with Mac behind me, his gun in my back. Our strides didn't match, and the steel barrel bumped sharply against my vertebrae every few steps. I wondered if it would go off accidentally. I envisioned myself among the paraplegic vets I'd seen down at the Vietnam Memorial Wall. Wheelchair athletes, some of them, with biceps as big as balloons. *Just let me live,* I thought urgently. I felt a sudden flood of love and affection for my family, for my gypsy-bird mother, my beautiful wisecracking nieces, even—surprisingly—my brother, Johnny. The news that he had boosted my latest verse at the J-E had stunned me almost as much as Mac's attack. I wondered if Johnny had actually read my poems—or had he simply been pushing them? But what if he *had* read them? I winced. There were a couple I'd just as soon he hadn't.

We marched uphill, climbing above the wind-stunted pines behind the trailer into a soft-floored forest of sizable Douglas firs and whitebark pines. I guessed we were on the north side of a ridge, because jams of deadfall still held long patches of unmelted snow, dirty as discarded Styrofoam. It looked solid enough to break; I fancied picking up a hunk and crumbling off pieces of it to mark my way back down. About as helpful as the old breadcrumb trick.

Once the forest opened: an avalanche had cut a wide swath down the mountainside, uprooting the trees and sweeping them along with their soil into a tangled barricade several hundred feet below us. All that was left was a vast slide of red shale boulders. We scrambled across it, small as ants on a gravel path, but I didn't risk looking around for a bearing. I was watching my footing, trying to stay ahead of Mac's gun, waiting for and dreading the chance to pull out my own.

I tried talking. "You didn't count on lividity, did you?" I said over my shoulder. "If you hadn't left her sitting in the car for so long after you bashed her, her blood wouldn't have drained into her lower legs. You could have hammered those holes in her and it would have looked like a bear attacked her while she was alive."

"It was a bear attack," he said easily. "Keep moving." He encouraged me with the barrel of his gun.

The wind picked up. Back in the trees, warm gusts spun the top of the pines against a lavender-gray sky. "Smells like rain," Mac observed cheerfully. A distant rumble of thunder answered. I was sweating inside my down vest, and thirsty. I concentrated on where I was putting my feet. I began to focus on fallen logs, to see them with extreme clarity: the faint grain of their smooth, silvered exteriors; the rich, rusty color of their disintegrating insides. I saw heartwood cracked into velvet chunks, like cinnamon charcoal, or shredded into soft spills of mulch which supported evergreen mats of kinnikinnick. I wasn't exactly *consoled* by these logs rotting into the forest floor, rotting into new life. But somewhere more profound than my fear, I felt connected to them.

When we stopped, my Timex said six-ten. We'd climbed at a

decent clip for over an hour—maybe three miles. The calculation seemed meaningless. Three miles to nowhere. There was no alpine meadow, no view of distant snowfields to expand the heart and provoke an "Ah" of surrender. There was only the banal repetition of pine trunks spiked with dead lower branches.

"This ought to do," Mac said. He looked around. "Over there," he ordered. The gun jabbed at my spine. We crackled through the dry underbrush to a large fir.

"Okay," he said.

I had started to turn around when he shoved me hard into the tree, mashing my nose against the ragged bark. An orange balloon of pain exploded behind my eyes. I gasped and swallowed back a cry. My eyes watered.

"Put your hands on the tree," I heard him order. "Higher."

Blindly, I raised my hands on the tree. Lifting my arms, I caught the stink of my own fear, pungent as rotten onions.

"Don't move," he said. I heard him stepping back several paces. Then I heard the rustle of nylon, the curt swish of a zipper opening. His backpack, I thought.

"God almighty," Dave said, his voice shocked.

"Here," Mac said. "Take this."

Feet moved heavily, snapping dry sticks. I could feel a slow trickling from my nose, blood or mucus.

"Okay, Lee," Mac instructed, "up you go."

What was he talking about? "Excuse me?" I said.

"Climb the tree." I heard a metallic click. The revolver's hammer. "Go on," he urged. "Pretend a bear's after you."

I thought about it for a long moment. Then I said, "No." Slowly I turned around to face him. "I'm not playing," I announced.

He was standing about ten feet away, hatless, his pale canvas jacket casually open. His handsome head was slightly cocked, as if my refusal had puzzled him. I saw that his gun was in his hand, still pointing my way, steadied on his left wrist. But something was wrong. With a dull thud of shock, I saw that his entire left arm was covered by a thick pelt of brown fur. A grizzly's fur. He was wearing a grizzly mitt. At the hand end of it, five slightly curved claws protruded like fingers.

"Put the gun down," I suggested. "After all, you don't want the forensic people to find a bullet in me." He took two steps toward me. "Wait!" I said. "Mac, I'm not a reporter. I don't care what you do, it's your own land, Mac. Mac, stop, don't do it!"

A loud crack of thunder interrupted. Mac glanced up at the darkening sky. The mitt's dark claws didn't look all that sharp, but the fur around them was matted with dried blood.

"That's what you used on Monica, isn't it?" I said, trying for a conversational tone.

But he wasn't interested in conversation. Like an athlete warming up, he loosened his shoulder, then swung the mitt in a practice arc. It looked heavy on the downswing, as if it were weighted. He let it swing back and forth, like a pendulum.

Dave stepped back, out of the way. He was holding a roll of duct tape.

"Do her feet," Mac instructed.

He swung again. There was a silent flash of lightning. His claws raked the electrified sky. Silhouetted against greenish light, for a split second he seemed half man, half beast. Then, in the moment of velvet darkness that followed, Dave dove at his brother's knees. The two of them crashed to the ground. The gun flew out of Mac's hand into the underbrush and fired on impact. The shot was deafening, disorienting. It took me several seconds to realize I wasn't hit. Then I remembered the .38 in the pocket of my vest. Fumbling, I pulled it out.

Mac roared with rage. He was back on his feet, swiping at Dave with the mitt.

"Run!" Dave yelled at me. He was rolling away from Mac when the grizzly claws caught his arm, tearing it open from shoulder to elbow. Dave let out a bellow of pain. I fired my gun into the air. Mac wheeled around, momentarily distracted. Then he saw me.

He stood there, coat open, his lean body casual and confident, like the boy star of a school team. The sardonic scowl was gone from his handsome face. There was concentration on his face, determination, but no glint of madness in his fine brown eyes. He might have been sizing up a knotty piece of firewood, maul in hand. I was nothing more than an object in his way. He let out a grunt and charged, grizzly arm poised, his pale coat flapping like moth wings, luminous in the prestorm twilight.

"Shoot!" Dave was yelling. "Shoot, for Christ's sake!"

I was screaming, "Stop!"

But he didn't. I aimed and shot and he kept on coming. I dropped down on one knee, got off another shot, then he was on top of me. I ducked down, gun still in hand, and tucked into a ball, instinctively protecting my head and the back of my neck with my arms. I remember thinking, *This is it.* There was an explosive crack and he landed on my back, heavy as a felled tree.

Some seconds later, Dave was pulling at me, pushing at Mac. I wondered if we'd been hit by lightning. Dave's face was white. His right shoulder sagged; the sleeve below it was soaked in blood.

"What happened?" I said. I sounded as if I had a cold. I found I could move. I touched my nose, looked at the blood on my hand, on the front of my shirt. I blinked. Hil was squatting beside me, peering at my nose.

I sat up. "Hil?" I wondered. "How'd you get here?"

"Walked. Same as you." He leaned in for a closer look, his breath sweet with gin. "He break it for you?"

I jerked my face away. "I don't get it. What are you *doing* here?"

His thin mouth twisted into a bitter smile. "Keepin' an eye on you."

Dave was kneeling over Mac, wounded arm dangling, his good hand probing his brother's neck. Mac looked white, too. His damp hair clung to his forehead in an irregular row of commas. His eyes and mouth were wide open. He wasn't moving at all. "He's dead," Dave said dully. He took his hand away from Mac's neck.

I looked at the .38 in my hand.

"Give it here," Hil said.

I let him take it. He spun out the cylinder and shook the remaining slugs into his hand.

I looked back at Mac. Lying there, his skin alabaster-white, his left arm covered in grizzly fur, he might have been an enchanted prince. In a fairy tale, a beautiful princess would have broken the spell with a kiss. In fairy tales, love always works.

Dave, using his good hand, tugged and yanked the grizzly mitt off Mac's arm, then angrily hurled it into the brush. I peered at Mac's chest. There was a small, off-center hole above his belt and a very large, messy one in the vicinity of his heart. I saw splinters of bone, transparent bubbles of blood. I groaned and burst into tears. "I thought I'd missed him. I thought I'd missed him!" I gasped at Dave.

"You didn't kill him," Dave said with extreme patience. He sounded tired.

I pressed my hands to my mouth. Squeaks came through my fingers.

Hil weighed my bullets in his hand. "No way you can stop a griz with these little mothers," he said. He reached into his breast pocket and took out a single brass mega-bullet. He held it up between thumb and forefinger, like a vial of medicine. "This here's what to use on old Honey Paws."

It took me a while to grasp that the big hole in Mac's chest was an exit wound made by a bullet from Hil's rifle. But if my brain was sluggish, it was still working. The fact that Hil's bullet had stopped Mac was, of course, a technicality. I had squeezed the trigger. Twice. I didn't feel particularly bad about it. Not then, at any rate. Perhaps it was shock settling in after my tears. Mostly I felt a numb surprise. Up until that moment, I had assumed that I could never kill a human being.

Dave's brain, however, was racing, taking the corners at full speed. He announced that Mac was going to disappear. I didn't object. Mac, after all, was his brother. If one death can cancel out another, then Mac had paid the debt. "Justice" had been served. In fact, Monica's ghost had been twice "avenged," if you counted the scapegoat grizzly sow. But whatever the score, I saw no need to advertise it. Leaving the law out of it would not only spare Dave and his family but, more selfishly, save me legal fees—and headlines.

"If he's gonna disappear," Hil said laconically, "it oughta be higher up. You don't want no tourists tripping over him the way she"—he glanced in my direction—"tripped over that griz up the canyon."

So Dave sent Hil back down for horses and shovels. "Go back with him," Dave said to me. "Go back with him and get out of here. Trudi and Lynn are staying the night in Helena. No one has to know you were here."

I shook my head. "Your farm manager saw me this afternoon. Besides, you're not going to be able to dig with that arm."

"Hil will do it."

I looked up at the darkening sky. "Don't forget the umbrellas," I said to Hil.

It was a long wait. I dug into a patch of snow and held clean handfuls of it against my nose. Then I washed Dave's arm with it, carefully peeling back the slashed shirt from the wound. The grizzly's claws had cut deeply into his biceps, exposing ribbons of pink muscle. With the help of Dave's pocket knife, I cut large butterfly stitches from the duct tape to pull the wounds together, but the pieces of tape kept slipping in the blood. Finally I gave up, tore my T-shirt into strips, and bound his arm as best I could. "You're going to need to see a doctor," I told him. He didn't say anything.

Fat drops of cold rain began to fall. I went over to Mac and closed his eyes. I tried to do it unobtrusively, but Dave saw me.

"What's the point?" he complained. It came out like a sob, full of grief and despair.

It rained hard and briefly, enough to soak us through, then moved on, obscuring the next ridge in a blurry sheet of white.

"It was Mac I talked to on the phone, wasn't it?" I asked Dave, trying to stop my teeth from chattering.

He gave a curt nod. His lips were blue, like those of a skinny kid who's spent too long in the swimming hole.

"You had a fight in the trailer?"

He shrugged. "We bumped around a bit. I tried to tell him that there was no way he was going to get the money out of the Japanese. I mean, even if it works out, we're talking about a process that takes years. It didn't register," he said bitterly. "Mac thought he could sell the place the way you sell a car. He has no idea what's involved, what it takes to keep the J-E running. When I think—" He broke off, his voice tight with emotion. "When I think of all the years Trudi spent breaking her ass—" He stopped again. "Then to end up with nothing—"

He retreated into silence. Drips from the pine boughs overhead ticked on his hat. Then he went on. "I was steamed. Really hot. But you know what he's like. He could sell green cheese to the man in the moon. I guess I wanted to believe him. He said he just wanted to scare you off, that all we needed was a bit more time. He swore he hadn't killed Monica. He said you were delusional, that after what happened last year up in the Bob, you were obsessed with murder."

To keep hypothermia at bay, we each walked our own brisk circles around the pines. Once Dave slowed down to ask, "You think he was using something?"

Like acid? Or PCP? Or Native American sorcery? I could see Mac's teasing smile: *Does it matter?* "You could find out with an autopsy," I suggested.

"No," he said firmly.

We went back to walking our private circles. By the time we heard horses snorting below us, it was almost dark. "I thought maybe he'd gotten lost," I said to Dave.

"Hil? Around here? Not a chance."

I taped Mac's ankles together. His hiking boots stood up at attention. Then I buttoned his coat, taped his arms to his sides, and rolled his wet, stiffening body onto a canvas tarp. The ground where he had lain was warm under my knees as I folded flaps of the canvas around him. Hil uncoiled a rope and laid a couple of looping hitches over the saddle on a gray mare. Then, awkwardly, the two of us hefted the body, stomach down, across the mare's back and tightened the ropes around it. The horse didn't seem to mind.

We mounted, Dave with help from Hil, and rode up through the woods until we emerged above the tree line on a high rocky bench. On all sides, dark walls of mountains banked against the night sky. In the west, a lemony afterglow sharpened the profile. Small stars emerged, unblinking behind a sheer veil of cloud. The horses' hooves rang against rock. Sparks flew from their shoes, as if they were apocalyptic steeds. Then, descending again into the trees, we finally stopped in a clearing studded with mounds of bear grass.

My feet felt frozen in my wet sneakers, but warmed up after ten minutes of digging. Hil and I took turns with a pick and a short shovel while Dave moved a battery lantern around for us. It took us two sweaty hours to get three feet down. We put Mac in the hole and stood around it, our damp faces bleached in the lantern light.

Dave, bandaged arm across his chest, took off his hat and bowed his head. Solemnly, Hil followed suit. Cowboys at graveside. Grade B-minus. I fought an urge to laugh. I looked up at the patch of night sky overhead and latched onto a new moon. It curled among the stars like a small, wet feather.

Finally Dave said, "The Sacred Paw was the best part of him." Then he looked expectantly at me.

Dave's words shocked me. His epitaph, if not damning, seemed too bleak, too impersonal. "People loved him," I said at last. "He'll be remembered," I added lamely. But it seemed to satisfy Dave. He scooped up a handful of dirt and dropped it into the grave. Pebbles, falling with the dirt, made a dull patter on the canvas. Hil and I picked up our shovels.

Once Mac's body was covered, filling in the hole was easier than digging it. I had the sense of tucking Mac in, and a very physical sense of completion. About halfway through, I remembered his root. I picked up my vest off the stony ground. The rain had turned it into an ice pack. I fished the root from its pocket and dropped it into the grave.

Hil stopped and leaned on his shovel. "What's that?"

"Bear magic. To inter with his bones."

We replanted clumps of displaced bear grass over Mac, then strewed armfuls of pine needles and deadwood to disguise the grave. Hil went to his saddlebags and brought back a full fifth of Tanqueray. He took a long swig and passed it to me. I didn't hesitate. The liquor was pleasantly sharp in my mouth and went down warmly. I passed it to Dave. Then Hil screwed the top back on and we walked back to the horses.

I was tying my shovel onto the gray mare's saddle when my arm brushed something soft and furry. I yelped and jumped back. The horse jerked nervously. "Whoa, there," Hil said on the other side of the horse. Dave raised the lantern. I saw Mac's grizzly mitt tied to the back of the saddle.

I couldn't believe it. "You're not taking that thing with you," I objected angrily to Hil.

"It's worth something," he said evenly from under the brim of his hat.

"But it's got Monica's blood all over it!"

He looked up and met my eyes. "Reckon it'll wash out."

Suddenly Dave was beside me. He thrust the lantern at me, then furiously, with one hand, unlashed the piece of fur and thrust it at me. "Bury it," he ordered.

Dave held the lantern for me. When I was done, he doused it.

"Hil," I said.

"Yo." He was over by his horse.

"You killed that bear in the canyon."

No answer.

"You knew it wasn't human. You knew there was no psycho on the loose. That's why you didn't go and get a gun. How much did you get for the skin, Hil? How much for that bear's gallbladder? How many penises does it take to keep you in fancy gin? *How many?*"

No one moved. Then Dave said in a tight voice, "Let's go." I held his horse, boosted him on.

We rode into the corral just before dawn. I changed into dry clothes, got in my red rental, and drove east into the sunrise.

Later that day I got on a flight out of Great Falls. Descending at Salt Lake to change planes, I saw lilacs blooming in suburban yards. Then I was in the air again, flying east into the spring, east into the dark. After a steamed-in-plastic dinner, the cabin was darkened for a Steve Martin movie. I rented headphones for four bucks. Watching Martin's amiable slapstick, I started weeping, blowing my nose into a paper napkin that smelled of chicken. The woman next to me kept her eyes fastened on the monitor, but I could feel her shrinking away from me in her seat. I pressed my face against the cool plastic window and grieved, wetly and silently, for the dead bears, for their vanishing wilderness, for Mac.

EPILOGUE

Three months later, early on a warm July morning, I was drinking java mocha in the mossy brick garden of "my" Georgetown mansion when an Associated Press story jumped out at me from a page of the *Washington Post.*

> CHOTEAU, Mt.—Six environmental activists were arrested for trespassing and destruction of property during a weekend protest staged at a proposed Chevron Oil Company drill site near Bear Paw Swamp. Armed with cans of green spray paint, the protesters defaced an oil company trailer containing dynamite and other seismic testing devices.
>
> A spokesman for Chevron Oil said that the company is sensitive to the unique ecology of the area and that all appropriate environmental safeguards will be employed during the test drilling. "These kind of sophomoric theatrics can only have a negative effect," he said.
>
> Several demonstrators wore bearskins. "We wish to call attention to the endangered status of the grizzly, which uses the swamp as a spring feeding ground," said Leonard Thunder Moon, a Blackfeet traditionalist. The grizzly plays a prominent role in the Blackfeet religion.
>
> Earlier this year, Bear Paw Swamp was the site of

New York heiress Monica Leeds's death. Last April, Leeds was attacked and killed by a grizzly sow. Family attorney Jon Putnam stated that Leeds, a freelance writer, was researching grizzlies for a book on the ecology of the Eastern Front of the Rocky Mountains. In June, the Leeds family announced the endowment of the Monica Leeds Environmental Studies Chair at Yale University.

The arrested activists at the swamp included Dr. Clare Jenkins, executive director of the Sacred Paw Institute, a nonprofit research center founded by environmentalist Evan Fife, who disappeared in the Bob Marshall Wilderness a week after Leeds's death. Jenkins stated that at the time of his disappearance, Fife had been working on a grizzly bear survey. "He believed that the state game wardens, in a misguided attempt to retaliate for Miss Leeds's death, killed the wrong grizzly. He was determined to locate the right one," Jenkins said.

Authorities believe that both Leeds and Fife were victims of the same bear. Fife's body has not been recovered.

AUTHOR'S NOTE

The J-E Ranch, Bear Paw Swamp and the Sacred Paw Institute exist only in my imagination. However, the existence of *Ursus arctos horribilis* is, in fact, threatened in Montana. In this story, I have tried to be accurate in describing real-life land-use issues and conflicts. In portraying the grizzly, I have relied on the research of and conversations with Dr. John Craighead, director of the Wildlife-Wildlands Institute in Missoula. I am also indebted to the following people for information: Mike Madel, bear management biologist; Dave Carr, manager of the Nature Conservancy's Pine Butte Preserve; Bob Yetter, president of the Rocky Mountain Front Advisory Council in Missoula; Woody Kipp, counselor for Native American Studies at the University of Montana; and Matthew Cohen, director of Travel Montana, State Commerce Department. Any mistakes in this book are my own.

Although fiction requires no bibliography, I would like to cite David Rockwell's powerful book *Giving Voice to Bear*. His account of Native American bear myths and rituals was a primary source of inspiration.

I am also grateful to the many friends who, in so many different ways, gave support and encouragement. In particular, thanks to Zella Erickson for insights into the guest ranch business, to Harry Papagan for his critical advice, and to Robin Pfau for helping me discover the territory of this tale.

Special thanks to my editor, Ruth Cavin.